The Keepers

Between the Lines

JJ Hull

Paranormal Crossroads & Publishing

The Keepers, Between the Lines

Copyright © 2011 by JJ Hull

ISBN 978-0-9846755-9-3

www.paranormalcrossroads.com

This work is fiction. All of the characters, organizations, and events portrayed in this novel are either products of the author's imagination or are used fictitiously.

The publisher does not have any control over and does not assume responsibility for author or third-party Web sites or their contents.

Image copyright Yaro, 2011 used under license from Shutterstock.com.

Table of Contents

1. Chapter One   9
2. Chapter Two   12
3. Chapter Three   19
4. Chapter Four   21
5. Chapter Five   24
6. Chapter Six   28
7. Chapter Seven   33
8. Chapter Eight   39
9. Chapter Nine   48
10. Chapter Ten   51
11. Chapter Eleven   57
12. Chapter Twelve   68
13. Chapter Thirteen   74
14. Chapter Fourteen   90
15. Chapter Fifteen   93
16. Chapter Sixteen   103
17. Chapter Seventeen   111
18. Chapter Eighteen   122
19. Chapter Nineteen   129
20. Chapter Twenty   153
21. Chaper Twenty-One   159
22. Chapter Twenty-Two   167
23. Chapter Twenty-Three   177
24. Chapter Twenty-Four   181
25. Chapter Twenty-Five   202
26. Chapter Twenty-Six   207
27. Chapter Twenty-Seven   215
28. Chapter Twenty-Eight   227

Dedicated to...

My family,
for supporting my dream.

The Keepers

Between the Lines

JJ Hull

The Saga Continues...

CHAPTER ONE

Elizabeth

I could feel his rapid, staggered breath on my face. My mind knew how wrong this was! However, my heart knew this was easy and right. We were one. Our lips met again and the complete world around us melted away. There was just he and I lost somewhere in the stars and moonlight. When I pulled back and looked into his face, I felt no regret.

"I guess that answers it," he said while looking deeply in my eyes as he squeezed my hand. "You are my girlfriend."

What! Oh, no. I didn't regret kissing him, but I was torn. I wasn't ready to be his girlfriend. However, words could not fully describe how deep inside I knew we were no longer two separate individuals but two parts of one soul. Oh my God, soul mates! I gave him an anxious glance and he questioned, "Do you not want to be my girlfriend?"

I opened my mouth to tell him why my mind somehow knew becoming his girlfriend was wrong but stopped when I thought of the simple word, soul mate. Of course, it had always felt easy and right when I was near him. He interrupted my thoughts, "Don't. I'm sorry, I just assumed... with the kiss, this is where we were heading." He pulled his hand from mine and I could see the hurt across his face for a brief moment before he turned away and pulled his legs up to him.

"Marvin, please look at me," I pleaded.

"No, you don't have to be my girlfriend," he stated as he waved his hand in my general direction.

I attempted to turn him towards me. He didn't budge so I moved to kneel before him where I could see his face. "I want to. When I am near you..."

"I complete you," Marvin finished my sentence. "Just as you complete me."

"But, I worry about losing you," I interjected. "If for some reason this doesn't work out..." I trailed off and looked away frowning.

"You think it will ruin our friendship?" Marvin questioned finishing my thought. I nodded as he gently turned my head to look at him. "Elizabeth, I know right here..." Marvin pointed to his heart. "This is right." Marvin paused. "We belong together. What we share goes way beyond friendship."

My mind understood a relationship with Marvin would be amazing. It understood we complimented each other with him taking in stride all my quirks and demons. He always made me feel safe. I wouldn't know what to do in a life that existed without him, without him to complete to me. However, I could not explain the anxious feeling of something else being on the horizon for me and that any commitment we made might have to later be broken. Soul mate or not, it would be cruel to Marvin to lead him on and prolong the inevitable. My gut knew why I had to put any realistic hope of a relationship off. Up to this moment, it was easy to deny what we had. Now, I knew what I had to do.

"Elizabeth?" Marvin asked with alarm written all over his face. "Do you trust me that this is right?"

I sat back letting my body lean on the rock and dirt ledge. I looked out over the cliff and said what I knew to be the truth, "I can't."

Instantly, I knew I was going to be sick. My whole body was screaming that this was wrong and in conflict with my mind which understood my need to let Marvin go.

"Why can't you?" Marvin returned.

I opened my mouth to explain but no sound came out. How could I explain my gut feeling? All I desired to do was to go back to minutes before when our lives seemed simpler.

Marvin let out a huge sigh and assumed, "There is someone else."

My head swung around and I was taken back by the shock and dejected look on his face. The answer to there being someone else was both yes and no. Instantly, the hesitation that crept up from somewhere in the far depth of my mind was Dustin. I rationally thought, why was I letting Dustin come between us? Dustin was dating Tiffany and had never shown any clear interest in me. It was only I who was drawn to him. Marvin had no idea about my fascination with Dustin. Tilly had made remarks about my getting love notes. Only they weren't love notes, they were some unknown person's journal entries. I couldn't explain Dustin or the journal entries to Marvin. If I told him everything, it would be too much!

I scooted between his legs and leaned over into his arms which he wrapped around me. With my head against his chest I could hear his heart beating. Our worlds were changed. We both understood we could never go back. He felt the undeniable bond too. My own heartbeat felt as if it were now beating in synch with Marvin's. They were two halves living in separate bodies but beating as one.

"Elizabeth," Marvin whispered as I felt the breath of his words on the top of my head. "Who…"

"There is no one else," I cut him off before he could ask. My attraction and fascination to Dustin was my choice. Why had I dreamed of Dustin when I had a dream coming true with Marvin? I would bury the eerie thought of Dustin in a deep place so his attraction would never see the light of day.

"Then why do you deny what we have?" Marvin asked.

I peered up into his eyes as a tear streamed down my face. I admitted out loud for the first time, "I am your girlfriend." The unspoken term, soul mate, crept into my mind. In this moment we both knew speaking this truth, that we were soul mates, was unnecessary. We both felt it from deep within.

He peered intently at me and wiped away my tear with his fingers. He gently kissed me sealing any worry with his confidence and my feeling that we were one. My mind conceded that this was right. If there was something being on the horizon for me, Marvin and I would face it together.

CHAPTER TWO

Tilly

As I rolled up to the edge of the golf course in Spring Park, I skidded the tail of my skateboard to a stop. The shortest way across the course to the Pine Hill Country Club was a straight bee-line across. I put my skateboard in my back pack and began the trek. My job tonight was to ensure Hank could follow the path which would lead him to Professor Kegley for his blind date. I would leave the chocolate covered strawberries at the country club for Hank and then hold the boat at the marina for him.

I was deeply worried about bailing on Elizabeth and leaving her at Harmony alone. Tiffany and her cronies were sure to eat her alive without me there to protect her. Unable to get to me, they first started picking on Trevor. The group, satisfied that they had humiliated him, moved on to Elizabeth. Cruel words and taunting demeanors were all fun and games to them. Their goal was to get at me through them.

Conductress Tiffany, the demon in curls and my nemesis, was purposely having Elizabeth stand before the mike. They all knew she couldn't sing and her placement was beyond cruel. Tomorrow night was payback time. I had a surprise for Tiffany. Trevor had taken my plans for the sound system and brilliantly tweaked it. He turned it into a sound system that was so tempermental it screeched at the sound of a human voice. Anyone singing would sound like a chipmunk. Absolutely, no one would know Elizabeth couldn't sing. It was over the top genius! Tiffany was priding herself in being the best conductress. Was she in for a surprise. She would want to crawl in a hole and never come out after this public humiliation.

The only thing I couldn't fix for Elizabeth was her robe. Why had Kegley issued her that monstrosity from the Harmony closet? She looked like she should be standing on streets begging for food. The robe wasn't even worth cutting into rags. Dreadful!

The country club was lit up like a flashing beacon beckoning come across the manicured grass. I was close enough now to see the patrons eating, drinking, socializing, and appearing happy and content. Since this was my parents' scene, I understood not all was as it seemed. People in false faces put on a show for the others they wished to impress. Their façade was thin and could be seen through if you took the time to look deeper.

My mother never had an urge to be domestic. Cooking was task number one that she wouldn't think of doing. We ate at the country club almost nightly. Of course I never sat with her and my father. The moment we entered through the front door as a family, I was shuffled off to the kitchen. I became a kitchen fixture for dinner. Why would my mother assume the kitchen staff was my baby sitter and always available to keep me at any moment? The only upside was that I was always fed well by my kitchen family.

As I ran to the back of the building, I neared the commercial door leading to the kitchen. It was cracked open as usual with a huge can of veggies jammed between the door and the door frame. I could hear the familiar tunes being hummed from within.

I opened the door and peered in. "Tilly," Jill said with a warm smile as she motioned for me to come in. I picked up a hair net as Jill rushed over to hug me. When she pulled back she asked, "What are you doing here?"

"I came to ask a favor," I said as I pulled the netting over my hair.

"Anything for my girl," stated Nathaniel from a far corner of the kitchen. This prompted him to sing a rendition of an Earth Plane song. Nathaniel was the pastry chef for the country club. His tenor voice was as sweet as his pastries. He could melt my cares away and had been doing so with his songs since I was a child.

I was lost in his song when Dalton whispered in my ear, "Brown eyes!" I swirled around and immediately fell right into his open arms. Dalton had his own favorite song to sing to me, thus the nickname. He was the head chef and a hard, don't mess with me, and set in his ways man with few friends. However, I had melted him long ago.

I must have been about four or five when I found him lying across his couch in his office complaining of a headache. I raised my tiny hand as far above my head as possible and brought it down with all my might hitting him smack dab in the forehead. Wow, the chase was on. I had given him headache number two. I hid under the big steel prepping table moving from end to end as he tried to angrily catch me. Eventually, he pulled up a chair and just watched me holding his aching head with both hands. I informed him from my safe spot that any headache of his was of his own making since he was in charge of the kitchen. His second headache from me was a wake up call. To this he chuckled saying I was an old soul in a small, irritating body. I always told him exactly what I thought from then on. He appreciated my candor.

When I pulled back, Dalton asked, "Mathilda Bradford, why has it taken you so long to come see us?"

"They keep me busy, all that school work," I sadly stated rolling my eyes.

"Are you attempting to pull our leg?" Lisa countered as she too was awaiting a hug. "You do homework? Ha!" Lisa handled the preparation work and the vegetable portion of the entrees. The only homework I didn't finish with Mrs. Summors was my spelling words. Lisa would always pick me up and plop me down on the counter beside her after I finished my meal and grill me. With my mothers total lack of interest in my schooling, I would not have learned to spell without Lisa.

"Or is it your social life? You never did let grass grow under your feet," Rick piped up from behind me. I turned to smile at him as he pulled me into a massive bear hug lifting me off my feet. Rick was the father figure in my life as far as guys were concerned. He always tried to give me advice and inquired about any guy he knew I was dating.

"I'm too old for you to worry about my social life," I countered feeling as if I was three.

"You will always be thirteen to me. Every pimple faced boy looking at you is fair game for one of my thumps!" Rick countered.

All my favorite faces were staring at me, minus one. Bruce. He was a quiet guy who only spoke when spoken too. He never initiated a conversation. "Where's Bruce?"

"We thought you might have heard," Jill said. "He ran off to start a cooking school."

"Really?" I questioned. "But he…"

"We asked the same thing," Rick interrupted. "He never talks to anyone, how was he going to stand before others and teach?"

"The Queen wishes the cheese on her vegetable lasagna to be less brown," a red faced, slender young lady stated as she pushed her way through the swinging doors which separated the dining room from the kitchen. "I sauntered over to take a look at the lasagna after she complained. I had to see, what on earth is wrong with the perfect lasagna." With one glance my way she asked, "Who are you?"

I stepped on the trash can foot pedal to assist her. She tossed the food into the trash and set the plate on the counter. "I'm Tilly," I said releasing the foot pedal.

"What am I, jinxed? One in the dining and one in the kitchen," she said as she walked around me. "I guess you'll be busting my chops for calling your mother names," she murmured under breath.

"Actually, I was the one who suggested she be called the Queen," I stated leaning back against a metal counter.

She scanned the faces in the room to see if there was a hint of truth in what I was saying.

Dalton assured her, "It's true. You don't have to worry about Tilly." Then he turned to me, "This is Rowan."

"I would say I'm pleased to meet you," Rowan stated as a short, blond pushed her way through the swinging door. "However, I work on the idea that respect is earned, not given." Rowan pushed past me to begin remaking the lasagna for my mother.

Behind her back, I could see an unhappy Jill rolling her eyes up and back in disbelief. She felt as I did, respect may be earned, but Rowan did nothing to earn it herself. She was rude!

The short blond reassured me, "Her bark is worse than her bite." Then she held out her hand to shake mine. "I'm Karen, the hostess."

"Hello, I'm Tilly," I returned.

"New employee?" Karen asked.

"Tilly is visiting," Dalton stated from behind the stove. "Do you need something?"

"I have a guest waiting who doesn't want a table," she began to explain. "He says he needs to pick up a special desert from the kitchen."

"What in the world is this about?" Nathaniel spouted. "No one placed a special order!"

"I know," I stated as I held up my hand waving for attention.

"What are you up too now?" Rick chuckled. Everyone had an inquisitive look upon their faces awaiting my response.

"You know about the special order?" Jill assumed.

I nodded and then said, "He's on a scavenger hunt for love. He only needs to pick up this special desert." I held up a brown paper bag. "Give this to him and he will be on his way."

"That simple, huh?" Nathaniel stated as he crossed the distance between us and peered inside the bag. "Two poorly dipped chocolate covered strawberries?" He then squinted to read the name printed all over the napkin. "Confectionery House." He peered at me, "These aren't any good! Why would you want to feed him these?" He handed me back the bag, "I could have made you scrumptious take me away into the moonlight chocolate covered strawberries."

"He appears to be in a hurry," Karen said as she took the bag form my hands interrupting, "No need Nathaniel!" She tuned and scurried back through the swinging door.

"Thank you!" I yelled after Karen while trying to ignore the shocked look on Nathaniel's face.

"Want me to make you some potato soup?" Lisa questioned.

"No, that's okay," I answered.

"Mac-n-cheese," Rick piped up. "It was always your favorite!"

"Actually, I'm afraid I need to leave all of you and stay one step ahead of him tonight.

"Well, goodbye! Your visit has been so lovely!" Rowan sarcastically stated.

Jill shot her a glare which clearly said to shut up. Then I was once again hugged as she said, "Come back soon! We are short on entertainment in here!"

"I agree. Don't let it be so long next time," Dalton said as he hugged me once more. "Stay away from the boys!"

I stepped towards the door and waved goodbye to the unhappy faces. Clearly they wanted me to stay so they could grill me on what was happening in my life. It had been a long time. I reassured them, "I'll stop by more often, I promise!"

I turned to hurry out the door. As the door banged back on the big vegetable can stuck in the door, I could hear Rowan, "I've told you not to prop that door open! You never know what might blow in. Including the Queen's princess!"

"Sometimes you can be so rude!" I heard Jill growl back.

"Get over it," Rowan returned. "I just call it as I see it!"

I hurried around the building, retrieving my skateboard from my backpack. The wheels and I hit the road. I once again rolled away into the grand scheme of things. I was off to the Table Rock Marina to hold the boat which would carry Hank across the lake to meet Kegley on Rock Island. She was already waiting with several comic book characters, hired actors, from Warrior Keeper. They were going to re-enact several scenes from the book for the professor and Hank. This had been Eric's, the living Keeper Warrior Dictionary, idea. I believed he wished he could be on the Rock Island for the show himself, a secret desire.

Hank would be following my several clue leaving stops. Obviously the napkin would lead him to the Confectionery House, his first stop. He would be given a fresh, big bag of chocolate covered strawberries. The bag itself would have a floral pick attached with a blank card. In the dome there was only one floral shop, so I assumed he would find his way there. At his second stop he would be handed a dozen white daisies. Both of these were purely my touch. Most women liked to receive chocolates and flowers. Kegley was no different!

If he looked closely into the bouquet of flowers he would notice the ribbon had the words, Table Rock Marina, printed on it. That is were I would be waiting to hand him the keys to the boat. This part of the plan didn't seem like such a bad idea when I had Harry to accompany me. All that dark, murky, open water would seem eerie to me, now alone.

My mind couldn't help but drift back to long ago, to my struggle at the dark waters edge during my earth life. I didn't like deep, cold, black water. It seemed to be a dark, frigid, and impersonal watery grave waiting for its victims. The Dweller who tried to murder me on the Earth Plane held me under it. Hopefully, the marina rental guy would be someone I could wrap around my finger and convince to hang out with me until Hank's arrival.

CHAPTER THREE

Elizabeth

"Marvin, I thought I was meeting you at the Administration Complex," I questioned as I stepped down the last stair.

His hands were behind his back, "I have a present for you." He pulled a huge, plain, white box from behind his back and held it out for me to take the lid off.

I was stunned when I removed the box lid. A new, silk choir robe was carefully packaged within. My fingers instantly traced the golden embroidered initials E.M.C. that danced across the right side. It was truly beautiful. I fully appreciated the robe after being fitted by Professor Kegley with a faded, too short robe from the Harmony closet. "Marvin, thank you," I said with a tear in my eyes.

"My girlfriend needs to stand out for having the best robe of the group," Marvin stated grinning ear to ear.

The silk, the fancy embroidery was remarkable in quality. How had he come up with it? Then it hit me! I squealed, "The Stitchery!" I threw my arms around him. He hugged me, pulling my feet off the ground. When he set me down, he again told me, "My girlfriend needs to stand out for having the best robe in the group."

"Professor Kegley didn't properly fit me because she knew, didn't she?" I questioned excited about such a thoughtful, luxurious gift.

A huge grin crossed his face as he said, "Go change and I will accompany you."

I raced up the stairs thinking of how kind he was to try to fill in where my family neglected me. He was fabulous just as the robe was fabulous. I dodged around girls in the hall and flung open my door. I didn't bother to close the door. I was too excited and could hardly wait to pull the robe from the box to examine it fully. It was a rare exquisite, fine silk in a vibrant green.

What strings did he pull to convince the robe maker to break his exclusive contract with Mrs. Raderton? The other concern was what to tell Tilly!

CHAPTER FOUR

Trevor

"Dude, are you really going through with this?" Eddie seriously asked me.

"I am," I answered as I placed the remote in my pocket under my robe.

"You and I already had a plan for revenge and we will be able to skate under the radar to pull it off," Eddie disagreed. "This is so public."

"This is a plan of Tillys," I reminded him.

Tilly did indeed like public spectacles. This was going to be a big, ugly one! She had a flair for public flaunting. However, like it or not, I was obligated to assist her. Her craziness was my craziness.

"Someone is going down for messing with the sound system," Eddie said under his breath. "I wouldn't want to be in your sound system shoes."

"I agree," I stated to his look of downright dismay. Making everyone sound like chipmunks wasn't the brightest idea. "What do you expect me to do? I watch Tilly's back, she watches mine!"

"Tell Tilly no!" Eddie exclaimed.

"You know I can't do that," I replied.

"I take it you did chicken out last night," Eddie replied.

I now understood. Eddie assumed when I went out last night to find Tilly, it was to nix the plan. However, this had never been my plan. First and foremost, I had a sinking feeling that she needed me. A feeling I just couldn't shake. It was a familiar gut wrenching edginess I hadn't felt since our last night on the Earth Plane. I hadn't spoken to Tilly since the run-in between her and Ruthanne over Ruthanne's brother Harry. It had been hours. Was she avoiding me? Tilly had backed down for me when Ruthanne demanded Tilly not see Harry and I knew it. Crappy is how I felt. I betrayed Tilly when I let Ruthanne win. I couldn't distinguish if this was the cause of my strong feelings last night when I went out to find her. I simply needed to make sure Tilly and I were okay. How could you make a betrayal right?

I found Tilly sitting on the boat dock at Table Rock Marina, alone and staring into the water. Upon seeing her, I understood my feeling. Dark, open water terrified Tilly and had done so every since her trauma on the Earth Plane at the hands of the Dweller who had tried to drown her. I walked up and sat down next to her and put my arm around her shoulders. I sat with her until the guy from the Hall of Babies showed up to get the boat. Tilly genuinely appreciated the company. It was just the two of us, like old times. We were solid…

"What will Ruthanne think when she finds out?" Eddie asked interrupting my thoughts with the jab. "You do have a woman to answer to other than Tilly!"

"I have no idea," I truthfully said as I plopped down on my bed. The mention of Ruthanne deflated me a little. She liked order and rules and would be extremely disappointed with me. I felt split between the two women I adored.

"What are you going to do with the two of them?" Eddie asked with a grin plastered across his face. "You will be forced to make a choice, sooner or later."

"What are you? The cross examiner?" I retorted to a silent Eddie as his smile faded. "Asking me a million useless questions this morning! I know I'm sandwiched! There is no way out!"

"Hey, don't get upset with me," Eddie matter of fact stated. "Bro, you're the one with self created chick problems."

"I don't have chick problems. I have told you that Ruthanne and Tilly both mean something different to me," I countered. "One is wheat bread and one is white. I like both!"

"Of course," Eddie sighed. "We're back to the mumbo jumbo about your bond from our childhood."

Eddie put on his ear buds, getting lost in his music. He always refused to really accept Tilly and me. In the end, I was glad to have the silence since he was disagreeable and nit picky today.

CHAPTER FIVE

Elizabeth

"You look a little green?" Marvin commented to me as we walked to the Administration Complex for the first Harmony performance.

"That would be because you have never heard me sing," I replied feeling my nerves growing the closer we got to the Complex. "I don't know what the professor was thinking when he made me join."

"I bet you sound like an angel," he reassured me.

"Well you can think that if you want," I replied and his hand grabbed mine. Whatever happened, I felt secure in his grip.

"Hey guys," yelled Tilly as she whizzed by on her skateboard followed by Eddie and Trevor. Slowly, stepping off, and flipping the board into her catching hand.

"Crash!" Eddie said as he came up beside us with Trevor following his lead.

Marvin didn't much care for Eddie's nickname for me and quickly gave him a dirty look.

Tilly had stopped not far ahead of us and looked at us like she had eaten a canary. As we walked closer she pointed to our joined hands, "This is new! What's with the hand holding?"

"She doesn't know?" Marvin asked.

"Of course she knows you're my boyfriend," I stated as I flashed a look of cool it!

"Er… Uh… I meant the robe," Tilly responded to my cue.

"Boyfriend?" I heard Dustin's mind question.
I turned. Dustin and Tiffany were approaching almost directly behind us. He heard my words.

"Elizabeth, you look a little green. Are you going to puke?" Dustin questioned as he bent his knees down to look at my face better. "Are you feeling okay?"

"How else would she look?" Tiffany spewed glancing at me from head to toe. She knew my robe equaled hers. "Someone left the Stitchery cage open. Sorry to say, even the brilliant green won't make others green with envy when she busts their ear drums. All that howling she will be doing."

"Stuff it Tiffany," spewed Tilly.

"Right, I'm escorting the mutt from the dog pound. She shouldn't talk about herself," I heard Dustin mind say.

Marvin pulled me close to him and put his arm around my shoulder and whispered, "Smile! She's jealous! You look better than her."

Hmm, how did both of them have the same opinion?

"Well?" Dustin questioned as he put his hand on my forehead. "Are you sick? Nauseous?"

Noticing Marvin's stance beginning to change, I pushed Dustin's hand away, "No, just nerves. You know, a little stage fright."

Dustin looked at me and I could see him trying to see if I was telling the truth while seeming not phased by Marvin's warning glares.

"She's fine," stated Marvin in a territorial way. "If she is sick or gets sick, I will take care of her."

"Sad, I'm sure he thinks he could take care of her," stated Dustin's mind. "For now, I'll play the part and let him mark his territory."

I looked from Marvin to Dustin. What was this about playing a part?

"No offense meant," Dustin said as he threw his hands up in front of him. "Elizabeth and I are just friends, and I was concerned. That's all."

To my relief, Tilly stepped right in the middle, grabbing both Marvin and my hand, pulling us further down the hill. Once a few steps away, Trevor handed her back her skateboard and we continued to walk in silence. Marvin still seemed tense and I reached over and grabbed his hand.

"Must I watch this? Do I barf now or later?" I heard Dustin's mind speak.

Dustin's choice was Tiffany! Marvin was good for me and there for me. I put my other hand on Marvin's arm and began to rub it while leaning in towards him. He looked down at me with loving eyes and I knew my world with him was right. I somehow needed to banish all longing for Dustin.

From somewhere behind I heard Tiffany question, "Where are you going?"

"I suddenly feel ill myself. Go on alone. I'll catch up with you later," Dustin apologized.

"I just can't watch the two of them," I heard his mind say.

Marvin chuckled under his breath and I asked, "What is so funny?"

"Only that Dustin seems to be a little jealous," stated Tilly looking back.

"Totally," interjected Eddie.

Marvin chuckled again as he gently tugged my pony-tail, "Maybe he was sending you those love notes."

"Would all of you stop! That is not funny," I said. I knew my world with Marvin was right. However, my attraction to Dustin was still gnawing at me and I was fighting it.

"Loosen up Elizabeth. It's funny that Tiffany can't keep Dustin from being attracted to you. It is also is funny that you are worrying so much about our performance tonight," Tilly stated with a devious look on her face. "The universe is on our side!"

"What did you do?" I asked knowing something was up due to her cheerful mood.

"She didn't do anything," smiled Trevor who rode off on his board and jumping his board on a bench. He rode it down the bench and back onto the ground trying to impress the onlookers with his talent.

"Don't mess with the performances! Professor Presnell will hang you out to dry if you embarrass her in front of the crowd," warned Marvin eyeing Trevor's cockiness.

"Whatever," said Tilly as she rolled her eyes. Then she looked at Marvin for a moment and shook her head, "I thought my mother had second thoughts and sent me my new robe. By the looks of Elizabeth's identical new silk, embroidered robe, you are the one to thank!"

"You're welcome," Marvin stated with a grin.

Tilly's head nodded with a true moment of acceptance between the two of them. She then peered at me, reaching out to touch my robe, saying, "Mine, however, isn't the quality of silk yours is." She was making an effort to make me feel special. I knew both robes were identical. She flashed me a grin. Then boards rolling across the pavement carried Tilly, Trevor, and Eddie away.

"You got her a robe too?" I inquired.

"She's your best friend," Marvin said with a shrug. "I know how much you care about her. You can enjoy them together." He turned to me and held my hands within his. "I meant every word when I said my girlfriend should have the best." He leaned down and pecked me on the lips. His eyes said it might have turned into a more passionate kiss if others weren't passing by.

CHAPTER SIX

Tilly

Elizabeth looked dreadfully sick and frightened as I discovered her at the back of our long line. I walked straight up to her, leaned over, and reassuringly whispered, "I meant what I said earlier. Don't worry!"

I could see the alarm building in her green sick look. She was wondering what I had done? Elizabeth began to ask, "Tilly..."

I stepped my foot on the top of hers. She knew if she didn't pay attention, I would press down on the top of her foot in a painful stomp. Her eyes darted to mine and I gave her a keep your mouth shut look.

"You're out of line," Rodger stated to me as he strolled down the line with the organizational list. "We gave you a small line placement number in hopes you could remember it."

"Rodger, back off!" I spewed and burst a wet pink bubble in his face.

"New robe?" Rodger asked Elizabeth in a sneering ridiculing tone.

She stared past him apparently too sick to respond. She was smart enough to know not to try to hold a conversation with him. Her placement in line was between Rodger and Janelle. Thus was my reason for standing here as long as possible.

"The other one suited her better," Janelle piped in before leaning up to give Rodger a peck on the lips. A grotesque image! She then focused her attention fully on Elizabeth taunting, "I meant that ratty robe fit your personal style!"

"Why don't you ask me about my new robe?" I baited Rodger and gave him my best flirtatious grin which I knew would infuriate Janelle.

"Because he doesn't talk to trash," Tiffany spewed as she walked up and stopped to peer at both Elizabeth and I. The frown upon her face satisfied me. I would definitely need to thank Marvin later. Tiffany spewed, "Janelle, Rodger, please make sure Elizabeth gets placed right in front of the mike. She should bless the room with her voice."

"Why do you desire to humiliate me?" Elizabeth weakly challenged.

"I told you in the beginning you should pick your friends better," Tiffany stated. "You chose the wrong friends." Before any response could be given, she turned and walked away.

Janelle leaned up and whispered to Elizabeth, "Don't forget all the longing, googly eyes you have made at Dustin. A little advice, girlfriends stick together and don't appreciate other girls vying for our boyfriend's attention!"

Elizabeth hastily whirled around I assumed to combat the statement with news of her hooking up with Marvin. However, Janelle was standing so close that Elizabeth flew right into the soda can Janelle was holding. It fell and sprayed all over the both of them.

Janelle screamed, "Look what you did!" She was swiping her hand down the front of her.

"What I did?" Elizabeth yelled back.

Rodger quickly moved around Elizabeth and was helping to wipe Janelle's robe with his hands as if he could squeegee away the wet splatters. Janelle whined, "Look at me!"

"It's okay, the robe isn't stained," Rodger stated to Janelle trying to calm her.

"But mine came from The Stitchery!" Janelle exclaimed. "Hers is a rip off copy!"

"Elizabeth's came from the Stitchery as well," Marvin stated as he walked up to us. "What happened?"

"Your dim witted girlfriend knocked my drink out of my hand. Now I have to go on stage looking like this!" Janelle spewed.

Elizabeth half in shock, peered down at the bottom half of her robe which was totally splattered with soda. I thought she looked panicked and much more nauseated than before. Elizabeth softly spoke, "I never meant to knock the soda out of your hand. I just turned around because you were teasing me. You were standing too close."

Marvin moved down to mimic Rodger's movements swiping soda from the robe's tail. There was nothing to be done to save the robe, leaving Marvin to stand and say, "Janelle is right about one thing."

"What?" I questioned as the line ahead of us started moving.

"You will have to go ahead and wear your wet robe on stage," Marvin added.

"Marvin, I'm so sorry," Elizabeth sniffled with tears welling up in her eyes. "Your gift."

"It's not stained, just wet!" Marvin disagreed. Then he enveloped Elizabeth in his arms in a comforting, calming hug. "We will send it to the cleaners after the performance. Besides, I came to wish you good luck and to hear my girl sing!"

"You're not mad about the robe?" Elizabeth questioned as he let go of her and took both of her hands into his.

"No!" Marvin assured her. "Robes come and go. Things come and go. It's you in my heart that is forever."

"Isn't that sick," Janelle spewed.

Ignoring Janelle, Marvin looked Elizabeth directly in the eyes and said, "Mad? Of course not. I still think you're the most beautiful girl in the room."

Janelle loudly made gagging sounds as she pointed her finger into her mouth.

"Switch with me," I spewed out.

"Huh?" Elizabeth and Marvin almost said simultaneously.

"I stand in back!" I happily said. "No one will see the stains. You can stand in front with my clean robe."

Their hands dropped as they peered at me like I was crazy. Of course, Elizabeth's had initials embroidered, but truly no one would see me. I was all but invisible since I was surrounded by tall guys whom I intended to flirt with. The stained robe would make them feel sorry for me. I could use it to my advantage.

"No way!" Janelle spewed. "She did this. She goes out looking just like me!" Then she focused on Elizabeth. "Why don't we tell Marvin what got you so rattled?

Elizabeth started, "Marvin, I was just telling her that…"

"Stop it!" I screeched at her. "You were alluding to your opinion that Elizabeth flirts with Tiffany's Dustin. She turned to put you in your place and inform you that she has a boyfriend." I took a step towards Janelle and pointed at her with a threatening stance. "Marvin is her boyfriend!" I took another step sticking my nose within one inch of her, forcing Janelle to step backwards. "She would never be interested in that pompous Dustin!" Again, I took another step, purposely invading her space. "You were standing so close that her elbow knocked the drink out of your hands!" With one final step forward, I spewed, "So stop it or you will have to deal with me!"

Rodger stepped in protectively forcing Janelle to take another step further back. I popped a bubble in his face and winked at him. He slightly blushed.

Elizabeth turned to Marvin, "It would suit her right to be the only one on stage with a dirty robe. However, I happen to like my robe and wouldn't trade it for the world, pop splatters or not." Then she turned to look at me, "Thanks, Tilly for the offer."

"No problem," I said with a look hoping to convey I was in control.

"Tilly," the piano playing young man called. "Your line has already gone on stage."

"So what," I stated as I walked toward the curtained stage entrance. I peered back and watched Marvin beaming at Elizabeth. She leaned over against him and I knew he was going to stay by her side until she went on stage. Something had changed overnight with the two of them. They seemed to be in synch. It was about time Elizabeth let someone besides me look out for her.

CHAPTER SEVEN

Elizabeth

Standing at the end of the stage, I could see comfort and pain walking towards me. Marvin and Rhett were walking towards Tilly, Trevor, and me in rapid motion. Heading toward us from a different direction was Mr. & Mrs. Bradford. Boy, did they look unhappy!

The performance had been a disaster! Anyone using a mike, screeched. You might have thought we were performing a comedy show by the amount of laughing in the audience. In the scheme of things, none of the party closing in appeared as unhappy as Professor Presnell. She was still at the side of the stage frantically hand gesturing. Mr. Solliday seemed to be joining her party.

Tilly had her robe lifted and was obviously digging in her pockets for gum. Trevor seemed to have the endless gum supply she was looking for. He held up the shiny, silver wrapper in his hands and she grabbed it mumbling, "Thanks!" With a fluid motion it was unwrapped and in her mouth.

"You might need two," Trevor stated as he held up another piece of gum. I cringed! It was going to be that bad!

"Miss Bradford, did you have anything to do with this?" Rhett asked in a stern voice.

Before either of us could answer Mrs. Bradford grabbed Tilly by the arm asking, "Did you do this?"

"I never touched the sound system," Tilly replied to all the peering eyes as she jerked her arm free.

"Don't be smart!" Mr. Bradford demanded. "Did you plan it? We know how you use people and guys in particular. Did you have one of your acquaintances carry out your plan?"

Mrs. Bradford turned her glare to me. When she spied Rhett her demeanor changed. Their eyes locked for a moment and I thought I saw a faint acknowledgement of each other. She nodded her head saying, "Rhett."

Rhett made the same motion calling Mrs. Bradford casually by her first name, "Olivia."

They knew each other. How? I was completely taken back when Rhett added, "There is no doubt whose daughter she is."

Mrs. Bradford seemed just as offended by this comment as Tilly. Her glare turned to me with her questioning him, "You assume Miss Cantrell had nothing to do with this?"

"She had nothing to do with this," Marvin interjected as he grabbed my hand.

"You would say anything, wouldn't you?" Mrs. Bradford spewed back at him.

Rhett's neck turned a deep shade of red and he huffed back at her, "Marvin wouldn't lie!"

"Yes, he is so utterly trustworthy," Mrs. Bradford sarcastically responded. She seemed satisfied that she had crawled under Rhett's skin so easily. "He hangs out with his Ghostie parents."

"As for you, young lady," Mrs. Bradford began sticking her finger in Tilly's face and shaking it.

"Give it a rest!" Tilly screeched at her mother. "I know the only reason you care. Your social status!"

"Mathilda, don't sass your mother," Mr. Bradford cautioned as he stepped up to the growing crowd, raising one eyebrow.

Tilly never missed a beat. She looked Mr. Bradford eye to eye and said, "I wouldn't if she remembered she was my mother."

"What nonsense are you blabbing about?" Mr. Bradford asked dismissing Tilly's statement. "We will always be your parents. It's you that chooses to alienate us!"

They stood staring at each other. You could cut the tension. No one was talking!

"What is going on?" Rhett asked watching the strange behavior on the part of the Bradford's.

"Whatever it is, it is none of your business," Mr. Bradford snapped at Rhett. "Tilly is our business." Mr. Bradford paused to point his long, skinny finger at Marvin. "Tighten up the reins on him. He's your business. You can't even control who he wallows in the mud with!"

"Leave Marvin and Elizabeth out of it, you don't want me embarrassing you by airing our dirty laundry?" Tilly taunted her parents. She turned to Rhett to spite them. "I was awarded the solo parts at the try-outs. Afterwards, my mother undermined my win and rallied for Tiffany to do the solos instead of me. She went to Professor Presnell and shredded me like I was unwanted trash!" In a flash Tilly's defiant demeanor was gone. The hurt was visible on Tilly's face.

"You didn't stand up for your own daughter?" Rhett asked as Trevor loudly huffed appearing genuinely mad about Tilly's hurt feelings. Rhett continued, "You took up Tiffany's cause?"

"Olivia!" Mr. Bradford sternly said in a lecturing voice. "You didn't?"

"Thomas Bradford, don't give me any grief! You know as well as I do Mathilda never takes anything seriously. This is my al ma-ma tar, my passion, and my face in the community. I wanted someone singing the solos that appreciated the position and would give it their all."

"I did intend to give it my all," Tilly quietly stated standing beside Mr. Bradford who seemed to have acknowledged that he saw her point for once in her life.

Mr. Bradford didn't look half as mad as Rhett. The words about Marvin had really infuriated him. If he planned on leveling the playing field, he had some work to do in this situation. Interrupting the painful conversation and awkward silence, Professor Presnell stormed over. On her heels was Mr. Solliday. He gave me a warm smile from across the circle as though secretly he found the situation amusing.

Professor Presnell's focus and anger were directed at Tilly and me. "Miss Bradford and Miss Cantrell! Both of you are to accompany me back to my office. Mr. and Mrs. Bradford, you had better come along as well."

Marvin instantly grabbed my hand and slid his body in-front of mine. Mr. Solliday took notice of Marvin's protective stance and I thought I saw a slight smile. Marvin politely said, "Professor, Elizabeth had nothing to do with this."

"Mr. Lagedge, as far as I'm concerned you will not interfere with the situation. You are wrongly trying to protect one of the guilty parties," Professor Presnell stated.

"Whether Tilly did it or not, who knows?" Marvin growled at the professor. "I can only say for certain that Elizabeth had nothing to do with this."

"The poor boy is blinded by love," Mrs. Bradford interjected. "Look at their hands, they're dating! He would say anything in her defense!"

"These two trainees, which are under my care, have a proven rebellious spirit and track record. Their antics will no longer be tolerated!" Professor Presnell announced heatedly and loudly for all concerned.

"Marvin wouldn't lie about this!" Rhett stated, disagreeing with both the professor and Mrs. Bradford. "His record is impeccable."

"Like you're a great judge of character," Mrs. Bradford said under her breath but loud enough for Rhett to hear.

"Shouldn't you be less worried about Elizabeth or Marvin and more worried about standing up for your own daughter?" Rhett growled at Mrs. Bradford. "You have your priorities are wrong!"

Mr. Solliday, having watched the whole exchange, took a step forward. "Miss Cantrell, your boyfriend has so gallantly stood up for you. I hope his trust isn't misplaced."

I started to say, "I really didn't…"

Mr. Solliday held up his hand to stop me from speaking. "Mr. Lagedge, would you accompany Miss Cantrell back to Keeper House."

"No way Albert!" Mrs. Bradford stated.

"I disagree with you, I have a right to hand out punishment," Professor Presnell stated hot under the collar. "Mr. Solliday you're…"

"Standing up for an innocent party." Rhett interrupted finishing the professors statement. "Elizabeth had nothing to do with this."

"Why are you even here and intruding on something that is none of your business?" Mrs. Bradford asked in a whiny and annoyed tone. "You are overstepping your boundary!"

"Because they are my students," Rhett said folding his arms. It was very evident he wasn't tucking his tail and running.

"Your students!" Mr. Bradford repeated.

"I believe the young ladies have been tasked with finding a ghost for Rhett," Mr. Solliday interjected. "They are indeed his students!"

"They've been separated from the student's training group?" Mr. Bradford asked wondering why.

"On who's orders?" Professor Presnell inquired with her red hot temper flaring as she threw a folder of sheet music to the floor.

"On mine," Mr. Solliday answered shutting the professor down.

"Isn't it great?" Tilly piped up. "I'm working for the Department of Ghosts!"

You could instantly see this insulted both of Tilly's parents because they felt anyone working for the Department of Ghosts was beneath them. Marvin began to tug on my hand wanting to vacate. I stood with my feet planted firmly. Even though I appreciated being excused from the firing squad, I would stand as long as possible with Tilly. Poor Tilly!

"Shall we," Professor Presnell stated and motioned for the group to continue towards the lift. "My office!"

Before they could abandon the three of us, Rhett interjected, "I would like to come along as an advocate for my students. They deserve representation!"

"No!" Mrs. Bradford strongly disagreed. "Absolutely not!"

"Rhett, this is not your concern," Professor Presnell said dismissing his request.

CHAPTER EIGHT

Tilly

We made our way in silence to Professor Presnell's office. What a rotten Saturday this turned out to be. The leprechaun midget snickered and marveled at the group dragging me to my apparent doom. Gawkers, whom we passed along the way, should have put their eyes back in their heads. If any of them believed for a solitary moment that I was in trouble, they were crazy. They were the gullible ones who should have been gawked at!

I entered into the putrid red office belonging to Professor Presnell and sat in one of the two new, red upholstered chairs before her desk. Yuck! The professor headed for her chair as, of all people, Rhett started to sit next to me. Was he attempting to pretend he was here for moral support?

"Not there," Presnell sternly warned looking over the rim of her red glasses. "Miss Raderton will be along."

He stood up straight and asked, "Why should she need to be present?"

"So she can have a front row seat!" I said under my breath.

"No," Presnell corrected me. "Miss Raderton was the party adversely affected. We should all hear the impact statement of the victim."

"Victim?" I repeated.

"Mathilda, can it," my mother said. "I've had all of your insolence I can take!"

"Let the show begin!" I said as I sat back in my seat. This was all a farce!

Tonight there were only two chairs sitting across from Presnell. It was obvious she hadn't considered she would have such a large crowd in her office after the performance. Also, I didn't remember her office being so small and cozy.

Rhett reluctantly leaned against the wall beside me, which was beside my mother. As if repelled by Rhett, she switched places with my father. Mr. Solliday was now standing beside my mother with an eyebrow raised as he seemed to notice the slight as well.

"While we await Miss Raderton, let me ask you, what do you know about what happened this evening?" Presnell asked gripping a pencil and tapping it on her desk to control or express her anger.

She was getting crafty by asking only what I knew, not if I did the deed myself. "I have no idea how the sound system works." Every eye was upon me. I corrected, "How could I know what happened?"

It was Rhett's reaction that caught my attention. I was sure I saw a hint of a smile on Rhett's face. That was odd since I felt he disliked me.

Even though it signaled the beginning of the show, a knock at the door temporarily diverted the attention away from me. I could use the time to think!

The room was so full that Presnell couldn't get around the desk to open the door. Rhett asked, "Shall I?"

"Yes, thank you," Presnell stated as she stood behind her desk waiting for Tiffany to enter and be seated.

Rhett squeezed behind my chair to open the door. My nemesis, the demon in curls, strutted in. I was aghast at her appearance. Her face was red where tears appeared to have trailed down her face. Considering she had made countless others cry as we grew up, I simply felt no remorse for her.

"Miss Raderton, please have a seat next to Tilly," Presnell said.

Tiffany fought the crowd to sit next to me. Her appearance was staged. I could tell it! Her acting skills rivaled mine.

Professor Presnell began, "Miss Raderton…"

"Do I have to do this now?" Tiffany blurted out in true drama queen fashion. Her hand slipped out of the purse she was clutching and then she wiped her face. Tears ensued as she spewed, "I'm just too upset! All that practicing and work."

"Everyone in the room appreciates all your hard work," my mother said as she pushed her way past my father, Rhett, and me. Giving Tiffany a warm hug she said to me, "Isn't that right Mathilda?"

"Oh for crying out loud," I said while shaking my head. "What real work did she do?"

Again Tiffany's hand made it inside her purse which was resting on her lap. After a moment she rubbed her face again and asked, "What work? I put my heart and soul into the performance." She glared at me from behind the tears. "You did it just to humiliate me!"

"Tiffany, you have been intolerable to deal with while you forced all your wants and ideas upon the rest of us. You dictated our robe color and placed all your friends in front. I seem to remember your thought process was only beauties should be seen," I spewed to the sounds of her fake sobbing.

"Miss Bradford, let me remind you it wasn't only her friends standing in front," Presnell interjected.

"Go ahead Tiffany. Tell them the truth about Elizabeth standing next to your click in front?" I demanded. "Elizabeth can't sing. She's tone deaf. She was placed next to the mike on purpose. The plan was humiliation!" Tiffany's teary eyed silence was beginning to crawl under my skin.

A new round of sobs and tears started.

"I can't say you picked the music or the frequency of our practices. Professor Kegley did that!" I took a deep breath, "My point is any monkey with half a brain could line up their friends and pick out a color. That is the total of your input!"

"Leadership is not easy and a lot of what a leader does is transparent," Rhett chimed in from beside me leaning over me and peering down at Tiffany for some reason.

"Leadership," I loudly retorted shaking my head. "Tiffany couldn't lead a blind person out of a paper bag!"

"Lies," Tiffany cried. "All lies." She dabbed her eyes and once more the flood gates opened and the water rolled.

"Play it however you want," I replied to Tiffany giving her no sympathy.

"Mathilda Bradford!" My father called in a reprimanding voice. "Have you no mercy?"

"No more!" My mother told me as she once again consoled Tiffany by putting her arm around her.

"Professor Zirak, would you mind escorting Miss Raderton back to Administration House?" Professor Presnell asked. "I don't see any need to subject her to anymore abuse."

It was the pot calling the kettle black! I wasn't the one who abused others.

As if following directions like a mindless puppet, Professor Zirak moved towards Tiffany and said in a sympathetic tone, "Sure."

As Tiffany rose, she picked up her purse by one handle leaving it gaping open for me to see inside. There was nothing in her bag but a zipped bag containing onion chunks and a mashed mess. This is how she was prompting herself to cry. As I peered up at her, she closed the purse and clasped both handles with her hand. Behind those fake tears her face screamed she got me!

Everyone waited in silence for Professor Zirak to lead Tiffany out of the red room. I hated to admit it, Tiffany's stoke of genius probably had landed me into some serious trouble.

"Miss Bradford, your lack of concern for Miss Raderton's feelings is shocking!" Presnell spewed. You could see the vein in her neck pulsate with anger.

"Don't reprimand me for telling the truth," I said for all concerned.

"Leading a group is a lot of work," Rhett again chimed in.

"Your problem is your mother spoiled you as a kid," my father said. "I told her you needed more supervision and structured discipline."

"Oh yes, my mother was always so attentive and spoiling me," I sarcastically replied. "She dumped me on anyone willing to put up with me."

"The matter at hand is punishing those responsible for sabotaging the sound system," Mr. Solliday stated from his position standing beside Presnell.

"I did not touch the sound system," I firmly stated. "I see no need for further discussion!"

"Miss Bradford, you may not have, as you put it, touched the sound system. However, I can't overlook the fact that you haven't denied knowing about the sabotage," Mr. Solliday stated while intently peering at me. "Can you indeed deny having knowledge?"

Darn! Lying to get out of trouble wasn't my style. The buck stopped here! My silence spoke volumes. I crossed my arms and with two fingers pretended I was zipping my lips.

"Albert, should we send her before the Council?" My mother asked totally oblivious to the fact she should be on my side as a parent.

"The Council?" Rhett asked before I could. Once again he was pretending to be concerned for me.

"She is bound to go back before them one day," my mother stated. "Why not just get over with it and get her out of all over lives. I believe in tough love!"

"Hold on," Rhett said in a raised voice back to pretending to care! "We have all been through training and involved in a prank a time or two, including you Olivia."

"Speak for yourself," Presnell retorted.

Rhett leaned forward placing his hands on her desk, "Maybe we weren't all as straight laced as you."

"I agree," my father spoke capturing everyones' attention. Under my mother's glare he said, "I agree with you dear. Mathilda is destined to end up back before the Council at some point. However, as much as I hate to admit it, I also agree with Rhett. It was just a prank."

"Not all pranks are funny," my mother returned. "She humiliated a sweet, kind, considerate girl. Are you forgetting Tiffany's pain?"

"Rhett I agree with you on another point. Leading others is a lot of responsibility and not easy. Something Tilly has never learned is being responsible for someone other than herself."

"What are you saying?" Presnell asked.

"What if Mathilda was placed in charge of the Harmony group?" My father suggested with a grin on his face. He was proud of this idea.

"No!" My mother and I both yelled at the same time. Finally, we agreed on something. We turned and looked each other in the eye.

The thought of this made the professor openly snicker and mutter, "Now I've heard it all!"

"Is it that funny to you?" I asked.

"I like the idea!" Rhett sated from beside me as he and my father exchanged a friendly look.

Professor Kegley, with tears in her eyes from a laughing fit said, "We would be the laughing stock of all the performances."

"Be serious," Rhett stated. "It's a choir and Tilly is a very capable young lady when she puts her mind to something. I have faith in her!"

"Yes, she has always been the most determined child when her mind is made up about something," my father agreed.

"The punishment should fit the crime," Mr. Solliday said giving me an intent stare. "Miss Bradford, you gave no thought of the planning and work that goes into a performance." I opened my mouth to disagree but Mr. Solliday cut me off. "Whether it was Miss Raderton or Professor Kegley's work makes no difference. You still gave it no thought. A fitting punishment is indeed for you to now lead the Harmony Choir."

"The problem is that I already told you, no!" I stated popping my gum in defiance.

"This is your punishment and there is no choice on your part," Mr. Solliday said. "You need to take this opportunity to learn responsibility and appreciate the work of others."

Silence fell over the room. My father and Rhett seemed pleased with themselves while my mother and Presnell were steaming. Presnell finally could take the thought of it no longer. She was as red as her office furnishings! "Albert, our performances are..."

"Now Miss Bradford's responsibility," Mr. Solliday stated finishing the professor's sentence and silencing any disagreement he had with the punishment.

"Well, the party has been great. Anything else?" I inquired as I stood.

Presnell looked as if she loathed me and was clearly exasperated with my punishment as she said, "There is nothing left to say."

"Except good luck with this new endeavor," Mr. Solliday politely stated.

I opened the door with Rhett following closely behind me. Once in the foyer, Rhett shut the door behind us as he asked me, "Did you forget to say goodbye to your parents?"

"Why bother!" I said. "They didn't bid me goodbye either." I sarcastically replied as we took a few steps out into the foyer.

"You were standing up for Elizabeth with your plan so she wouldn't be embarrassed, weren't you?" Rhett pointedly asked.

"Why are you worrying about my motivation?" I inquired.

Rhett paused observing me before saying, "I saw the onions in Miss Raderton's purse."

"You saw?" I blurted out.

"Yes," Rhett simply replied.

We now had an understanding. A bonding moment. "Anything I might have planned or done was executed to protect my best friend from humiliation. I didn't feel it hurt to take Tiffany down a notch! She picks relentlessly on everyone!" He gave me a disapproving, but understanding glare. "Before you ask, Elizabeth knew nothing."

"I wasn't going to ask," Rhett stated.

"Because of Marvin?" I asked to his affirmative nod. "Well, he is straight laced."

Rhett opened his mouth to defend Marvin and shut it changing his mind.

"I was beginning to believe you were a friend who was actually going to help me," I stated.

"That was my intention," Rhett stated.

"That is until you agreed with them about my leading Harmony," I amended. "I should have known you were out to stick it to me too. You are just another version of my parents."

Rhett let out a huge sigh and appeared pained, "Tilly, your father is a great leader."

"Leader of schmucks!" I said. "Besides, what does my father's leadership abilities have to do with me?"

"You're probably a natural," Rhett stated. "This is a gift!" I rolled my eyes as he threw up his hands in exasperation as Rhett countered, "That's all I'm saying."

I began to climb the first step when Rhett tried to give me a pep talk adding, "Give leading the group an honest try."

"I'll put into it what I want too," I assured him. "I give what I get!"

"That may be the problem," Rhett returned.

CHAPTER NINE

Elizabeth

"How bad is it?" I asked Tilly who had never looked more upset.

"Bad," Tilly responded.

"Why did you mix up the sound system so everyone sounded like chipmunks as they sang?" I questioned.

"I didn't," Tilly responded. "But, it was funny!"

I ignored the last comment and decided to conquer the bigger problem when I pointed out, "Okay, technically you didn't. However, you did plan it, so technically you are guilty,"

"Elizabeth, they punished me by putting me in charge of Harmony!" Tilly stated as she threw her body onto the twin, cushy bed. "They said I need to learn how to plan for events since I didn't seem to have any idea what it took to put an event together."

I had never heard of anything more ridiculous. Who in their right mind would put the Harmony Choir in Tilly's command? Did they want her to fail? Instantly, I had my answer. "Tilly, we must make this absolutely the best training session ever for Harmony."

"Right," Tilly replied.

"Don't you see what they are doing?" I questioned.

"Only giving me another responsibility I don't care anything about," Tilly stated.

"Wrong, you are going to make this your number one priority!" I responded.

"Oh, I am, am I?" Tilly sarcastically answered. "And what army is going to make me do this?"

"Stop, and listen to me," I demanded as she rose and then plopped down into the chair under the window. "Look between the lines! They want you to fail. Professor Presnell has been trying to get rid of you, well us, from day one. They don't think you will put the effort into this that it takes. We need to rebel by making this the best session in history!"

She sat quite for a few moments smacking her gum and blowing a bubble or two. I wondered if her ears were filled with cotton. She did not hear me, or seemed not too. I waited for her response, but finally decided it was not going to come and crawled into my bed.

"You are right. However, I despise Harmony," she quietly stated.

I rolled over to look at her. "If your mother was not an integral part of the group, you would not feel this way. Forget your mother! This isn't about her, it is about you succeeding and sticking it to Professor Presnell, Tiffany, and Janelle.

"You really are my best friend! You see right through the wall I put up," Tilly stated. "You definitely have my back on this one."

She was right, I did see the real her and I assured her, "I will help you with the choir."

"You know, I should be mad at you," Tilly stated.

"Mad?" I questioned.

"You didn't tell me about your boyfriend," Tilly replied. "He's a cutie, but definitely not my type."

"Oh," I signed. "Our relationship is new and iffy. I am still trying to figure out if it's permanent."

"Forgiven this time, but the next time you have news, I must be told," Tilly stated and got quiet again. "I personally think he's good for you."

"What makes you say that?" I asked out of curiosity.

"The two of you just look right together. Anyone looking at the way he gazes at you can see he is in love with you," Tilly stated.

"Hmm," was all I could say to that. I collapsed on my own bed and watched Tilly practicing her smile in the mirror and then pretending she was a choir director conducting an imaginary musical masterpiece. Out of habit I inhaled a deep breath, taking in the delightful smell of my backpack which smelled strongly of Dustin's cologne. Up to this moment I had been happy Dustin had carried it for me and left his mark. Now my mind understood anything that reminded me of him I needed to discard. First step was to no longer sleep with it. However, one sniff transported me into a peaceful relaxed stated. Maybe I would tuck it under my pillow one last time. My inner tug of war was still going.

CHAPTER TEN

Elizabeth

“Wake up sleepy head!” Tilly said amused as she tossed a pillow at me from above my head. Then she sprang up on my mattress and proceeded to jump on my bed.

“What is it?” I complained. “I want to sleep in.”

“Not this morning,” Tilly sang. “You have a love note!”

“What note?” I questioned as I squinted to view what she was holding. I was startled to see she was holding a familiar beige envelope with my name printed across the front. I sprung to my feet and onto the bed, “Give me that!”

She jumped from my bed to hers, “I guess the love notes truly aren’t from Marvin then!”

As I moved from one side of my bed and ready to spring to hers, she would move slightly to the other end. I was desperate to get the envelope before she possibly peeked.

“I thought I was the only one who had more than one man?” Tilly said freely enjoying playing keep away. Her smile and giggles gushed from her.

I sat down on my bed noticing it was still dark outside. The effort to get the envelope from her was fruitless. “Tilly, I don’t know who they’re from.” I glanced at the clock and it was only 4:30 in the morning. “May I have it please?"

"The plot thickens!" Tilly exclaimed. "I was right, you have a secret admirer. I love a mystery!"

"Hand it to me," I now demanded.

Tilly hopped off her bed saying, "You are no fun tonight." Then she held it up to the light to try to peek through the envelope.

"Don't play games with me Tilly, not at 4:30 in the morning," I answered as she mercifully placed the envelope in my hand. "Why are you up so early anyway?"

"Well, you see," Tilly hem-hawed. "I'm a much lighter sleeper than you. Someone was tossing rocks to hit our window. I know I shouldn't have, but I crawled out the window to see who it was. I thought it was Harry having second thoughts."

"Second thoughts?" I questioned. Then in pure horror I asked, "Wait, you crawled down not knowing who was at the bottom?"

"Elizabeth, we live in the Hall of Knowledge. This is the safest place in the dome," Tilly reasoned. "Anyway, I found a note and I really did believe it was from Harry. To me it seemed reminiscent of the scavenger hunt we put together for the professor."

"So you went to find Harry?" I assumed.

"Of course," Tilly replied. "What could be more exciting than a romantic rendezvous in the middle of the night! I scurried over to Grand Hall, but never found Harry. Instead, you know the cute guard?"

I nodded.

She continued, "He was just getting off work. We went to see the famous pop up band, White Crew. Did you know there is an underground pop up club in the dome?"

"Why would I have any knowledge of that?" I shot back thinking she was nuts if she thought I was into staying out all night listening to loud music and dancing.

"True, a little off your scope," Tilly sighed. "I should have discovered it a long time ago. You should have heard the music! It wasn't boring like what we sing in Harmony."

I pulled the pillow over my head stuffing the note beneath my body. It never ceased to amaze me what Tilly could get into.

Tilly started pacing back and forth between the beds. "That's it!" Tilly exclaimed. "We need to spice up Harmony. We should adopt that type of music!"

She was incredible. All she could think about was the music she heard. "Let me get this right," I began uncovering my head. "You left due to a note which led you to no one and you left me sleeping here alone with an open window."

"Are you back to being a worry wart?" Tilly retorted. "Again, I repeat myself, we live in Keeper House! This place is heavily guarded."

"Guarded?" I shook my head in disbelief. "I have never seen guards walking around. And if there were invisible guards around, why haven't they stopped you?"

"Stop me?" Tilly laughed. "I have all of them wrapped around my little finger. They all look the other way in hopes of getting a date with me. I am fine! Who could blame them for standing back and drooling over me."

"Tell me this, where did you find this note?" I questioned as I retrieved it from beneath me and waved it in the air.

"On the night stand between our beds," Tilly replied. "My guess is that Destiny sneaks them in."

Some stranger had been standing over me while I slept. I shivered and broke out in a cold sweat.

Tilly moved towards the door leading me to ask, "Where are you going now?"

"I'm going to shower," Tilly said. "I worked up a real sweat with all that dancing." Then she smiled a devilish grin at me. "Read the love letter while I'm gone. I want to hear all the details when I get back!"

I sat in my bed scared of the windows in my bedroom. Someone had lured Tilly out proving even those I trusted could unknowingly put me in danger.

I didn't look for a return address. I already knew their wouldn't be one. I simply ripped the envelope open.

Journal Entry #181

It turned out Tina did not want Grace to do her maid work. She demanded another slave do this for her. She finds daily joy in finding new ways to torture Grace. I have to wonder what Grace did to her to deserve such treatment. Tina is short and cross with others, but chooses to torture no one else but Grace.

The latest was to send her just beyond our grounds into the barren land and watch from safety as Grace deals with all kinds of different dangers. I suppose to Tina, it is like watching a new horror movie everyday with the characters, other than Grace, changing. No harm has yet to befall her. I believe this is due to Collin watching and the forces around the grounds being aware of his presence. They put her in just enough danger to make her scared and run from the darkness that surrounds her. Her character is not the same as it once was, kind and loving. She seems to be a shell of whom she was before.

I have never met another who can be so thoughtless. Tina fully understands what can actually happen outside the grounds. Not to mention Grace is old enough to be her grandmother. I would help Grace if I could do anything and I believe Tina sees through me and knows this. I try to stay out of her cross hairs.

Journal #189

Today started out to be a joyous occasion. Wilmena and her daughter Rebecca arrived from the Earth Plane with their guards, Brutiss and Sumner. Wilmena had taken a personal role in finding the woman that had stolen her wayward brother away from his duty. She was not successful but Piper was uncharacteristically happy with the return of her family and began to indulge the two.

For entirely different reasons, Tina must have seen Rebecca and Sumner as threats. Rebecca, who was raised in our world, already had her place cemented in Piper's thoughts and mind. Upon her return, it was apparent that she had returned to her place as reigning princess. Piper listened to all of Rebecca's new adventures on the Earth Plane and hung on every word. Rebecca quickly demanded the attention of everyone around, leaving Tina no one to meet her perceived needs. Sumner unhinged Tina's entire world because Tina had thought she was Collin's whole world. In actuality, Collin had always been attracted to Sumner. When she realized their attraction, she looked heartbroken. He was Sumner's constant companion and Tina's entire day was lost in the eyes of Sumner.

Eventually, Collin realized Tina was missing and panicked. Sumner wanted to help us find her, but he saw her as now the reason he had misplaced the most important thing to him. We all understand the compulsion to protect, but he carried it too far and hurt Sumner. I helped him search and found her wandering around the edge of the grounds. She wanted me to go away but I called for Collin and he was very relieved to see her. She played the pouting child well, making him feel guilty. I believe she has decided one day he will be more than a guard to her.

Piper was waiting for us and seemed upset with Collin. Tina had a tantrum screaming that it wasn't his fault. I can only guess she was trying to protect him. She turned on the fake tears, or maybe they were real this time, and began saying they didn't like her anymore. She fell to the ground and continued about being a spoiled brat until the "real" family came home. Piper instantly consoled her. Much to the horror of Rebecca who instantly looked as if the they were to be arch enemies. Collin was waved over to take her to her room and then return. Rebecca and Sumner were told to befriend Tina. Collin was warned about his fate if he should loose her again. I caught Tina peeking from the hall, wearing a huge smile. She had done what she wanted and got them all into trouble and ensured that tomorrow she would no longer be ignored.

All the journal entries were forming a story. There were two girls. Tina, the evil and cruel sister, and Bethany, the girl spared going through the Black Arch, were the grandchildren of the Dweller royalty, Deward and Piper. Tina had made herself at home amongst the Dwellers. I saw that now.

As the story progressed, it was becoming more dreadful. The Dweller writer and I did agree that Tina was evil, cruel, and spoiled. The second girl who didn't get sent to the Dwellers was lucky and didn't know it. The writer had alluded to her having a conscious. The treatment of Grace would bother her as much as it did me.

I couldn't imagine what the author and I had in common or why the journal entries were being left for me. Why were they so important that someone would lure Tilly out? They were going to great lengths to get the notes to me. I understood what I needed to discover my past. The key to this mystery as well as many others had to lie in my past.

CHAPTER ELEVEN

Tilly

"Ready to go to the slaughter," I laughed.

"Oh, it's not funny," Elizabeth sighed. "Professor Zirak really will slaughter me today at brunch. My unfinished assignments are adding up."

"Don't sweat it," I said and then popped a big bubble. "You do know I didn't complete my assignment to observe a Keeper making their life plan, don't you?"

"Yeah, yeah!" Elizabeth said as she tossed her backpack across her back. She had slept with that backpack every night and I was baffled at her reaction to it today. Was I really seeing her hold her breath? Up to this moment, she had always deeply inhaled the putrid smell as if it were some great smelling men's cologne. The problem was, it wasn't. It smelled like rotting garbage! When she noticed my peering eyes, she moved to hold open the door saying, "Grab your stuff and let's go down."

"Hey!" Destiny said as she popped her head through the open door.

Instantly, Elizabeth's eyes shut as her face read the regret of getting caught by Destiny. She wasn't anyone's favorite nosy neighbor. Every week Destiny tried to force Elizabeth to sit next to her at brunch.

"I'm so glad I caught you! We can go down to brunch together! Hope you did your homework this week," Destiny half giggled with a serious undertone. She then paused when she actually looked at Elizabeth who was flush from a lack of air. "Geez! Are you having trouble breathing or something?

Are you asthmatic?"

Even though I knew something wasn't right, I spouted, "Nothing is wrong with Elizabeth!"

"Are you her mother? Is she three and can't talk for herself?" Destiny retorted with her hands crossed across her chest.

"I'm fine!" Elizabeth said to Destiny. Elizabeth let the backpack fall from her back into her hands. Then she stared at it. Anyone watching could see her internal struggle as she said, "Tilly, we can get rid of my backpack. You are right, it stinks!"

"You have been adamant you were keeping it," I contradicted with my eyes focused on her. Feeling taken back with her words, I asked, "Why now?"

"Why get rid of it? It looks new," Destiny interrupted peering at the bag and then sniffing the air.

Elizabeth unhappily replied holding it at arms length, "It's just time."

"Marvin must have realized how much it smells today, huh?" I lightly probed since miss nosy neighbor was standing in the doorway.

"Smell?" Destiny repeated as she leaned over and took a big whiff.

Elizabeth flashed me a forced smile as I added to keep it light in front of Destiny, "Marvin is crazy about you! However, he's dating you not your smelly backpack."

"I get the point!" Elizabeth reminded me, rolling her eyes.

I took the backpack from Elizabeth, opened it, and handed Elizabeth the notebook inside. Being close enough to hold it made my stomach turn. I quickly handed it off to Destiny, "Here you go! It's all yours!"

Elizabeth faltered a little as she looked at Destiny with her backpack. Destiny seemed oblivious as to how much it smelled. She definitely didn't have the nose of a bloodhound. She also seemed unaware of how much the bag smelled either. The bag and her fit well together.

"Seriously? I would love to have it! You really don't mind?" Destiny stated to Elizabeth.

"I can't keep it any longer," Elizabeth mumbled appearing genuinely sorry to see Destiny with it. "Take it!" Then she turned to me and the look on her face read that she had lost her best friend. "Come on, let's go!"

I picked up my notebook and held the door open for Elizabeth to leave the room before myself. I was a little peeved that our nosy neighbor hadn't come to ask me to sit next to her! Girls didn't like me for some reason. I followed Elizabeth and Destiny down the hall, stairs, and past the professors office. Destiny mindlessly chattered on about real life in the Hall of Records. Poor Elizabeth! At some point, she had agreed to go catch some real life, whatever that meant, with Destiny as a ploy to get away from her. However, Destiny was persistent. The whole time Elizabeth's focus was eerily on the backpack hanging on Destiny's shoulder. It was as though it charmed her.

As we entered the common room, I was faced with a huge smiling Kim. Since befriending her, I felt her stuttering had improved. Kim only needed a friend who believed in her. Luckily, my seat was saved right next to her. I moved away from Destiny's relentless chatter to sit next to Kim as she whispered to me, "H... Hello."

"Hey," I replied as I pulled my chair out and plopped down.

Trevor was already seated to my other side and leaned over, "Need to talk about last night?"

Kim leaned over to hear my response. "Nothing worth talking about happened," I stated trying to blow it off.

"You're going to be a great conductress," Trevor whispered with a reassuring grin. He always did his homework.

"Seriously?" I stated. It was time to spin the story my way. "They thought placing me in charge of Harmony would be a punishment. I just bypassed Tiffany. She will be seething." This was the simple truth. She deserved everything she got. "Isn't it fabulous?"

Professor Zirak rushed into the room and tossed a stack of papers on the table in front of him. His demeanor demanded everyone's attention. "Good evening!" He called as he instantly focused in on Elizabeth. "Please pass your extra essays on the life theme of caregiver to me." Papers shuffled from person to person all around the room making their way to Zirak. The papers moved along with eye darts shooting at Elizabeth from all around the table. Everyone was skeptical of whether or not Elizabeth was ready to talk about her life theme. "Miss Cantrell, let's start off by running down your assignments. Are you prepared to discuss your life theme?" Zirak intently stared her down.

Elizabeth sighed, "I'm not."

"In that case, since Miss Cantrell has chosen not to complete her assignment, I will be assigning an additional essay. This week please write on the life theme of the leader!" Zirak stated loudly and in a stout demanding voice.

"Great! Just great!" Shannon exploded. "Why didn't you just do your assignment? You are selfish!"

"Miss Ventine, I won't allow outbursts! Sit down!" Zirak reprimanded. "Please pass your assignment on your individual life plan to me." He watched Elizabeth intently as she sat motionless having nothing to turn in. "Miss Cantrell, are you not prepared to turn in this week's assignment on your life plan?"

"Why are you doing this?" Elizabeth returned as the papers ceased to shuffle. "You and I discussed this last week."

Zirak stood with a stone cold expression and seemed to be contemplating his next move. You could have heard a pin drop as everyone was awaiting his response. "Miss Cantrell, I have been patient with you and given you several weeks to complete the most basic assignments. We will discuss your punishment privately in my office directly after our brunch today." He paused before saying, "I believe your training class will share in your dismay. Every week this training class will write a brief two page essay on a topic of one aspect of the life plan until Miss Cantrell completes her work about her own individual life plan. The topic this week will be your successes."

This was bad! Shannon stood and glared at Elizabeth, "You are so self centered!"

Around the room mouths fell open as Zirak demanded, "Miss Ventine, sit down! I'll see you after brunch as well."

The room fell silent as Zirak began, "Keep passing your life plan assignment, please. In addition, I need your essays on the Keeper which you viewed planning their life plans at the Hall of Babies. Miss Cantrell, tell me you did this assignment!"

"I'm the one who didn't do this assignment!" I loudly stated trying to deflect attention from Elizabeth. I ignored Destiny who loudly huffed and those who groaned imagining the work I was about to cause them.

"Miss Bradford, Professor Kegley explained to me you worked on a special project for her this week," Zirak began. "She said you did a great job but that it was time consuming. You have a free pass this week, a courtesy between professors."

His lack of cracking down on me made me unhappy.

"Thank you," Zirak stated as he stacked up the papers which had been passed to him. "Did all of you take the opportunity to go to the Hall of Babies and view the young man who visited his Earth Plane parents?" Heads nodded from around the table. "This was an opportunity to preview what we will be working on over the next couple of weeks, communicating with the Humlings we are helping."

"Can anyone furnish me a brief description of ways to communicate?" Zirak asked.

"D…D…Dr…Dreams," Kim stuttered. She was so bright and no one knew it because of her stuttering. As she sheepishly glanced my way for approval, I gave her a warm smile.

"Electronic avenues," Destiny chimed in.

"Personal visits," Trevor said. "Both during sleep, as we viewed with the young man, and visits during their waking hours."

"All three are valid ways to communicate. Very good," Zirak complimented. "Can anyone tell me what a Keeper would communicate?" The piano boy raised his hand and Zirak called on him, "Mr. Shepard."

"You communicate information about their life plan," he stated.

Zirak was boring me to tears. I pulled out my notebook and began to doodle while listening.

"Yes," Zirak agreed. "We communicate reminders to help them stay on their earth life's path. We also provide warnings, if they use their free will and stray from their chosen path. However, we never go beyond a warning. They always have free will to make their own choices. After all, life on the Earth Plane is about learning lessons and some of the best lessons are learned from mistakes when we make poor choices."

Elizabeth elbowed me sharply. I turned and mouthed, "What!"

She pointed to the Professor. When I glanced up, I noticed he had paused and was intently watching me before saying, "Miss Bradford, maybe you can tell me how Humlings communicate with us."

"They ask," I replied and rolled my eyes and popped a bubble.

"You need to be specific," Destiny blurted out.

"Is there ever a time when you can't hear them?" Zirak asked.

Was he trying to trick me? I hadn't paid attention to know whether Mrs. VanCues could be heard all the time. "No," I answered guessing.

"Wrong!" Destiny chimed in with a smug grin. "You can't hear them when they pray to God. Those conversations are private."

"Thank you Miss Nabor," Zirak complimented. "Miss Bradford, as I just proved, you don't know everything. You need to pay attention because you are on the bottom of the grading curve."

When Zirak looked away, I stuck my tongue out at Destiny.

"As we saw with the young man who visited his earth parents, the most effective way of communicating is through dreams," Zirak continued. "When a Humling dreams on the Earth Plane, they are most open to our messages. We can answer their requests and give direction. You watched the young man use a dream portal. How many of you have seen the dream portal in your office at the Keeper Complex?"

Nods from all around the table. I looked at Elizabeth who shrugged. She hadn't seen it either. Zirak continued looking in our direction, "If you haven't noticed, it is in your assigned office. Please look on Thursday." He slightly shook his head side to side showing disgust at my apparent lack of knowledge. "The dream portal in your office is generally only used by the Head Keeper assigned to the Humling. Keeping a constant in their dreams enables them to more readily receive the message."

Kim jotted down a note to me, "Family members can visit the other side, can't they?"

I leaned over to say, "Yes."

"Ladies, is there something you would like to share," Zirak inquired.

Kim looked at her feet as she felt embarrassed and put on the spot. She felt the need to answer, "I was ask... ask... asking T... T... Till..."

"She asked me if family members can visit..." I finished for her.

"Of course," Zirak answered. "Family members can schedule a visit to their loved ones at the Hall of Babies. They can use one of their dream portals." He picked up the stack of papers which he brought into brunch with him. "Take one and pass it on. There are three types of dreams."

"Release, Wish, and Prediction," Trevor interrupted.

"Yes," Zirak smiled. "All three are listed on the page that is being passed around. I want each of you to define the three types of dreams this week and give a personal example or one of your Humling that your office is assigned too."

Elizabeth breathed out loudly a sigh of relief.

"In addition, on Thursday and Friday when you are in your assigned office, I want you to locate your dream portal and write a paragraph about how your offices use the portal," Zirak stated and then glanced at us. "I would like you to log five verbal requests the Humling made and the five corresponding answers given to them by the Head Keeper in their dreams." Zirak then asked, "Does anyone have questions about this assignment?" When no one said a word Zirak's hands clamped together while he said, "Great! With the exception of Miss Ventine and Miss Cantrell, brunch is waiting in the kitchen. Ladies, I would like to see you in my office immediately."

Elizabeth jumped up and left the room in a hurry seeming rattled. I followed her lead and was hot on her trail. She walked past the Professors office towards the staircase. I yelled after her, "Where are you going?"

She stopped on the first step leading upstairs groaning, "I explained it all to him over the last couple of weeks," Elizabeth groaned. "Why bother to do it again?"

"You better change your mind and attitude or you'll be at the bottom of the grading curve with me," I informed her.

"You're on the bottom of the curve too?" Trevor asked as he walked up behind us. "What are you doing, Elizabeth, running away?"

"Exactly!" Elizabeth answered.

"That's not a good idea," Trevor said with seriousness to his voice.

With that, Elizabeth huffed and pushed forward up the staircase.

"She should have simply done her assignments," Trevor stated watching her feet disappear.

I disliked keeping secrets from Trevor almost as much as I disliked telling half-truths to Mrs. Summors. Trevor knew she had a memory fog, but he had no idea its extent. Also, he had no idea about the locket she wore around her neck. I wanted to correct him. Her doing her assignments wasn't as simple as he made it sound. She remembered nothing! The only thing stopping me was my owing Elizabeth silence. I pledged not to tell anyone. Then, there was my personal belief that a girl shouldn't tell everything she knew!

"I need to talk to you!" Trevor leaned over and whispered. "May we take a walk?"

"Right now?" I said as I peered up the stairs knowing Elizabeth needed me.

"I'll go up and get Elizabeth, Professor," Destiny yelled as she pushed her way past us. Of course she was anxious to stick her nose in where it didn't belong.

I started to take a step up the stairs to intervene. Trevor lightly placed his hand on my arm saying, "It's important!" I paused as he continued, "It won't take long and Elizabeth is sure to need you more after she gets handed her punishment from Professor Zirak."

He always had a way of being level headed and making sense. "I guess I won't be any use to her while she is being raked over the coals by Zirak. Make it quick?"

Trevor nodded. In silence, I followed Trevor out the door of Keeper House, down the corridor and stairs, across the foyer and out the front door of the Hall of knowledge. I knew him. His uneasy silence meant he had something serious on his mind. Once on the front lawn, I followed him until he sat down under a tree which was secluded by an ivy and rock wall.

"Spit it out," I said as I sat down beside him and leaned my back against the rock wall.

"I need to talk to you about Ruthanne," Trevor solemnly stated.

"Ruthanne?" I repeated. She wasn't exactly what I wanted to talk about today.

"I need a favor," Trevor stated hesitantly.

"I already dumped Harry," I said rolling my eyes. "What does she want today?"

Trevor pulled his legs up in front of him and picked grass between them. "It isn't what Ruthanne wants," Trevor corrected me. "I need you to ask Ruthanne to help you with the organization of the Harmony group." He appeared tense and uncomfortable with his own request.

"Why?" I retorted.

"Do I have to have a reason?" Trevor questioned in return looking uneasy. He forgot how well I knew him. He only got snappy when he didn't want to fully tell me his thoughts.

"You said you need me too," I answered. "So yes, you need a reason. Especially since you want me to trust my new foe Ruthanne with the organizational details of the Harmony group? My necks on the line." I mused while popping a bubble.

"Please do this for me," Trevor said in an exasperated beg and pleading eyes.

"I thought your girlfriend's stunt over her brother was cute," I stated. "I was actually…"

"I already told you how sorry I was," Trevor said interrupting me and looking away. "I was torn over taking her side."

"I already accepted your apology," I reminded him.

"I need you to listen. I've thought about this all night and I have to tell you," Trevor said as he took my shoulders and turned me so I looked directly in his eyes.

"Tell me what?" I questioned feeling jittery about what was about to hit me.

"You know what you mean to me." I started to open my mouth as he spit out, "No Tilly. Listen!" He then looked away. "The thing is Ruthanne makes me happy."

"I already know that," I countered feeling relieved and a hint of regret that I couldn't be the one to make him happy. His happiness was what I cared about and was the reason why I hadn't demanded that he stop dating Ruthanne. I was tolerating their relationship. I quietly called, "Trevor." When he turned to face me, I knew exactly what I felt. "You are not a boy toy like the guys I date. I would never play with you." I also understood what he needed to hear. My permission. "I'm telling you I want you to be happy!"

He smiled and shook his head, "All I have ever wanted for you is happiness!"

I settled my back against the wall and leaned my head over on his arm. He sighed placing his hand on my knee saying, "What are we going to do with each other?"

"We will continue to dance on the edge of the cliff," I answered. We sat in silence enjoying each others closeness. No one understood us like we understood each other. We had made the best decision for us both. As much as each of us desired to make the other happy, we weren't going to make the dive off the cliff together. I would continue to tolerate Ruthanne and he would continue to tolerate my dating. "I suppose you want out of the middle?"

"It would be much easier if you would make an effort to make friends with Ruthanne," Trevor stated. "You and I are forever. However, forever would be more pleasant if you and Ruthanne were friends and not enemies in the present."

"It's still asking a lot," I said raising my head to look at him. It wasn't the end of the world though. "I will ask Ruthanne to be my right hand woman!" Trevor flashed me a thankful grin. "I have to ask if you believe Tiffany and Janelle will get to her. I can't afford any hint of sabotage concerning Harmony!"

"You will quickly find the two of you have common ground in regards to your feelings about them," Trevor seriously stated.

That was yet to be proven to me.

CHAPTER TWELVE

Elizabeth

As I threw myself on my bed, upset, I instantly regretted giving Destiny my backpack yesterday. After my first day of punishment, I needed the intoxicating scent of Dustin. It would have been a great comfort as I sprawled upon my bed intent on having a good cry. I still felt the desire to deeply inhale the strong scent and let it take me away to daydreaming of him. Getting away from my new punishment even for a moment might be worth being totally lost in Dustin's scent.

What a mistake I had made! Even Tilly believed my letting go of the backpack was strange. It was written all over her face. I couldn't tell her I had made the decision to let go of Dustin. He wasn't mine and never would be. Why pine away after him when Marvin and I were made for each other. If Marvin and I were so perfect, how could I be thinking of Dustin? Just as the smell of the backpack had enticed me, I also realized that in Dustin's presence I would still be overwhelmingly drawn to him. My obsession hit me in the face. What was I going to do? The tears began to roll down my cheeks when I heard the door open.

Depressed, I ignored it. If it were the note leaving Dweller, he could have me this evening.

"That bad, huh?" Tilly questioned breaking into my world of self despair.

"Basically, my new part time job sucks!" I mumbled as the tears continued to roll down my face and I wiped its mess on the back of my hand. "The couple hours I have to spend in the Hall of Records filing every day is unbearable."

"Shannon is that bad to be around?" Tilly asked sitting down on the bed edge next to me.

"I can't even put it into words," I replied flopping over and pulling my pillow over my head to try to hide my misery.

"Marvin stopped by earlier," Tilly stated. "I sent him over your way. Did he pop in?"

More tears streamed down my face as I thought of the scene which unfolded earlier. "He did," I said with a sucked in loud sniffle. "Mrs. Summors replacement rudely informed Marvin that I was working and that work hours were not social time. She chased him off telling him he would need an appointment to see me and the earliest opening would be in ten days."

Tilly moved to sit on her bed, watching me as the tears once more rolled down my cheeks in despair.

I asked her, "Just let me have a minute, would you?"

Tilly shook her head and slowly moved to rummage through her closet tossing clothes upon her bed. Apparently, she was planning her outfit for her evening date. If Tilly were in my shoes there would be no tears. Tilly should be a roll model for anyone down and out. There was no punishment anyone could impose on her that she couldn't take in stride. Nothing fazed her. Here I was crying over my pitiful day. Tilly wouldn't cry. She would figure out a way to use the time at the Hall of Records to benefit her. She would have a plan!

If Tilly were me, she would use her time to get dirt on Tiffany. She was so rotten she was bound to have a few skeletons in her closet. Tilly would find them if she had access and time to dig. She would read books, chapters, or anything that was restricted, just for bragging rights that she had done so. She would have an angle for using any information to aid her in a huge plot of some kind. Then she would rope Trevor into going along and build whatever was necessary. I couldn't help but giggle through my tears at his willingness to follow Tilly's every move.

"You're giggling?" Tilly asked breaking up my thoughts. "First crying, now giggling?"

"I was thinking about what you would do if you were spending as much time as I am in the Hall of Records," I replied.

"First, I would break all the rules," Tilly smiled with a devious grin. "You need to embrace the concept of throwing caution to the wind and using opportunities presented to you. I would figure out a way to make anyone who stood in my way pay for doing so. Like Miss come back in ten days!"

"That is pretty much what I was thinking you would say," I replied with a slight smile forgetting to cry for a moment.

Tilly's confident smile at the thought, turned into a worried look, "Don't sweat it! We will figure something out." She turned back to delving in her closet continuing, "We will either get you out of hot water or get Shannon into more so her punishment will change and she will be yanked up and threw into a deeper punishment pit!"

"My lack of memory has caused this!" I interrupted. Tilly turned to intently stare at me. "The only way out of all of this mess is to figure out who I really am." I sat up on the side of my bed.

"Don't do anything drastic," Tilly warned holding a pink tiny T-shirt up to herself and then discarding it.

I plopped my head back down on my pillow smiling inside. Of all the people to tell me not to do something drastic, it wasn't thrill seeking Tilly. She lived on the edge and most of what she did could be viewed as drastic.

As if someone had hit me over the head, my path was suddenly clear. I would use my daily time at the Hall of Records to look up Elizabeth Kaswell. I felt the locket around my neck coolly caressing my skin. The locket had become part of my daily routine without my giving it much thought over the last couple of weeks. I closed my eyes and could see the initials E.M.K. engraved just inside the locket and opposite of the picture of me with my family. Certainty was the one word describing how positive I was that Elizabeth Kaswell and Elizabeth Cantrell were one in the same. Both names described me. I only needed to be able to prove it to uncover my past.

Tilly seemed content, after unloading half her closet, with her final choice as she moved to the window. Peering out she asked, "I have to ask you. Did you cut the ladder yesterday so I wouldn't leave you alone last night?"

Even though I hadn't, what a great idea! I simply hadn't thought about. I truthfully answered, "Of course I didn't."

"I hope you understand I had to ask!" Tilly stated as she pulled off her favorite high heeled boots. "You spend so much time worrying we aren't safe, you are starting to make me a little skittish."

I wanted to scream at her that we weren't safe! However, that would lead down a path I wasn't ready to take. My hand delivered journal entries were still mine, and mine alone. Tilly would sense their danger and I feared what she might do. I smiled as her word, drastic, popped into my head. She would do something drastic if she read the notes contents!

Tilly moved to primp in the mirror. We still had Harmony practice to go to. She usually waited till afterwards to primp for her dates. I had to ask, "Aren't you getting date ready early?"

"Oh no," she replied. "I've canceled practice tonight."

"Professor Presnell just let you cancel it?" I questioned in shock at her action. What was Tilly thinking? We were already neck deep in trouble and about to drown.

Tilly just shrugged her shoulders with a smile which read it wasn't that simple.

"Did you ask Professor Presnell at some point today?" I inquired.

"No," Tilly answered as she moved to her makeup table. "You were with me all day! We sat and listened to Presnell drone on like a broken record about the workings of the Council, remember?"

Tilly may have thought she droned on. However, I found the topic of great interest. I could visualize the two girls from the journal going before the Council of six Keepers and three Humlings with the children's future depending on their decision. The tale was intriguing with one ending badly and well for the other.

In my opinion, Professor Presnell hadn't gone into enough detail. I had questions about the Black Arch, myself. There were two arches. The Council controlled one that I was aware of. According to the journal, the Dwellers controlled the other, my new interest. I asked, "Could you refresh my memory? Today, I didn't hear Professor Presnell say a lot about the Black Arch. Could you tell me what you know about it?"

"What about it?" Tilly asked.

"Are there two Black Arches?" I asked getting straight to the point.

"I have never heard of anything like that!" Tilly stated inquisitively peering at me.

"Hmm…" I hummed. She sat at her makeup table staring at me in her mirror, leading me to change the subject before she started asking questions. "Professor Presnell isn't likely to be happy that you canceled practice."

"Throw caution to the wind!" Tilly reminded me still studying me. I could tell she had filed my odd question about two arches away in the depths of her memory. She added, "Don't be a worry wart!"

"I'm sure they didn't put you in charge so that you could cancel practice," I mumbled a protest. "If we don't make Harmony succeed we are toast!"

"I'm going to see White Crew in a pop up club tonight," Tilly stated as she returned to staring at herself in the mirror. "I told Professor Kegley I was researching new music. Kegley can worry about Presnell."

"Clubbing is hardly research," I mumbled.

"That is a matter of opinion," Tilly replied. "You should take the opportunity to sneak out and see Marvin tonight. You look like you need a diversion to take your mind off your problems." She turned with a hopeful grin, "I would be happy to do another makeover!"

I cringed when I thought of how fake I looked last time. I was lucky to have an excuse. "Marvin is coaching the kid's basketball with Jessie tonight," I replied. "They have a game." I peered at the open window. "The ladder is fixed?"

"Yeah, Trevor took care of it," Tilly matter of fact stated rising from her primping. "Want to go with me?"

"Be a third wheel with whatever guy will be accompanying you?" I returned. "No, I'll be fine here."

Tilly seemed a little disappointed that I wasn't going along for the ride tonight. She bit her lip slightly when she was disappointed. Returning to finish her primping, she dropped the subject. My staying in this room alone wasn't really going to be comfortable. Unfortunately, I would be awake when she left and when she came back. Sleep deprivation was becoming my friend.

CHAPTER THIRTEEN

Trevor

Where was she? I had sat awaiting Tilly's return home for hours. I glanced at the clock on Eddie's bedside table. It was only 3:00 A.M. Tilly was likely to be another couple of hours. I was edgy. Eddie was lucky to be wired to be able to sleep no matter what was going on around him. Nothing ever worried him enough to have a sleepless night.

I heard a soft knock and a muffled voice, "Trevor."

I moved to open the door and peeked my head out. Elizabeth was nervously standing in the middle of the dimly lit hall. I stepped out and peered down the boy's hall and luckily all the other doors were closed. No one was watching! I grabbed her by the hand and pulled her into my room. As I shut the door I inquired, "What are you doing here at this time of night?"

"Sorry to barge in on you," Elizabeth began as she looked around the room in a small turn. "You did tell me once to come up anytime I needed to talk." She faintly smiled at me hoping I would remember my offer. "I really need a favor."

"You must to chance getting caught on the boy's floor," I said under my breath. "You look exhausted. Why aren't you sleeping?"

"You're obviously not sleeping either!" Elizabeth countered pointing to my unmade bed.

I picked up a book on my desk stating, "I was reading."

Elizabeth sat on the edge of my bed asking, "May I ask you to do something for me, but not tell anyone I asked you to do it?"

I pulled out the chair to my desk, sat, and waited for her to begin. Elizabeth was hard to figure out. At times she had guts of steel and at other times she put off this hurt puppy persona. As the silence drug on, I felt like a shrink waiting for Elizabeth to spill the beans about what was on her mind.

"I want to know about the Black Arch but I don't have guts enough to ask," she blurted out.

I certainly hadn't expected that to subject to pop from her mouth. She must have had questions after Professor Presnell's lecture today. Elizabeth was always inquisitive about how things worked. "You want me to ask in class today?" I questioned.

"Please!" Elizabeth begged.

"Why?" I asked.

"You're the only one of us that sits on the good side that Professor Presnell teaches. Haven't you noticed she doesn't answer questions for the bad side of the class?" Elizabeth answered.

"I believe Professor Presnell calls it the un-trainable side," I corrected.

"Either way it boils down to the bad side of class," Elizabeth sighed.

"What exactly do you want to know?" I asked trying to narrow down a large topic before deciding whether or not to agree.

"Well… We all know the Council can send us there. The thing is I don't understand how the Dwellers work. How do they travel back and forth? What if my Humling meets one on the Earth Plane? What will I do?"

"Have you asked Marvin?" I questioned thinking he was more knowledgeable than myself.

"No," Elizabeth shortly answered dropping her head and blinking her puppy dog eyes at me.

"And why not?" I countered.

"Marvin is so over protective," Elizabeth sighed. "He would throw a fit if he thought I wanted information about Dwellers. Like my learning about them could bring harm to me."

"If Marvin is reluctant, he must have a reason," I stated tipping back on the rear two legs of my chair in a balancing act as I studied her.

"Only that he is an overprotective boyfriend!" Elizabeth said under her breath as Eddie rolled over in his bed.

Okay," I responded to move the conversation along. I wanted to get back to my place as guard at the window. "I'll ask."

Elizabeth flung her arms around my neck causing the back of the chair to roughly hit the desk. "Thank you!"

Eddie rolled over and his head lifted from his pillow. The thud had alarmingly waked him. "Crash? Wow, when did this all happen?" He questioned with a smirk. Then, he rolled his body over clearly wanting to block us out. He placed his ear buds in. "Sorry to interrupt." Then he chuckled. "Wait till Ruthanne finds out. Man, your chick problems are growing."

With that Elizabeth appeared to have realized what her being in our room with her arms wrapped around my neck must look like. She moved towards the door. I quickly stepped in front of her. Eddie finding her was one thing. He was simply poking fun at me and would never breathe a word of her visit to anyone. Someone else discovering her was another situation all together. I began, "You're welcome to stay as long as you want, however you can't leave by the hall. There is too much of a chance you will get caught."

"Then how will I get back down to my room?" Elizabeth questioned.

I pointed towards the window with a cocky grin. Elizabeth sighed, "You fixed the ladder again."

"Yup," I stated as I moved to look out the window at the ladder which was awaiting Tilly's arrival. "That's my job!"

"It's you job?" Elizabeth asked shaking her head. "Do you personally ever use it for more than coming down to our room?"

"No, it's basically all for Tilly," I stated knowing that I supplied the ladder so she could date. Her serial dating was my fault. I could never make her fully happy. Sometimes I wondered what there was about me that was lacking.

"You never use it to sneak off with Ruthanne?" Elizabeth questioned as she scooted across my bed to peer out the window and down.

"No!" I quickly answered. "Ruthanne doesn't share Tilly's overwhelming need for adventure. She's quiet, kind, and nurturing." I couldn't help but think to myself she was also vulnerable and defenseless most of the time. However, Ruthanne had no idea how beautiful she was. "Ruthanne likes to follow the rules. She wouldn't dream of going on a date with me if she knew I had sneaked out to see her or after curfew." I paused and thought about how the two of them couldn't be more opposite! Tilly was loud, independent, assertive, comfortable in her own skin, and strong minded not caring what others thought of her. I found myself speaking my mind when I said, "Tilly on the other hand is a force to reckon with. You know her well enough by now to know you can't cage her."

"Very true," Elizabeth agreed shaking her head.

"If she didn't have the ladder, she would definitely find a different way to escape," I chuckled. "I prefer to know she is leaving and arriving safely."

"So, you keep her escape route in working order for her," Elizabeth surmised.

"Like I said, that's my job," I repeated wondering why I was telling Elizabeth this. "I need to know she won't resort to more drastic measures. However, you take the cake using the boy's hall to come here." I paused and shot Elizabeth a smug grin. "It's my job to watch over her, not you!"

"You better not let her hear you say that," Elizabeth stated straightening her ponytail and considering what courage it would take to step out a third floor window and mount that ladder.

"I know," I agreed moving to sit on the side of my bed by the window. "It really isn't you cutting the ladder, is it?"

"No," Elizabeth replied once again looking out the window. "Watching Tilly pace last night racking her brain about how to get out was nerve wrecking." Elizabeth seemed deep in thought. I understood. Watching Tilly backed into a corner was scary since you never could predict her fight or flight response.

I pulled out Tilly's black and white checked skater shoes and a small container of polish. If I went ahead and finished my project, I could send them down with Elizabeth and not have to sneak the shoes back into Tilly's shoe rack.

"What are you doing with Tilly's shoes?" Elizabeth questioned.

"Putting shoe goo on them!" I responded as I opened the small container and began to rub the invisible polish on the bottom of Tilly's shoes. "It helps her feet stick to the board."

"She couldn't put this on herself?" Elizabeth asked. When I didn't respond, she blurted out, "You are the one who took care of her on the Earth Plane, aren't you?"

I sighed realizing Elizabeth knew too much already! I didn't want to discuss the details of our life together on the Earth Plane. If Tilly wanted her to know, she would tell her. However, with Elizabeth, if you didn't answer her, she would dig. "When I came into her life on the Earth Plane, I did my best to have her back. We grew up here at home together as children. Our bond has transcended our two worlds leading to our unique friendship here and on the Earth Plane. I have no regrets."

Elizabeth seemed to speak her thoughts as she said, "You are still on duty at your post. Only now your post is now your window."

"Exactly," I agreed. "With the ladder, I know she is safe in her bed at night."

"You stay up," Elizabeth asked in astonishment.

I now had clearly said too much. "I have never admitted that out loud to anyone before!" I said as I stood. It was time for Elizabeth to go to her own room.

"I'm not going to tell anyone!" Elizabeth stood assuring me. "You wouldn't want Tilly to find that little tid bit of information out. That would be like your father waiting up for you. She doesn't like to feel caged!"

"You are right," I agreed. I guess that's why I let myself admit all of this to Elizabeth. "You know her well enough not to tell her." I paced a few steps at the foot of the two beds and continued, "Tilly assumes the bell wakes me. However, I am a sound sleeper. I sit up and study at night. Once I know she is in, I pull the ladder up. Then I go to bed."

Elizabeth seemed deep in thought before saying, "You're her angel whom she doesn't know she has!"

"Elizabeth," I stated. "I thought you knew me. I am no angel." I walked to the window and pushed it open. "Being no angel, I think it's time that you head back down."

"Oh!" Elizabeth said. "Well... Okay." She moved to the window and stopped straddling the window seal. "You will ask tomorrow, right?"

"I will," I replied to her relieved smile. "Good night."

"Good night!" Elizabeth happily said until she looked over the edge and hesitated.

I watched her slowly slide over to place her legs on the rungs of the ladder and cling to the window seal with her white knuckles. I had a new realization of why Elizabeth took such a dangerous route to my room. She must be scared of heights. I held the ladder and tried my best to steady it as it moved from side to side as she slowly made her way down. Then the top of her head disappeared through their window, directly below mine.

I settled back into my chair feeling tired and worn out. Then I began to read….

My book fell to the wooden floor with a deep thud awaking me from my sleep. I peered around the room. Eddie was still sleeping. The light was still on and the ladder still out. The sunrise was in full effect as I turned to catch the time. 6:57 A.M. I had fallen asleep! Not only had I not known when of if Tilly came in, I was late getting to my early morning appointment.

My only saving grace was that I was still dressed. I pulled the ladder up securing it beside my window. I shut the window as Eddie was waking, "Dude, was Tilly out all night?"

"No," I sighed as I pushed my stuff inside my backpack.

"Didn't you tell me you'd be gone this morning when I got up?" Eddie asked.

"I fell asleep late and overslept," I answered.

"Crashed huh," Eddie said as he set up rubbing and scratching his chest in male fashion. "What was up with Elizabeth?"

"She needed a favor!" I said as I slung the backpack over my back. "I'm late, can we talk later?"

Eddie grinned a smug grin, "Later."

I darted through Keeper House and the Hall of Knowledge as quickly as I could since I was almost too late. If I waited another entire day, I thought I might just loose my nerve. My plan for taking on the Queen herself was a huge gamble. Once outside, I dropped my board to the ground and rode away.

Watching the scene after our stunt the other night, I knew Mr. and Mrs. Bradford had thrown in the towel and were ready to wash their hands of Tilly. My suspicions were correct. Mrs. Bradford was willing to let Tilly go before the Council. She was done. Mr. Bradford would follow Mrs. Bradford's lead when it came right down to it. Although it went without saying, Tilly had never lied about her parent's lack of true concern for her.

No one knew that I was a self made spy who was listening. I parked myself in the massive testing room across the foyer from Professor Presnell's office. Eddie and I had set up a bugging device in Professor Presnell's red decorated office on our first night at the Hall of Knowledge. The only complication was that the radio receiver had to be close to the device to pick up what was being said. We couldn't use it from Keeper House. A limitation Eddie and I intended to work out at some point. However, it worked well enough to let me listen to the conversation taking place in Professor Presnell's office.

I heard Tiffany's dramatic acting. Helplessly listening to Tilly spout the truth about Tiffany, I was even more spurred on to enact the plan that Eddie and I had in place. Tiffany deserved what she had coming.

I had believed, as did everyone else, that Tilly only wanted the solo parts to knock Tiffany out of them. When I saw her spilling the beans to Rhett about her mother choosing Tiffany over her, I knew she had bluffed us all. Tilly was hurt about her mother's actions. Her mother hadn't gifted her with that fancy new robe which she was so excited about. It had been a gift from Marvin who obtained her and Elizabeth both one. I saw the disappointment on her face about this as well. To top it all off, I listened to Mrs. Bradford not stand up for Tilly when it was important to do so in Professor Presnell's office. The problem with all of this was that Tilly, deep down, wanted a relationship with her mother. I would not stand by, knowing this, and not take action. No one would hurt Tilly so deeply, not as long as I was around.

This is how I found myself on my collision path with Mrs. Bradford. I entered my familiar childhood neighborhood, Pine Hills. I was declaring war on the Queen. When in war, you had to have a good weapon. I knew Tilly's Aunt Isobelle couldn't stand her mother, something about them getting into it during training. What better place to start to dig up dirt. What I found, though, was beyond the realm of what I believed even the Queen was capable of.

It was so painful that breathing a word of it to Tilly would unravel her whole world. I went straight to Dad to ask his opinion about the whole situation. Dad's warning that I should tell Tilly just kept ringing in my ears. He left the final decision, to tell or not to tell, up to me. He would respect my decision either way. I did try to take his advice the other night. However, when I looked into her eyes, I knew I couldn't be the one that delivered the blow. She simply meant too much to me to hurt her so badly. When I lost my guts, I played it off like I wanted to talk about Ruthanne. Although this conversation needed to be had as well, it was by far less important.

It now made sense to me why her mother treated her like she did and why Mr. Bradford ignored her in most circumstances. I made an alternate plan and now knew exactly why Mrs. Bradford would cave to it. Dad wasn't likely to agree with my decision to not tell Tilly, but he would be disappointed in my blackmailing Mrs. Bradford. Regardless though, my mind was made up. Mrs. Bradford should pay Tilly for her nightmare of a childhood. You reap what you sow.

Tilly's house was a spacious, colonial home with a series of six white pillars lining the front. The property surrounding the grand house was enclosed by a wrought iron fence and completely cold and bare. No trees, grass, or hint of anything living in the yard was to be seen. Only well manicured rock gardens. Long ago Tilly and I had named this spatial home, Ice Castle. I made my way to the door realizing this was my first time to step foot on this property alone. This was an non-welcoming place.

I knocked as hard as my fist could bang on the door, expending some nervous energy. The door creaked open to reveal a disheveled Mrs. Bradford. She was still in her robe, wore fuzzy house slippers, and stood with drooping curlers in her hair.

"Mr. Stillholm, what do you want at this early hour," Mrs. Bradford asked half asleep in a confused stare.

"I need to talk with you about Tilly," I stated. "May I come in?"

"Oh great! What did she do now?" Mrs. Bradford asked with a sigh motioning for me to come in. "Whatever it is, I don't want the neighbors hearing!"

I moved through the door stating, "Does it have to be she did something?"

"You still have on those rose colored glasses," Mrs. Bradford stated. "Why are you still wasting your time pining away after her? Even though she will one day be stuck with you, she didn't want you on the Earth Plane and doesn't really want you now!"

"Our relationship is complicated," I stated pausing. "It is clearly something you don't understand. However, our relationship is not why I am here!"

"Then what do you wish to talk about?" Mrs. Bradford inquired. "My relationship with my daughter?"

"Exactly! You need to improve your relationship with Tilly. Actually, your going to start being nice. You are going to take Tilly shopping because she likes to shop and do mother daughter things. You are going to support her every endeavor!" I growled at Mrs. Bradford as I invaded her space, standing in her face. She backed across the room.

"She has Elizabeth for that!" Mrs. Bradford screeched back at me. "My dream would be to disown Mathilda."

"You may not want her, but she wants you!" I countered in a raised voice. "You are even going to be nice to Elizabeth!"

"Your threatening demeanor isn't enough to make me do anything," Mrs. Bradford said. "I'll just ring for security and you are out of here. I'll have Mr.

Bradford ensure you go before the Council."

"I haven't threatened you yet," I warned her. "Let me ask. You prize your social status, don't you?" With no response I sat down in her floral chair. "You are married to Mr. Bradford and he provides the social status which you enjoy. You have no great social background on your own. You climbed the ladder using him. You are a parasite!"

"Get out Trevor," Mrs. Bradford said as she headed for the door.

"You should sit down because we are going to talk!" I stated. "Imagine what your life would be without Mr. Bradford if he suddenly had a change of heart over your finely kept secret."

"Get to the point or get out!" Mrs. Bradford demanded still standing holding the door open.

"I understand the night before you married Mr. Bradford you made a rash decision!" I stated. "I know all the details!"

Her hand and arm on the door knob went limp. She made her way to the couch like a robot and sat down. She stared off into space and for the first time ever was speechless. "How did you find out?"

"I didn't know if it was true until your reaction now!" I began. "I started digging when you hurt Tilly by supporting Tiffany for the solos."

"Why do you want to unravel my life?" She asked. "It is Tilly who is the problem and always has been. She's trash!"

"I could care less about your opinion or life beyond Tilly needing you," I stated. "This is the deal. I will keep your secret. In return, you will be the mother Tilly has always dreamed of having. You will be there in every way. Lastly, you will keep our deal a secret. Take it or leave it! Otherwise I will go straight to your husband."

"You're not worried that I might beat you to it and go tell Tilly and Mr. Bradford myself," Mrs. Bradford asked testing me.

"You are a selfish, manipulating, self centered woman. You and I both know the social scene to you is more important than Tilly or Mr. Bradford.

You won't rock your boat!" I spewed.

"Get out!" Mrs. Bradford yelled at the top of her lungs.

I calmly stood and sauntered to the door taunting her, "I'll see you at Harmony practice this evening."

"Right!" Mrs. Bradford sarcastically retorted.

"Oh I'll see you! You would surely want to support your daughter on her first night as conductress. I suggest you bring her the multi-flavor pack of gum from that specialty shop in The City!" I replied walking past her as she held the door open for me to exit. I placed my hand squarely on the door telling her over my shoulder, "The choice is yours, Harmony or Pine Hill Country Club. The country club will be packed tonight and make a great audience for me to use the mike and tell Mr. Bradford and all your friends your dirty little secret!"

I took one more step out and she slammed the door behind me. I couldn't help but grin thinking I had won. I dethroned the Queen. My only regret is not being able to share this win with Tilly. She would have loved this moment. Mrs. Bradford was no longer the untouchable adult.

Perfectly happy with myself, I strolled down the old neighborhood towards my own home. All the houses were stately along this far end of the golf course. My family home was here first. All the other homes grew up around it when we were enclosed in the dome. We were the only Keepers living amongst the Administration crowd who loved the golf course and the country club.

My family home was a two story Victorian with a huge front porch. As I walked up the sidewalk I couldn't miss the old familiar toys happily reclaiming their spot in the yard and on the porch. Baby Henry had arrived and the toys were already awaiting him to play. My parents saved everything. Eddie and I had all the toys in the world to play with on that huge porch. Now they were Henry's. I chuckled when I thought about the ritzy neighbors who complained and complained about all the toys saying they were eye sores.

Setting on the steps was my favorite toy. I loved that faded, rusted, metal, yellow dump truck. The day of its arrival would forever be etched into my memory because it attracted a small, spit fire, toe head blond girl to it. Eddie and I were happily digging holes in the yard, scooping dirt into the back of the dump truck, and making a mountain under our favorite tree. Our boy's only tree was complete with a tire swing which we couldn't yet reach the seat. We were building a ramp.

While methodically working on our mountain which would lead to the swing's seat, neither of us noticed the small girl who was standing watching us. She interrupted, shaking her head, saying, "Boys. You're never going to reach that tire swing, even if you dig to China."

I was always the leader and couldn't believe someone would dare question my brilliant plan.

"Why don't you just stand on your wagon?" She simply asked while pointing at our perfectly good red wagon parked under the next tree. "Besides, I need that dump truck to hold my princess." She held out two gross looking dolls dressed all in pink. "Don't worry, those holes you dug we can use them as lakes, pools, or maybe a hot spa for my princess. Ooo, better yet, they can be alligator pits to toss the mean villain into."

"You have a villain too?" I asked.

"No silly, whoever doesn't do what I say is the villain," she matter of fact said like we were crazy. Then she boldly stated, "I'm Tilly and this is Princess Apple and her Maiden Peach." Tilly pointed directly at me, "You can be the chauffeur…"

"He's Trevor and I'm Eddie," Eddie piped up.

"Nice to meet you," Tilly curtly said. "Want a piece of gum?" She held up the gum adding, "I'll give you a piece if you do what I want."

"What is it you want?" Eddie asked.

"You are going to play dolls with me," Tilly matter of fact stated with a devilish grin.

I couldn't help recall that all our Tilly-Trevor madness began that day. Mom took Tilly down the street to find her home once dark fell. As I climbed the couple steps to the porch, I recalled how many times Tilly had also ascended the couple steps to visit during the years of our childhood. They were as many as I had chauffeured those ugly dolls around! From the beginning, Tilly was the apple of my eye and we always played what she wanted. I opened the front door, almost bumping into my Dad. "Hey dad!"

"Hello, son!" Dad said giving me a happy hug and a couple slaps on the back. "Why aren't you at training?"

"Just needed a home-cooked breakfast!" I stated sniffing, hoping for the smell of something delicious.

"Good luck," Dad said as he held up his brown paper bag. "No bacon! The baby cried all night and I'm late to work. Your Mom slept in, so muffins it is!"

"Nothing hot?" I huffed.

"Not today," Dad said. He looked me squarely in the eye. "Everything okay with Tilly?"

"I've decided I'm not telling her," I replied.

"I gave you my opinion," Dad hesitated with clearly more to say.

"Look who the cat drug in," Sis stated. "You're here. You can hold him while I change."

She held the baby out and I settled him awkwardly into my arms trying to remember the whole time to balance his head. Had they forgot that I adamantly refused to hold him the last time I was home? He was breakable!

Dad answered my worried face, "Don't worry and rock him a little if he wakes up. See you later."

I watched helplessly as Dad left me standing with the baby in my arms. I wandered into the kitchen hoping to pawn Henry off on anyone awake. My stomach growled with the thoughts of eggs and bacon. I hadn't expected to be baby rocking. I found Mom with her back to me stuffing clothes into the washer. I called, "Mom."

"Trevor!" Mom exclaimed as she moved to half hug me around Henry.

"I came in hopes of having breakfast!" I stated.

"Sorry, we overslept this morning," Mom sighed. "I'll get you a bag and throw in some muffins." Mom moved to pour herself a cup of coffee, oblivious to my awkwardness with Henry.

"Where is everyone?" I questioned.

"Sleeping, I suppose." Mom paused before seriously saying, "Honey, I'm glad you came by. I have something to talk to you about!"

"I'll take Henry now," Sis said as she reappeared holding her hands out for the baby. She focused her goofy grin on the baby saying in baby talk, "There's my itsy bitsy muffin boy!"

"Yuck!" I said in protest as the baby spit up in the transition. "That's just sick!" I added as the white, sour, smelly goo dripped from my hand.

"Get over it," Mom said as she handed me a tea towel to wipe my hand.

"Disgusting!" I said under my breath as I instantly wiped it away with the towel. I moved to wash my hand in the kitchen sink.

"Anyway," Mom said putting a few muffins in a brown paper bag for me. "I met your Ruthanne." My eyes darted to hers. Mom held up her hands, "By accident. Totally by accident. Don't look at me like that. Anyway, she was having lunch with her Mom at her Mom's desk when I went to file my paperwork at the Administration Complex. She introduced herself to me. She is so polite and… nice."

"Did you expect my girlfriend not to be nice?" I inquired.

"You never told us you were into red heads," Sis teased me.

"The thing is…" Mom hesitated as she glanced my sisters way. "You can't date both Ruthanne and Tilly."

"Mom, he doesn't want to talk to you about all the women in his love life!" Sis added cringing and making a face.

"Okay, time to run!" I muttered. Sis was right that this was not a conversation I wanted to have with Mom.

Mom stopped to look at me directly and inquired, "Are you dating Ruthanne to make Tilly jealous?"

"Tilly and I are only friends!" I corrected her.

Sis snorted a little at my comment saying, "Better watch out, red heads usually have a temper over their men."

Mom gave her a disapproving look and then she turned to me, "You do know that Tilly is like one of our children. Your Dad and I love her like a daughter. We've been there for her whenever she needed us."

"I know!" I agreed. "I appreciate it and so does she."

"I just think it's not nice to toy with Ruthanne's affections!" Mom stated as she went back to filling the paper bag.

I could feel my irritation growing as I proposed in a raised voice, "You think its okay for Tilly to date others, but it's not okay for me to do the same?"

The baby gave a whimper after my raised harsh outburst. My Sis focused in on me with her tired eyes, clearly irritated for waking the baby, saying, "Crying out loud, just commit to Tilly already! It is your place to ask! Don't get irritated at us for Tilly's dating habits."

The truth was Tilly always had a spot in our household, with or without me. Tilly and I both understood our relationship. Why couldn't others? I questioned in return, "Why can't anyone believe we are just friends?"

"Honey, the two of you have always been thick as thieves. After the Earth Plane..." Mom sighed. "I can't help but wonder if there is anyplace for Ruthanne in your life. You do no the saying, two is company and three is a crowd. And what about the Council?" Mom handed me the brown paper bag adding, "All I'm asking is that if you are ready to commit to Tilly, then let Ruthanne go!"

I would rather rock the baby than stand here talking about my love life with Mom and my sister for even a moment longer. Both of them were giving me a look that said they thought I wasn't being truthful with them. Time to go! "Mom thanks for the muffins," I said shaking the bag slightly. I leaned over and kissed her on the cheek. "Love you."

"Love you," Mom replied.

I slightly waved goodbye to my face making Sis who was too engrossed in the baby now to really pay attention.

CHAPTER FOURTEEN

Trevor

I strolled into the lions den for the second day this week. Since we were covering the Council, class at the Hall of Records had been canceled to allow for the two day session with Professor Presnell. She was busily giving her lecture to the trainable side of the class. Feeling Ruthanne's staring eyes, I tried to not pay attention to Tilly as she blew me a flirtatious kiss when I passed. Eddie had his ear buds in and Elizabeth was straining to hear and attempting to take notes. Presnell didn't notice me until I walked into her line of sight. Like a cat pouncing she demanded, "Where have you been?"

"I'm sorry I was late," I quickly and seriously apologized. Then I took my place at the desk beside Ruthanne.

Presnell intently glared at me from behind those hideous red glasses, before countering, "Did you not hear my question, or are you choosing not to answer it?"

"I had trouble sleeping last night!" I told her. It was telling the truth without telling the whole truth.

"Mr. Stillholm, you better acquire a descent alarm clock to wake you!" Presnell scolded me. She then walked over to Eddie, on the un-trainable side of class, who was lost in his music and doodling. He never saw her coming. Elizabeth tapped him on the shoulder. When he looked up he saw the professor and took out his ear buds. "Mr. Eddie Stillholm! You are to ensure you bring your room mate, the other Stillholm, with you each time you come to my class," demanded Presnell confiscating his ear buds.

Eddie looked at me oblivious to what had gone on before the professor demanded his attention. I shook my head slightly yes. Eddie caught my suggestion and agreed, "Yes, ma'am."

Presnell glared at him before turning to walk away to continue her lecture.

When I glanced the other way, Ruthanne was watching me. I grinned at her as she sheepishly returned the smile. As she gave me that amazing smile, I knew why the other girls picked on her. With her long flowing red hair, perfect skin, and natural curves, she was a goddess. I understood why the other girls were jealous of her natural beauty. Her best feature was her soft, quiet demeanor. She was very down to earth and easy to talk to. I trusted her, but I didn't deserve her. I didn't feel I was her equal because I had secrets.

Ruthanne interrupted my thoughts of her. She sighed and pointed towards the un-trainable side of the room. I turned to see Elizabeth inquisitively peering at me. I could read her mind. She was waiting for me to ask her questions.

"Excuse me," I interrupted raising my hand.

"Mr. Stillholm!" Presnell reluctantly acknowledged my raised hand. Her hands flew to her hips while she tapped her foot impatiently.

"Professor, can you tell me about the Black Arch?" I asked as I caught a glance of shock on Ruthanne's face.

"First your late, then you ask me about the Black Arch!" Presnell pointedly stated. "Are you not taking my class seriously?"

I began to answer, "Yes..."

"Unless you have a good reason for asking," Presnell interrupted. "I will move you over there!" Presnell pointed to the un-trainable side of the room.

"I simply wanted to know how Dwellers travel," I responded.

I noticed the room suddenly felt icy and tense as though I had asked about the great unpardonable subject of the darkest kind.

"Again, are you ignoring my question?" Presnell asked.

"Professor!" Elizabeth interrupted by yelling across the room wildly waving her hand.

Her head swiveled to shoot darts at Elizabeth. "Miss Cantrell! I will not tolerate outbursts!"

Then I watched Elizabeth do the unthinkable. She stood. "Professor, we should all have knowledge about Dwellers! It's imperative we understand them. Isn't the purpose of training to gain knowledge so we can help those we assist on the Earth Plane?"

Presnell let out an exasperated sigh as she turned back to me saying, "It was Miss Cantrell who put you up to asking?" I didn't answer knowing she was baiting me. My silence seemed to speak volumes. "I should have known it was conspiracy."

"I wouldn't coerce or expect Trevor to stand up for me!" Elizabeth once again yelled from across the room. "I would have asked myself if I were allowed to ask questions."

"Miss Cantrell, if you have questions you should ask yourself!" Presnell stated.

"Right!" Tilly joined in. "You wouldn't answer us if we asked. You only teach what you consider to be the trainable side of class!"

"Since the three of you seem to be so inquisitive," Presnell smiled with her red lips beaming. "I will look forward to visiting with you in private this afternoon." She peered around and continued, "Everyone else in this room will be free to go to lunch and not return this afternoon." She then turned to me with her finger pointing to the un-trainable side, "Mr. Stillholm, move!"

This certainly hadn't panned out the way I had hoped.

CHAPTER FIFTEEN

Elizabeth

A knock came at the classroom door. Professor Presnell glanced at her red watch over the rim of her red glasses while she went to see who it was. When the door opened, it was Mr. Solliday standing there waiting to be greeted. Professor Presnell held out her hand as she said, "Please come in."

"Thank you!" Mr. Solliday returned.

The Professor then turned to the class, "Unless you are Miss Bradford, Miss Cantrell, or Mr. Stillholm, you are free for the rest of the afternoon. Class is dismissed."

I now understood why Tiffany had been smirking at us all morning. Professor Presnell had sent her to deliver a hand-written message which she must have read. Tiffany knew Mr. Solliday was coming because we had inquired about Dwellers.

Tiffany passed, stopping before Tilly's desk spouting, "I truly hope not to see you after today."

"Likewise!" Tilly retorted with a look of contempt on her face.

They were interrupted by Mr. Solliday clearing his throat from his place beside the door. He had heard their exchange and had a less than amused look on his face.

The Professor turned to look at the three of us sitting on the bad side sighing. Then he waved us to move to the good side of class saying, "Please sit in the first three desks here in the front row."

We moved to the desks as Professor Presnell pulled two chairs and positioned them directly in front and facing us. I was surprised not to see anger in those eyes of hers. Instead was deep resignment, like she knew she would eventually have to answer unwanted questions.

She and Mr. Solliday took their seats. The Professor began, "Miss Cantrell, I am uncomfortable with your line of questions about Dwellers. I invited Mr. Solliday as a third party to…"

"Wouldn't he be the fifth party?" Tilly interrupted with a wide grin. I couldn't gauge how much trouble we were in. Tilly was fearless as usual.

Professor Presnell was embarrassed by her student's remark and was turning a rosy pink. Given enough time with Tilly crawling under her skin, she would turn a deeper shade of red and match her loud red dress.

"Let us focus on the questions the three of you have," Mr. Solliday stated refocusing everyone's attention.

I squared my shoulders and sat as tall as I could in hopes of having more presence before them. "Mr. Solliday. I am the only one with serious questions," I stated hoping to divert the attention from Tilly and Trevor. "Trevor inquired for me and Tilly…"

"I can't keep my mouth shut," Tilly stated finishing my sentence while loudly smacking her gum and offering me a stick.

I shook my head no. I could swear I saw Mr. Solliday smiling at Tilly's comment. He then asked, "Can any of you present me with a general description of a Dweller?"

"A Dweller is someone who is influenced by the dark and not the light," Trevor stated as if reading from a textbook.

"Yes," Mr. Solliday agreed nodding his head affirmatively. "Dwellers choose to embrace any form of darkness and shun any form of goodness or light. Do each of you understand how Dwellers of the dark are kept separated from Humlings and Keepers of the light here at Home?"

"If found here, they are sent through the Black Arch," I answered thinking about the girls from the journals. Dark Tina met her fate when she was sent through the Black Arch.

"The Black Arch is the portal separating our two worlds," Mr. Solliday agreed.

"I believe all three of you may end up before the Council at some point if you continue all of your antics. That is the first step toward darkness and the arch," Professor Presnell said under her breath clearly still agitated and aiming the remark towards Tilly.

"Professor, these three trainees have a lot of spirit, but I don't see darkness in them," Mr. Solliday disagreed with her. "Like those on the Earth Plane, everyone here has free will and chooses their path, whether it be good or bad. If we choose to bask in evil tasks, actions, and thoughts, we create darkness in our lives. Those dark souls go before the Council. Only dark souls who have turned their back on the light and God are sent through the Black Arch."

"Are they really absolutely kept separate from us?" I inquired before Professor Presnell could respond to Mr. Solliday. "Most portals you can enter two ways, going and coming. Do you know whether Dwellers can travel back and forth through the arch like a door?"

"The Black Arch serves as a portal connecting our two worlds. However, it is highly guarded!" The Professor began to answer. "I can assure you, no Dweller is returning here out of the Black Arch. It is like a one way street."

"So, the Black Arch only goes one way," Mr. Solliday concurred. For a moment, I thought I saw hint of sorrow behind his eyes.

As much as I pitied Mr. Solliday being an old soul who appeared tired, I had to have as many questions answered as possible. "If they can't return, then why do we live in the dome for protection?" I inquired.

"The blame for those who disappeared years ago lies with the Humlings. Everyone knows that!" The professor stated.

"No," I seriously disagreed. "The disappearances were a long time ago, but the Dwellers had to be able to enter our world." I paused realizing the professor wasn't going to dignify this with a response. "How do they enter our world now?"

"What makes you think Dwellers are traveling into our world?" Mr. Solliday seriously inquired.

I knew they were. The Dweller from the journal had not only traveled into our world, he had made it home. "Who says their not? Who is the authority on this? Are we living in a bubble thinking we are safe?" I shot back.

"Do you believe you have seen a Dweller?" Professor Presnell asked rolling her eyes and looking at me like I was crazy.

I was resigned to get to the bottom of the journal pages meaning. "Are there those who work both sides?"

"Both sides?" Trevor repeated now sharing the professors look like I must be crazy. "Like spies? Sleepers?"

"There are those who are more likely than others to be influenced by both the black of darkness and white of light!" Mr. Solliday stated. "They simply haven't decided where they belong."

"So, they are gray," I said speaking my mind. "Can Dwellers and Keepers marry and have children?"

"Children?" The professor repeated astonished at my revelation. "All Dwellers are sent through the Black Arch. There is no mixing of dark and light here in the dome. Gray children are a ridiculous thought!"

"Just because they are sent, does that really mean they can't intermingle before and have children?" I countered.

"Do you really think God would bless a dark Dweller with a new soul?" Professor Presnell answered in a snippy voice.

"Isn't it possible the new souls, or Dweller's children, wouldn't necessarily be dark? Couldn't they be gray?" I again countered. "White would be in the gene pool!"

"Souls are only given to those who walk in the light!" Mr. Solliday corrected me looking deeply saddened.

"All this talk and your questions are frivolous and a waste of time. No Keeper would want to have children with a Dweller!" The professor summed up.

"Is their a second Black Arch?" I continued ignoring Tilly's gaping mouth and the professor's indignation.

"Where is this girl coming from?" Tilly mumbled. "Elizabeth, don't you have better things to think about?"

The professor and Mr. Solliday simply stared at me. It was Mr. Solliday who broke the uncomfortable silence by asking, "Miss Cantrell, what is the reasoning behind all of your inquires?"

"Just something I read," I said with a shrug of my shoulders.

"I thought the collection of dark works were restricted from viewing," Professor Presnell stated turning to Mr. Solliday with a shocked look on her face.

"There is a whole set of books on dark works?" Tilly blurted out with the familiar devious grin. "And just where are these housed?"

"Miss Bradford, don't even get any idea about trying to obtain or read them!" The professor stated. "They are only viewed by chosen council members."

"It is my understanding that the Dwellers do have a process for riding themselves of unwanted ones," Mr. Solliday stated. "I'm sorry. I can't tell you what they call it."

"How does it work?" I asked.

"They send the offending party into an eternity of reincarnations on the Earth Plane," Mr. Solliday sighed with the sadness returning to his face.

"They don't ever progress and return here as light or return to the Dwellers?" Trevor inquired.

"No," Mr. Solliday answered. "The moment they die on the Earth Plane, their dark soul recycles right back into an Earth Plane baby. An example of this is an earth's sociopath."

97

"Are they in our nursery?" I asked aloud before thinking.

Mr. Solliday just looked at me with an unreadable stare.

"Elizabeth, the nursery is another one of those fairy folk tales our parents have told us," Tilly sighed. "We've been to the Hall of Babies. Did you see a nursery?"

I didn't answer.

"Miss Cantrell, have we answered all of your questions?" Mr. Solliday questioned.

"I guess so…" I sighed.

Mr. Solliday turned to Professor Presnell asking, "May I help you with anything else before I journey over to the Hall of Records?"

"You're stopping by the Hall of Records?" Professor Presnell questioned.

"Yes, I exchange my books every Tuesday," Mr. Solliday added. "I'm an avid reader."

"Miss Cantrell will be going there today as she does everyday," the professor began.

"You like to read books?" Mr. Solliday inquired with a friendly grin.

"Oh no," the professor corrected him before I had a chance to answer. "She files there a couple hours everyday. It's a punishment from Professor Zirak."

"Punishment for…?" Mr. Solliday asked turning to look at me with a questioning look.

"Not turning in my assignments," I unhappily stated. Professor Presnell had said this on purpose to embarrass me.

"Oh, I see," Mr. Solliday said. "Professor, were you hinting for me to escort Miss Cantrell to the Hall of Records?"

"That would be perfect," Professor Presnell stated. "It will ensure she doesn't get into trouble with Miss Bradford and Mr. Stillholm this afternoon. She will be one less unruly student I have to worry about."

Mr. Solliday and the professor began to stand from their seats as Professor Presnell said, "I will see you out." Then she turned to Tilly and Trevor, "The two of you are to wait for my return."

I stood and purposely took my time gathering my book and notebook. As I watched the two of them move towards the door, I couldn't help but think how much I really missed having a backpack.

"What was all that about?" Tilly whispered and popped a big bubble. "Are you playing with their minds for some reason?"

"It was definitely interesting," Trevor said shaking his head. "However, you should have told us you were reading some crazy book!"

"Elizabeth, this time you have took your paranoia too far!" Tilly returned. "You now have Solliday and Presnell zoned in on you thinking you are a schizo or something!"

I had tried to get them out of my hot water. It hadn't worked. I turned to Trevor saying, "I'm sorry I dragged you into this mess."

"You didn't drag me in," Trevor disagreed. "I made up my own mind to help you. You didn't twist my arm."

"Can you tell me why?" Tilly sarcastically requested of Trevor. "Why did you buy into Elizabeth's paranoia?"

"It just seemed like the right thing to do," Trevor sighed. "Elizabeth is my friend too!"

I could see the professor looking sharply back over her shoulder at me. With a quick, "I'll catch you later. Sorry!" I began to make my way to the door. I waved bye to my friends from over my shoulder. The tides had turned and now I was the one getting a get out of jail pass and leaving with Mr. Solliday.

"Thank you for coming and helping me deal with this off the wall subject,"

I heard the professor say to Mr. Solliday as I neared the door.

"I was glad to be of assistance," Mr. Solliday replied. "Send me a note any-time." He looked at me as I passed through the door. "Miss Cantrell, have you eaten?"

The professor's eyes darted angrily to Mr. Solliday as he said, "Do the train-ees not get to eat lunch when they are being punished?"

The professor looked aghast with the thought that Mr. Solliday would want to have lunch with me. She responded, "Of course they get to eat lunch, but…"

"Great!" Mr. Solliday retorted cutting her off before she could voice her objection. "I'm starved, are you Elizabeth?"

"Well, I guess," I mumbled. Maybe Trevor and Tilly were now the lucky ones. Saying the wrong thing over lunch to him could land me in serious hot water. I began to realize he wasn't my only audience. Mr. Solliday had several gentlemen that seemed to be following us. I assumed they were his security.

"Shall we?" Mr. Solliday asked extending his hand out before him, gestur-ing for us to start our walk. Professor Presnell crossed her arms across her chest as we began to move. "Miss Cantrell, your questions were very de-tailed."

"Too detailed," I added. "Trevor and Tilly deep-down believe I'm crazy."

"I doubt that," Mr. Solliday stated walking beside me. "They seem to be your true friends." His steps faltered before a nondescript door. He pulled an access card out and slid it into the electronic lock beside the door. As it swung open he held his hand for me to enter first.

I stepped into a small, private lift. Mr. Solliday stated to the operator, "My visitor and I would like to go to the cafeteria in the Hall of Records Com-plex."

The suited man answered, "Yes sir."

Mr. Solliday then turned to me, "I thought I would save us a few steps. I've always been fascinated by lifts here and on the Earth Plane." He had a huge grin on his face like a kid showing off his new toy. "Where were we...? Oh yes, your friends. True friends would never think you were crazy. They will always be there for you when you need them the most. You can confide in them and they lift your spirits. Doesn't this define your friends well?"

"It does," I slowly replied. "Others don't share my opinion about Trevor and Tilly."

"I prefer those around me that I trust to have some spunk," Mr. Solliday said to my surprise. "Your friend, Miss Bradford, reminds me of someone I know."

"Someone you trust?" I inquired.

"More than most," Mr. Solliday concurred. "He was a spitfire as a child himself." He had a broad smile across his face as he was temporarily lost in his memories. When he glanced back at me, he asked, "Did you have more questions?"

"Is it possible that a Dweller could change from dark to light?" I blurted out.

"A true Dweller that worships evil, no," Mr. Solliday answered. "Your theory of a Dweller that is a shade of gray is also unlikely. It would be unwise for a person to hold out hope for this."

"I know you know how they travel," I declared opening a can of worms between the two of us.

"Dwellers can be crafty. They are our enemy and have used a variety of different methods to get into our world," Mr. Solliday stated. "None of their methods currently matter, since we have countered every measure. Their travel here is very unlikely." We walked a few steps before he requested, "Anytime you think of additional questions, I would like you to direct them to me. The professor isn't an expert in this field."

"Why?" I asked. "Why should I inquire only of you?"

"You need to understand that Keepers and Humlings don't often spend time worrying, thinking, or asking questions about Dwellers," Mr. Solliday replied. Negative thoughts breed negativity in our lives. When you bring a topic like this up in class, it makes others uncomfortable."

"Is everyone better off ignoring the thought that Dwellers exist?" I pointedly asked.

"Everyone knows they exist, but constant thought of them is the first step in allowing negative thoughts to enter into your life," Mr. Solliday countered.

He was guarded in talking about them and wanted me to be the same. The problem was that I knew the Dwellers were leaving me notes. They could still travel. I needed to get to the bottom of it!

The lift had come to a stop. Mr. Solliday captured my attention when he said, "One more thing before we leave the lift, I want you to have this." He held out his card for his private lift.

"Why would you give me this?" I asked.

"You never know when a time will arise to use it," Mr. Solliday grinned. "I am asking you to come to me with any further concerns about Dwellers. Don't upset your professor. She is easily provoked! This card will bring you directly to my office." He held the card out and I reluctantly took it and wondered what his motive was.

"How will I find your door?" I asked since I hadn't paid much attention to its location.

"They're like magic," Mr. Solliday grinned. "You only have to touch the card and think of a door and one will appear. Think of mine and it will appear. This is a rare Keeper secret that I trust you with."

Incredible! Tilly would love this. However, I was making a mental note to keep this piece of magic to myself.

CHAPTER SIXTEEN

Tilly

There it was! Why had it not been shelved back where it belonged? According to the computer, the book Communicating Through Dreams wasn't on hold. However, it had been placed on the reserved cart. I thought of Mrs. Summors. She would be shocked that I was checking out a book for homework. I also felt she ran a much more organized library. I picked up the book and began to scan it into the computer.

"May I ask you what you think you are doing?" Asked Mrs. Summor's replacement.

"I could ask you the same thing?" I retorted.

"Attitude!" She huffed as her hands flew to her hips. "Let me guess. You are Mathilda Bradford."

"Yes, and you are?" I responded.

"Not someone you will be able to run over. Your mother hired me specifically to replace the old lady you were in cahoots with!" She replied.

"What?" I questioned.

"Your mother told me how the old lady and you steam rolled everyone!" She replied.

"We did no such thing!" I growled. I could feel Elizabeth grab my arm.

"Mrs. Summors is…"

"Mrs. Summors condoned your behavior," she interrupted. "If she had done so on the Earth Plane she would have been thrown into jail for aiding and abetting a criminal."

Elizabeth pushed past me and stood between me and the counter. She was red as she spouted, "That's going a little too far! Tilly is not a criminal! Who in the heck do you think you are?"

Now it was I who grabbed her arm as I shouted, "You had better zip it and…"

"And what?" The new librarian interrupted me again. "You'll run to your mommy?"

No way! I answered her, "No! I'll…"

"Run to daddy?" She spouted without letting me finish my thought. I stared at her as our eyes dueled. I broke the silence saying, "No, I can take care of you myself!"

"Oh please," she stated as she rounded the counter to sit on her stool and began to stack the chapter returns. "What could you do to me? Let me add, it would be laughable to see you complain about me. I have a stellar record and you… Let's just say I hear it definitely isn't spotless."

"Hello ladies!" A familiar voice echoed from behind me. Tiffany then stepped up and leaned against the counter beside me stating, "I hope there is not a problem. Carmen, my newest friend, did you enjoy the real life the other night?"

"Sure did!" Carmen replied sharing an overly warm smirk with demon in curls.

"Watching the couple's romance unfold in real life was very informative," Janelle stated.

All three giggled as if it must have been a private joke which we weren't privy too.

"Do you have my copy of Communicating Through Dreams," Tiffany asked.

"It's right here," Carmen stated as she pointed to the book in my hands.

"Not this copy," I challenged. "I was here first!"

"It was reserved for Tiffany," Janelle stated as she rolled her eyes.

"It wasn't on the reserved list," I challenged everyone involved. "I looked."

"You looked?" Tiffany chimed in.

"You found that book on the reserved cart," Carmen stated. "I placed it there myself."

"Just placing it on the cart doesn't make it reserved," I challenged her. "You are supposed to enter it in the system."

Carmen dropped the book in her hands, stood, and spewed, "This is my job, not yours. I will run this desk as I see fit. Reserved books will be entered as I have the time. Do not monkey with my computer!" She stood from her stool and pointed her finger directly at me. "I'm not going to take any crap off of the likes of you! Your mother has already informed me of your pushy and Tilly first behavior."

I started to slap her hand out of my face but Elizabeth grabbed my arm.

I never broke my stare as Carmen continued, "This is your warning! Stay out of my way, out from behind my desk, and out of my library."

"Or what?" I challenged.

"I will find creative ways to make your life miserable," Carmen threatened.

I swung the book in my hands at Carmen hoping to knock her silly. I missed so I pulled back and began my second swing at her.

My effort fell short as from nowhere a strong set of hands caught my arm. "Hey! Stop!" I heard Andy spout at me.

Now that my focus was no longer solely on Carmen, I noticed Mike was barricading Elizabeth from coming to my aid. At the same time, he was drooling over Janelle. Two separate boys were standing beside Tiffany and Janelle as though they were body guards. They sported a stupid smile. This was Tiffany, Janelle, and Carmen's plan. I had fallen for it. They new I needed the book and planned this to get me in trouble.

Andy turned me towards him still holding my arm and asked, "What in the world is this all about?"

"Tilly was stealing a book which I reserved," Tiffany stated with a smirk that read I got you again.

"You can have it!" I said and tossed it onto the counter.

Andy was still intently peering at me positioned between myself and Tiffany. "I never fully realized how strong you are," Tiffany said catching Andy off guard as she wrapped her hands coyly around his bicep. Both Andy and I were shocked! She then gave Andy a coy, flirtatious smile. "Yuck!" I muttered.

In a huff, I grabbed Andy's hand and pulled him away from Tiffany's claws. We walked to the far end of the room, next to the lift, before stopping.

Andy immediately began, "You shouldn't provoke them!"

I gave him my best puppy dog look saying, "But it's so fun to crawl under their skin!"

"I'm serious!" Andy seriously stated.

"So am I!" I retorted. "Serious about going on a date tonight."

He stood shaking his head like I was unbelievable saying, "You were just in a cat fight and your interest is in asking me for a date?"

I leaned in and fiddled with the collar of his grey sweater vest, "Does my itsy bitsy library fiasco have to be important at this moment?"

"Tilly, you are in trouble," Andy stated pushing my hand down.

I stepped back and threw my hands up saying, "So what? I'm always in trouble over something."

"Exactly!" Andy agreed as the lift dinged. "Nothing with you ever changes."

"Why does that surprise you? She is Tilly!" Mike said under his breath as he and a distracted Elizabeth stopped beside us. Mike had a grip on her arm.

"How much trouble do you think we are in?" Elizabeth nervously asked while peering over her shoulder.

"You personally are not in any trouble," I assured Elizabeth as I glanced over my shoulder. Tiffany had moved on. Anyone within a ten mile radius couldn't have missed the public display of affection between her and Dustin. Her arms were around his neck and his were around her waist. I had turned just in time to see him lean down and give her a sickening kiss. Where was Mrs. Summors when I needed her!

Elizabeth let out a sigh and stormed off after forcing Mike's hand from her arm and viewing Dustin's kiss. I glanced at Andy, pointing and saying, "I better go after her. Do we have a date tonight?" He simply shook his head as my fingers danced across his arm as I stepped away.

Elizabeth was speeding away. I chased her to the red carpet pathway next to the outer wall. I grabbed her arm, forcing her to stop.

"I've got to get out of here," Elizabeth stated. "Don't ask me why!"

"What about filing?" I asked holding both of her arms preventing her from high tailing it like a deer in fright!

"What about it?" Elizabeth asked in return pushing my arms and hands away. She was skittish.

"Elizabeth! Stop and consider, you may really be in trouble if you don't do your time," I roughly stated wondering whether my friend had lost it today. First she had asked sticky questions about Dwellers. Now she was shucking her punishment. "What is going on with you today?"

"Can't we just chalk it up to a bad day?" Elizabeth asked in a sour mood.

Whatever was going on in her head it was apparent that she wasn't ready to talk about it. "I'll let you have your bad day! However, I won't let you get into trouble. Go back!" Elizabeth started to object but I interrupted, "You asked me how much trouble you were in and I told you none. Well, I tried twice to whack that snob up side the head. I'm sure to be in trouble. One of us has to be a rock to help the other."

"Your mother," Elizabeth stated returning to reality. "I won't make you face her alone."

"Thank you," I replied.

Out of nowhere I suddenly could hear my mother calling, "Mathilda Bradford! Mathilda! You come out of your hiding place in the bookcases immediately!"

The moment was so reminiscent of my days of playing hide and seek from my mother. I was grown now. If I didn't want to be found, she still had no hope. I would relish the chance to play with her. However, I had Elizabeth to consider.

"We better go," Elizabeth stated nervously.

We crept through the book cases until we reached the end of the first set of shelves. I stepped out into the center of the opening, waiting for my mother to soon spot me. It didn't take long. She stepped out glaring at me from a few isles down. I offered Elizabeth a stick of gum as I murmured, "Get ready!"

My mother had a trail of individuals hot on her heels including; Tiffany, Janelle, and Carmen. As they approached, I could physically see my mother take a huge, deep breath. Then she plastered a smile across her face which appeared to take an extreme amount of effort. As the entourage stopped before Elizabeth and me, she began, "Now girls, I know we seemed to have had a misunderstanding."

Carmen instantly objected, "It was more…"

"As I said, a misunderstanding!" My mother stated firmly cutting her off. "I expect all of you to grow up and get along." She paused and proceeded to point her finger around the circle adding, "I'm talking to all of you! I expect you to become good friends."

"Friends?" Tiffany retorted in a huff. "What fairy tale are you living in?"

My mother let out a sigh, "Yes friends. Tilly and you have been good friends since childhood."

"Is that what you would call it?" Janelle sarcastically asked.

"You are not going to reprimand her for assaulting me?" Carmen pointedly questioned visibly red and angry.

"Did she actually hit you?" My mother huffed.

"No, but she did try!" Carmen loudly said.

"No harm, no foul," my mother summed up. "No assault to punish for!"

Tiffany seemed unable to control her anger. I wasn't sure if it was my mother standing up for me or the fact she had the gall to call us friends. Tiffany spouted, "My mother will never stand for this!"

Tiffany had always been my mother's favorite and she appeared taken back by Tiffany's harsh tone and demeanor to her. Her smile faded as she spewed, "Your mother wouldn't dare speak out against me or try anything!"

Silence fell. There was truth in my mothers unspoken threat. The last time another female threatened and challenged my mother, she considered it all out war. Ashley, a Humling, ran the tennis center in which my mother had been taking lessons for a couple of months. A weekend came when the tennis center had planned a tournament and cancelled open play. My mother was enraged with Ashley who denied her a court to play on. First she tried to have her simply fired. When this didn't work my mother made it well known that the tennis center was to be boycotted. In the end, Ashley did loose her job and was sent back to the world of the Humlings.

The truth was that my mother's friends weren't really friends. They were people she collected to enhance her status. She truly lived a lonely life. By the looks on the faces around the circle, we all agreed on one thing. An alien had taken over my mother's body making her say things she normally wouldn't say.

I was the only one gutsy enough to ask, "Why?"

I watched as my mother seemed to be searching within herself for an answer. She finally muttered, "Instead of pranks, can't we simply get along?" She swung her hands around, "That's all. Carmen get back to work. Tiffany, get that book checked out if you want it." All, go!" As the others started to disburse she turned to Elizabeth saying, "We really should at some point take you shopping. That frumpy look you sport during your leisure time is regrettable, to say the least." Then another forced smile.

"Umm… Okay," Elizabeth hesitantly agreed.

"That pony tail has got to go too! I'm going to take you to my hairdresser." My mother let out a huge sigh as if letting out her frustration with all of us. "I'll see you later dear," my mother stated before walking away leaving me speechless.

CHAPTER SEVENTEEN

Elizabeth

The only thing standing in my way of seeing Marvin was Harmony practice. This was our first practice since Tilly took over. I was sure it was going to be trying and I was already exhausted. Today had been full of surprises like Mr. Solliday seeming so much like a real person, not to mention the 180 of Mrs. Bradford. Then there was the filing. Carmen made me do the filing for myself and Shannon who had the afternoon off. The day was filled with exhaustive events. Relaxing in Marvin's arms would be a welcome comfort. That wasn't possible.

Leo interrupted my thoughts, "Hall of Knowledge."

"Thank you," I said to him as he held up a familiar brown paper bag for me to take. "Leo, it isn't necessary for you to give me gingerbread everyday."

"Yes it is," Leo disagreed. "It's healthy for you!" Then he grinned and held up one of his little arms to flex his muscle. "I'm healthy and fit! I eat gingerbread!"

I took the bag from his hand again saying, "Thank you." I gave him a warm smile.

Leo returned the warm grin as I exited the lift into the foyer. Instantly, I was faced with a new dilemma. Eddie was standing at the top of the staircase firmly holding a rolling cart in place while watching Trevor struggle to carry a heavy box up the staircase.

I walked over to the multiple boxes still needing to be carried up and tried to lift one. They were extremely heavy. As Trevor came down to get another box, I asked, "What are you guys doing?"

"Just trying to move these boxes," replied Trevor.

"I would help you but they are heavy," I replied.

"They sure are," replied Trevor straining to pick up another.

"What's in them?" I questioned. Curiosity was my downfall.

"Must you know everything?" Questioned Trevor in a short tone.

"Whatever Trevor!" I replied as I started up the stairs. I didn't like to be cut short by anyone, not even Trevor.

I could hear Eddie mumbling to Trevor, "We should ask Crash for help."

"Hey, Elizabeth. I'm sorry I snapped at you," Trevor apologized as he climbed the stairs to stand next to me. He whispered, "I'm really frustrated at trying to carry these up the stairs by myself."

"You want my help?" I questioned.

"Could you stand at the top to steady the rolling cart while we bring them up?" Trevor questioned.

"Sure," I responded. "As long as you are fast. We do have Harmony practice tonight."

"Your not the only one who hopes to do this fast," Trevor stated as he walked back down the stairs. A light bulb must have gone off inside his head as he turned to ask, "Where did Tilly decide to hold practice tonight?"

"The saints are using Grand Hall tonight for a private performance," I stated to Trevor's impatient stare. "We will be practicing in the common room at Keeper House tonight."

I watched as he and Eddie exchanged what appeared to be a look of panic. I now was curious what his last comment about being fast meant. Trevor always had a reason for everything he did.

"Bro," was all Eddie mumbled.

As I watched them carry the boxes, I held onto the cart as they slowly stacked six boxes on top of it. They quickly thanked me and pushed them away. I watched their frenzy and speedy demeanor.

"What are you up too?" Dustin asked as he strolled up to me from behind, watching the boys pushing the cart away.

I took a deep breath in and Dustin tickled my senses.

I couldn't help but close my eyes. *I was startled when Dustin spoke in my head, "Earth to Elizabeth. Did she not hear me?"*

Instantly, I opened my eyes to see him intently studying me. He again asked, "The boxes... What's going on?"

"Their delivering them, I guess. I have Harmony Practice and I'm late," I sputtered.

"I though Harmony Practice was cancelled tonight?" Dustin questioned with a serious look on his face.

"No it was just moved to Keeper House. It seems we are having an organizational meeting," I corrected him. "Besides, shouldn't you be with your girlfriend?"

"I am late picking her up," Dustin sighed.

I couldn't help the grin that spread across my face. I asked the obvious, "Tiffany won't be at Harmony tonight?"

"As mad as she was this afternoon, you are fortunate and should be thankful for her absence," Dustin's mind said.

Then he spoke aloud, "All of Administration House is going to watch the private performance by The Saints."

I happily added, "Well have fun!"

"Yeah! Fun," Dustin's mind smirked.

I bounced around him and felt as if I really should be doing cart-wheels down the hall. By her absence, Tilly and I both had just received a get out of jail free card! Without Tiffany there, Tilly would have more freedom to set up Harmony the way she wanted it set up. The windows in the Keeper corridor were open and the breeze further calmed my nerves. Life was looking up!

I opened the door to Keeper House and boy was I surprised! There was wall to wall, shoulder to shoulder, mass of excited young adult Keepers. You couldn't stir them with a stick. What was going on? I pushed and said, "Excuse me." Over and over until I was standing at the edge of what had been our comfortable common room. Our couches on one side and dining area on the other were gone. The back of the room, flanked by our kitchen was piled high with anything and everything to get it out of the way. What I saw resembled the eye of a tornado.

What else should I have expected? Tilly had managed to place a portable stage on the side of the room that normally housed our couches and chairs. Warming up on the cramped stage was a full rock band. Each member wore revealing dark clothes. It was one, which Tilly was flirting with, that caught my attention the most. He was tall, unshaven, wore earrings, and had dark, long hair. He was wearing black tight jeans, a thick studded belt, and only a plaid vest as a shirt. He was strutting his stuff and totally taken with Tilly. His other band members were watching the two of them. Who was I kidding? By the looks of it, all the band members were smitten with Tilly. Otherwise, how could she have gotten them to do something so ridiculous as to set up a stage in such a small place for trainees? I was sure this wasn't their normal scene.

The room itself was dark with the only lights being the stage lights. Behind me was a packed crowd jammed like sardines in a can where the dining table should set. All had expectant odd looks on their faces. To my horror, the dining table had been stacked on one of our couches with the other couch then stacked on top of the dining table. It looked like a couch and dining table sandwich which was shoved against the opposite wall. I noticed the stuttering Kim girl standing near me. I asked, "Where are the dining chairs?"

She tentatively smiled at me, "All ch… ch… chairs in P… P…"

"The professor's office," I sighed. She nodded. How did Tilly wrangle the professor into that? Then I immediately answered my own question. She hadn't asked permission for any of this.

The kitchen was full of people as well. I didn't know half of the well dressed people standing there and had no idea how many Tilly had invited. The far out individuals must be roadies. Did Tilly think Harmony was an invitation to throw a party and bring a pop up band? The room was shrinking as more people piled in. There was electricity in the air, an excitement I hadn't experienced. The guitarist was warming up running chords up and down his electric instrument. You couldn't move or breathe.

I spotted Professor Zirak standing at the edge of the stage with his arms crossed across his chest. He didn't look too happy.

"Oi!" The rocker stated into the mike. "Oi!"

Silence fell over the room as the rocker handed over the mike to Tilly who appeared pleased to have all eyes upon her. She began, "Welcome to Harmony! Tonight I have invited special guests to perform for you. This is White Crew."

All the strangers in the room erupted into loud cheering with arm in the air waving. The excitement was contagious. Tilly was drawn to the group because they were edgy. They were underground! The pop up band which she had been sneaking out to see. They were forbidden.

The tall rocker held up his hand to quiet the crowd and then once again smiled at Tilly, allowing her to have the stage.

"I have a vision for Harmony," Tilly beamed at all of us. "I want to discontinue using our boring choir music and give everyone something they can really rock too!"

Again the cheers went through the roof! As I peered around, my fellow Harmony trainees were clapping but the cheering wasn't coming from them. Tilly had invited all patrons of the underground group to come. My fellow trainees appeared as shocked as I was over Tilly's unpredictable, but predictable plan.

Tilly held up her hands to hush the crowds. "Before we get the party started, I have a few business items to announce," Tilly stated. "Every group or band needs a manager."

The tall band member leaned over, "My dear, you are the natural leader."

He fed right into her ego as she answered, "Of course I will still lead the general direction of the group. But I do need a manager to handle the administration end of Harmony." With that she paused to give him a flirtatious grin, running her hands down his bare chest, before looking back out into the crowd. "I have chosen Ruthanne to be the band manager. Where is Ruthanne?"

Ruthanne was shoved from person to person until she was standing at the edge of the stage appearing frightened to have anything to do with this scheme.

Still looking a little baffled at Tilly choosing her, Tilly asked, "Ruthanne, do you accept?"

"She does," Trevor yelled as he shoved his way to stand beside Ruthanne. He grabbed her hand and smiled down at her. She started to speak and he slightly shook his head no. Then he leaned over and whispered something in her ear.

"Great!" Tilly stated. "Over the next week I will be filling the key positions…"

"What is all of this?" Professor Presnell screamed at the top of her lungs like a parent who had walked into a party being thrown in their home. The mice had played, but the cat had returned. I knew this party was over.

Professor Presnell climbed up on the stage as Tilly put the mike in the mike holder. "Professor Zirak, why are you letting a trainee throw a party?" Professor Presnell asked loudly when she spotted him standing next to the stage. She quickly scanned the off beat, wild members of the band and their flashy equipment and lighting. She cringed.

The rocker leaned over to the mike saying, "Nice to meet you too!" The crowd went wild with excitement at just the sound of his voice. He hit a short loud running chord on his guitar.

"A band? A band in Keeper House!" Professor Presnell spewed. This is unprofessional! Professor Zirak, I will see you get called on the carpet for this!"

"Riot! Riot! Riot!" Yelled one of the band members. The drummer and then he ran a series of runs on his drums. The crowds once more went wild!

"Professor Zirak had nothing to do with this," Tilly interrupted smacking a fresh piece of gum. "He was out when I let the band in and we set up."

"What would make you think this was okay?" Professor Presnell spewed as she turned a darker shade of red as the crowd continued to vibrating their bodies to the sounds of the drum beats.

"Is this not an official Harmony Practice?" Tilly returned.

"Of course it is," Professor Kegley replied. With such a huge crowd, I had missed her arrival altogether.

"Are you in on this too?" Professor Presnell loudly asked Professor Kegley over the drummers beat.

"Am I not the conductress of Harmony?" Tilly questioned demanding Professor Presnell's attention.

"Yes, but that doesn't give you the latitude to throw a party," Professor Presnell stated yelling.

"I'm not throwing a party," Tilly mused. "Harmony is going in a new direction under my leadership. I'm showing my fellow trainees the new genre of music I am choosing for Harmony."

The drums silenced and the band leader yelled, "Are you ready to party?"

The professor again turned to look at the gruff, half dressed band members. "Absolutely not!"

The leader yelled, "Absolutely not! Absolutely not! Absolutely not! We are ready to bring the house down! Let's rock!"

The crowd went wild again. Professor Presnell turned off the microphones switch giving them an angry glare. The crowd started to "Boo."

"Oh no!" Mrs. Bradford said with and exasperated tone from beside me.

I shut my eyes for a moment and took a deep breath. I squared my shoulders and looked right at her saying, "If you came to give Tilly a hard time you can leave."

Mrs. Bradford forced that smile from today back on her face as she said in a sticky sweet tone, "Why would you think I came to give Mathilda a hard time? I'm here to support her and give her this gift on her first night as conductress."

I looked to see what the present was. She was holding the largest package of gum I had ever seen. What did she want? My staring at her seemed to make her uncomfortable as she moved away from me and towards the stage. I followed on her heels as we pushed past the puzzled on lookers.

"Good evening, Mr. Stillholm," Mrs. Bradford stated as she passed Trevor giving him a knowing look.

"Hey," I stated as I momentarily stopped by Trevor and Ruthanne. "What's up with Mrs. Bradford?"

"Did you see that strange look?" Ruthanne added.

"You haven't seen weird!" I said. "Today at the Hall of Records she actually helped Tilly and me."

"That is a little strange," Trevor agreed grinning. I looked at him for a moment. Had I really saw a hint of mischievousness. He looked back at me, "What?"

I shook my head and pushed past several bystanders to make my way to where the three professors, Tilly, and Mrs. Bradford were now huddled.

At this point the band leader held one black gloved hand in the air yelling, "Do we need mikes?"

The crowd went wild and answered, "No!"

"It was Mr. Solliday who put me in charge and I won't hesitate to ask to see him," Tilly spewed over the loud crowd.

"It's not going to come to that," Professor Zirak stated. "Professor Presnell, can't we work out a compromise?"

The band leader pointed to the drummer to hit it again. With every beat the crowd vibrated starting to pulse up and down in their stance.

"You can't be serious!" Professor Presnell answered yelling and holding her ears. She was beat red and the vein in her neck was pulsating showing her anger.

"Miss Bradford, this is a lot to take in," Professor Zirak began also yelling. "Maybe you should get your plans together and bring it to us for review." Tilly started to talk but he held up one finger in front of her face. "Since the next performance is a mere nine or ten days away, why don't you continue to use the normal music."

The drummer's rolls and beats once more quieted.

"So you can tell me after the next performance that I still can't take the group in the direction I want it to go? No thank you!" Tilly sternly shouted.

Professor Presnell grinned and I've got you smile. "If you can have a successful show using our regular choir music at the upcoming Harmony performance, I will guarantee you here in front of my two colleagues that you can use any type of music you wish for future upcoming events. Would you agree to use the choir music?"

Tilly studied her. I assumed trying to figure out what her angle was. "You truly don't think I can lead no matter what type of music is played, do you?"

"That is the first intelligent thing you have said during this whole conversation!" Professor Presnell spewed loudly.

"Can we play music?" Yelled the band leader. The crowd went wild.

I could see the raw determination cross Tilly's face as she loudly agreed, "You're on! Your music this time, mine from then on."

The band leader pointed to his steel guitarist who jumped to his feet and did a number on his strings sending electronic shock waves through the crowd.

"In addition, Administration house is to have their own song," Professor Presnell shouted.

"That wasn't part of the deal," Professor Kegley shouted.

"It wasn't," Tilly agreed loudly over the crowd. "I don't mind to let them sing. However, it will be the worst part of the show!"

"Miss Bradford," Professor Zirak said in a reprimanding loud, stern tone.

Tilly for the first time seemed to notice her mother as she asked, "What do you want?"

As Trevor and Ruthanne walked up behind Mrs. Bradford she yelled, "To say congratulations and give you a present for your first night as acting conductress." She handed the large package of gum over to Tilly.

The crowd was about to explode as the steel guitarist finished, put his guitar down, and started contorting his body in some sort of dance across the stage.

Before Tilly could respond Professor Presnell interrupted asking, "Ruthanne, why are you here? I thought you were sick."

Ruthanne stood dumbstruck as how to respond. Tiffany and Janelle always claimed she was sick when they had adventures so that they wouldn't have to be seen with her. She would be left behind to do their homework for them. However, Ruthanne could never rat them out. She had to live with them.

"Never mind," Professor Presnell said. "You are in my house and I will deal with you later! As for the rest of you, clean up!"

"Not before everyone has the opportunity to hear at least one song," Tilly rebelliously disagreed.

The band leader yelled again with one arm in the air, "One song!"

The crowd picked up the chant and the crowd repeated it louder and louder.

"Not tonight," Professor Presnell yelled trying to sternly put her foot down.

Tilly smiled a fake smile saying, "Okay, then I will invite them back when…"

"Just stop!" Professor Presnell stated as she threw up her hands. She turned to Professor Zirak demanding, "One song. Then you get your trainees to put this house back the way it should be!" In almost the same breath she turned to Ruthanne, "You are not staying. You will be accompanying me to Grand Hall for what is left of the performance."

Tilly never missed a beat! She turned to the mike, turned it on, and yelled, "Are we ready to rock?"

The crowd erupted as she handed the mike to the rocker. Then she plopped down on the edge of the stage and looked up at them all. The drummer started a loud, thudding beat. Then the electric guitar squealed. The keyboard played a catchy tune and the song began. The rocker was mesmerizing as he belted out the lyrics while bouncing and letting the song's beat move through him. The strangers in the room were singing along with him and there was electricity in the air.

Zirak allowed the band to play on into the night. Eventually Marvin came to find me. With his arms around me I relaxed and enjoyed the craziness which Tilly had created.

CHAPTER EIGHTEEN

Elizabeth

Someone was loudly banging on our door. I sat up and looked over at Tilly who was amazingly still asleep. I threw my blanket off and made my way to the door. The light from the hall was bright and blinding as it hurt my tired, red, sleepy eyes. As I squinted, Destiny was standing peering in. "What do you want?" I questioned in an annoyed tone for being woke up.

"Where's Tilly?" Destiny questioned while trying to sneak a peak past me.

"I assume still sleeping," I growled as I stepped into the hall. "What?"

"Whatever you two have done, you're in trouble again!" Destiny stated with a hint of a grin on her face.

"Why would you say that?" I questioned.

"Professor Presnell wants to see you in her office, immediately!" Destiny stated with a catty grin.

"Why is it, you're always the one to know when we are wanted by one of the professors?" I marveled out loud.

"I'm not nosy, if that is what you are suggesting!" Destiny stated clearly offended.

"Yeah," I replied. "You just happen to be always at the right place at the right time?"

"Don't blame me because the two of you always have a scheme going," Destiny haughtily clarified for me. "If you didn't stay up to all hours of the night, you would have been up this morning at a decent hour. You would have been downstairs when Tiffany knocked and you would have heard her relay the message from Professor Presnell yourself."

I opened my bedroom door and stepped back into my room, without stating another word to Destiny. It wasn't worth my time or effort.

I moved over to shake Tilly to wake her saying, "Wake up! Professor Presnell wants us."

"Go away," Tilly mumbled as she pushed my hand away with hers.

I pulled at her blankets demanding, "Get up!"

Tilly rolled over as I turned on the night stand light. Instantly she covered her eyes and protested, "The alarm clock hasn't gone off! What do you want? Turn the light back off!"

"It isn't what I want," I began. "Professor Presnell is demanding to see us."

"Guess she wants to renege on our deal," Tilly sighed.

"You are probably right," I sighed.

"Well, at least we had one great night last night!" Tilly said as she stood and stretched her arms above her head.

I moved to slip on my usual sweats and T-shirt while Tilly moved to primp at her make-up table. When I was entirely dressed and finished tying my shoe laces, I asked, "Are you trying to irritate the professor by making her wait?"

"Don't get so excited," Tilly said in an annoyed tone. "It's good to keep her waiting."

Another knock came at the door. Tilly and I both said together, "Destiny."

With a smile exchanged between us, we ignored the door.

"You had better hurry or they might send Destiny in to check on us!" I half-teased.

Tilly fluttered around and dressed. Then like lightening, we were out the door, through the Keeper corridor, down the staircase, and before Presnell's office door. I knocked on Presnell's office door hearing her say, "Come in."

We stepped through the door and she gestured for us to have a seat in the two red upholstered chairs facing her desk. Then she proceeded to ignore us. Every vein in her neck and head were wildly pulsing as she sat writing and filling out some type of report.

Tilly leaned her head back on the chair and closed her eyes to catnap. She had no fear!

I on the other hand, peered around the red room. Presnell had new wallpaper which went from the chair rail to the ceiling. Her pattern choice was her unusual madness. Red bird wallpaper! It was atrocious! I did have to marvel at her deep devotion to the color red. She basked in it. I found it to be overwhelming.

In the distant echoes, I could hear my fellow trainees in the foyer awaiting the lift. It dawned on me how long we had been sitting here. Our fellow trainees were off to the start of their own day while we were waiting a bashing to commence from Presnell. We were presumptuous to believe that we got off easy for Tilly's stunt last night.

I was surprised when another knock came at the door and Presnell said, "Come in."

An older gentleman carrying a small metal cage entered the door. He plopped it down on top of Presnell's desk saying, "Good morning. I'm Charlie with Animal control and at your service on this beautiful morning."

"There is nothing beautiful about today!" Presnell said in an annoyed, raised voice.

"Well sure there is," Charlie began unaware of Presnell's foul mood. "The sun in shining and the..." He stopped when Presnell glared at him with those super critical eyes.

"In case you haven't noticed," Presnell spewed. "The sun always shines." She stood handing him the stack of paperwork she had so diligently been filling out. "It's all in order. I want them removed now!"

Charlie no longer smiled. She had put out the sunshine in his day. He grabbed the paperwork from her and politely said, "Yes ma'am, that is what I am here for."

"Administration House is the door to the right down the Administration corridor," Presnell stated.

Charlie picked up his metal cage and turning to exit said, "Thank you ma'am."

"Got bugs, do you?" Tilly muttered in a giggle. "Or does Charlie the exterminator and you have something going!"

"Ladies, tell me about the frogs," Professor Presnell demanded not hearing Tilly's muttered statement.

"Frogs?" I questioned dumfounded.

"The frogs which were placed into the bathroom of Administration House?" Professor Presnell harshly stated.

"Someone put frogs in your house?" Tilly asked as she looked down at her feet. She was trying to control her giggling with a huge smile across her face.

"Silence!" Screamed the Professor who looked as if she would skin alive the prankster who had done this. Her glare at Tilly left no doubt in my mind. She thought Tilly had produced the plague of frogs. "Miss Cantrell, do you know if Miss Bradford had anything to do with this?"

"Professor, I had Harmony practice last night," Tilly stated with a giggle interrupting.

"You listened to that trashy band play a song. That is hardly Harmony practice," Presnell disagreed with an icy voice.

I paused for a moment wondering if Tilly could have been involved. If she was involved, she said nothing to me about it. Tilly was definitely in last night. Harmony practiced in our house. Presnell was staring at me waiting. Calmly, I stated, "Oh no, I can guarantee she didn't have anything to do with this."

"Then, I am to assume that if you can guarantee it was not Miss Bradford, you know who did this?" Professor Presnell pointedly asked.

I could tell she believed she had twisted my words against me. This made me nervous. What game was she playing? I tried to correct my statement, "I meant … I know Tilly did not do it because I am her room mate and she was home all of last night with me."

The professor stared deeply at me making me fidget. I tried to avoid eye contact with her. Relief came over me when Professor Zirak flung open the door to come inside. Professor Presnell didn't seem happy to see him at all. Clearly annoyed with his arrival, she spewed, "Professor Zirak, is this the example you set for your trainees. You have entered my office rudely without knocking."

"Ah, Professor Presnell, forgive me," Stated Zirak. "I was just in such a hurry to see what my two trainees had done which would cause you to take time out of your busy day to question them."

"Someone put hundreds of hip pity, hop pity frogs in Administration House's bathroom!" Tilly relayed to him trying not to burst out laughing. She clearly was holding back belly laughter which would not be welcomed.

"Frogs?" Professor Zirak repeated. "If a few frogs made their way into your house, you can't blame these two for that."

"Not a few frogs," Presnell disagreed with her neck veins pulsing. "Hundreds of frogs!" With her nostrils flaring she spewed, "I truly believe your trainees are behind this latest atrocity! Miss Bradford must be guilty. She is not trying to deny it! Listen to her giggling and gloating!"

"I did not put the frogs in your bathroom," stated Tilly very slowly. Her shoulders shook as laughter once again overtook her. "Really. I can't speak to deny it, because if I open my mouth, laughter is all that will come out!"

"Tilly, quiet," demanded Professor Zirak as he gave her a stern look. Tilly had taken two deep breaths to try to calm her laughter looking at her feet. "What was the time line for this?" Questioned Professor Zirak.

"At some point last evening," Professor Presnell replied.

I could hear a mousy, light squeaking sound come from Tilly. I then noticed that Professor Zirak had stepped on Tilly's foot to remind her to be quiet. "With all due respect, it would be impossible that they accomplished a feat like that last night," stated Zirak.

"You are ready to swear they never left Keeper House last night?" Questioned Professor Presnell.

"That is exactly what I am prepared to tell you," stated Professor Zirak as he shook his head. "Remember the band? It took most of the night to get Keeper House back to normal. The crowd lingered and lingered. I was in my office very late and personally watched Tilly and Elizabeth put all the furniture back as they found it. It was well after midnight." Stated the professor.

We all sat as the minutes dragged on for what seemed like hours. I could see the wheels turning in Professor Presnell's head. Her face suddenly brightened, "Were any of the other professors with you, after the band left?"

"Allene!" Professor Zirak exclaimed in a raised voice. "Are you really questioning my integrity?"

"Of course not," Professor Presnell stammered seeing she had stopped on his righteous indignation.

"Unless you have proof that my two trainees had something to do with this, I demand that you let them go to their class. You have made them late," Professor Zirak stated to Professor Presnell as he stood towering over all of us.

"Very well," the professor spewed standing to match Professor Zirak's posture. "Until I have further proof, your two trainees are excused."

"May I be of further assistance in this matter?" Asked Professor Zirak.

"Not unless you are willing to admit these two did this!" Growled Professor Presnell.

"Thank you Professor Presnell!" Professor Zirak stated politely while smirking at his win.

I followed Tilly out the door and into the foyer.

"Ladies," Professor Zirak called. "I would like to warn the two of you that if I find out you did have anything to do with this, you will no longer be apart of Keeper House. This is below the standards of the house. Do you both understand?"

"Yes sir," I answered.

"Don't get your knickers in a bunch," Tilly giggled. "I really have no idea…" Tilly was once again belly laughing as she turned to walk towards the staircase.

"Where are you going?" Zirak questioned.

"To change into our uniforms," Tilly answered.

"Both of you are already late," Zirak sighed. "Don't waste time. Go on to class in what you have on."

Tilly peered down at her usual tight skirt, revealing shirt, and knee boots. She was pleased and smiled at the thought of wearing her seductive get up to class. Probably thinking she would run into Andy. She answered, "Yes sir! Whatever you say. I do look fabulous today!"

I, on the other hand, was clothed in my raggedy, comfortable sweats, an oversized T-shirt, and tennis shoes. I was sure to gather some turned up nose looks today. Oh well, at least I didn't look like a marsh mellow in my all white uniform. I tentatively smiled at the professor as we passed by him to await the lift.

CHAPTER NINETEEN

Elizabeth

The lift door dinged, opened, and we stepped through saying, "Destination Four."

Leo smiled at me and a second later growled at Tilly. She opened her mouth to say something in return to his frown. However, I caught her eye and shook my head no. I had requested that she try not to pester Leo since he was my friend too. She had reluctantly agreed not to bother him in my presence.

I stepped to the back of the lift unable to get away from Tilly's escaping giggles. She was still marveling at the Administration House's frog problem when she asked, "She did say hundreds, didn't she?"

"She did!" I agreed letting myself imagine hundreds of frogs jumping around a bathroom."

"I've met my match," Tilly giggled. "Whoever pulled this off was good. I bow to their genius!" Tilly paused and appeared deep in thought. "You know, it took some planning to move hundreds of frogs."

"Oh crap!" I muttered. Why had I not seen it? I knew exactly who had done this. Worse yet, I had helped them. Trevor, Eddie, and I had moved all those heavy boxes last night. Trevor would have known that Administration House was empty. He was dating Ruthanne and knew how to get into her house as well. This didn't seem so amusing to me anymore.

"Destination four, Hall of Ghosts," Leo said as he tugged at my baggy T-shirt. I smiled down at him as he offered me another brown paper bag of gingerbread.

"Leo, I can't accept another bag," I said holding up my hand in front of me.

"Sure you can," Leo disagreed. "I want to keep you healthy!"

"Does gingerbread have some health benefit that only you know about?" Tilly questioned with a smirk. "Did you go to medical school?"

Leo peered past me with a growl.

I took the brown bag out of his hands and said to regain his attention, "Thank you Leo. I know you have my best interests at heart."

"You're welcome!" Leo rang back.

I backed out of the lift into the Elephant Room and waved at him as the door shut.

"I wouldn't eat that crap if I were you," Tilly stated. "It might be poisoned."

"He might poison you," I countered. "I'm safe though. He likes me!"

"Why are the two of you late?" Rhett yelled at us as he rounded a corner and spotted us.

"Good morning to you too," Tilly mumbled as we turned to face Rhett.

"Well?" Rhett demanded.

"Professor Presnell thought we played a prank on Administration House," I replied. "We have been in her office."

He looked directly at Tilly asking, "Did you?"

"No," Tilly said as a giggle escaped her. "It was a fantastic prank and I wish I had thought of it!" Tilly then leaned over, belly laughed, and then did a hip pity hop like a frog.

Rhett's questioning face turned to me. I explained, "Someone put frogs in their bathroom."

"They were excited over a few frogs?" Rhett retorted seeming amused himself at their wimpiness.

"Not a few," Tilly choked out. "Hundreds or hip pity hop pity tree climbing frogs! They were probably even on the ceiling."

I could see the amusement in his eyes. "So you've had a good laugh at their expense this morning. Now we need to buckle down and get to work. Are the two of you any closer to finding your three ghosts?"

"None," I sighed.

"That figures!" Rhett said under his breath. "Today is you lucky day. My team will be assisting you for the next couple of hours."

"Your team?" Tilly repeated.

"Well, three of them," Rhett replied with a smile. "Use your time with them wisely."

"Where will you be?" I questioned.

"Obviously, you haven't seen my desk this week," Rhett said. "I'm buried in paperwork. I need a couple hours to dig out before the office is on my case. Not to mention, I need to give the two of you a grade. You are not going to fail on my watch. What would others think if I couldn't teach you?"

"If you pawn us off on your crew, is it really you who is teaching us?" Tilly defiantly questioned in a sticky sweet voice.

Rhett just peered at her while shaking his finger at her. Obviously deciding not to respond, he turned and waved for us to follow him. Standing along the wall in front of Rhett's office was an odd pairing of personalities. I could see a cowboy, a beach bum, one that looked pressed and stiff, and a construction worker type. This was going to be an interesting morning.

The gentleman who was wearing pristine clothing stepped forward questioning, "Ladies, where are your coats?"

Maybe I was crazy, but I felt as if his stare was focused on me. I knew I appeared a little disheveled in my sweats and pony tail. He kept looking me over from head to toe, again and again like I wasn't what he expected.

Tilly interrupted his awkward stare as she answered loudly enough for all ears, "We were detained this morning. Falsely accused of putting hundreds of frogs..." She once again couldn't control her giggling or her hands. She put her hand on the chest of the beach bum guy. He was the youngest of all of them and was obviously going to be her target!

This forced all eyes upon me as I once again finished, "Administration house had hundreds of frogs placed in their bathroom overnight."

"Like I would touch a slimy pond frog!" Tilly squealed. "A great idea though. Brilliant!"

"That still doesn't explain why you have come dressed for summer," the pressed man stated shaking his head.

"By the time we were dismissed by Professor Presnell, Professor Zirak told us to come straight here," I sighed. "Because we were late."

I couldn't miss the disapproving glance Rhett was giving beach bum guy. Tilly was oblivious to Rhett's stare. Her focus was beach bum guy and working her magic. The construction guy was watching too in pure fascination.

"Cryin' out loud," the cowboy interrupted. "Conrad, you aren't intendin' to mosey down with us, let her borrow your coat!"

Rhett followed the cowboy's suggestion as he held out his coat to Tilly causing her to take a few steps away from beach guy. The pressed man, Conrad, reluctantly held his out for me. Under his stare I said, "Thank you."

Conrad smiled at me and politely said, "You are welcome." He turned and disappeared through Rhett's office door.

Rhett handed the cowboy a clipboard saying, "The three are listed." Then he turned to us, "Good luck!" Conrad appeared in the door with a file of some sort forcing Rhett to disappear through the office door with him.

"So you are Marvin's gal?" The cowboy asked in a friendly tone.

"In the flesh," Tilly answered for me as she winked at beach bum guy.

I held out my hand saying, "I'm Elizabeth. It is nice to meet you."

"Skip the formalities," Tilly said from beside me as she pushed my hand down and popped a stick of gum into her mouth. "I'm Tilly and this is Elizabeth. You are?"

"Billy," the cowboy answered.

"And you?" Tilly asked pointing to the next in line.

"I'm Luke," the plaid flannel construction worker type replied with a grin that said he was fascinated with Tilly.

She pointed to beach bum type standing next to her and gave him a flirtatious smile. "And finally, you are?"

"Too old for you to cotton up too," interrupted Billy who was now giving the same type of warning glare that Rhett had been giving.

"I'm Jason!" The beach bum guy answered as he moved to stand between myself and Billy.

"Now we're all acquainted!" Billy stated with a satisfied look. "It's round up time!"

Tilly huffed a little and was clearly irritated at being told no concerning Jason. Then Jason actually moving away from her was an insult. She returned Billy's glare while popping a huge bubble. "Let's just get this over with!"

All three of them exchanged looks with each other over Tilly's sudden change of mood. Billy then looked at the top paper on the clipboard reading, "Staci Diamond."

"Staci lives in a small town called Shell Knob," I began. "It is nestled in the Mark Twain National Forrest and sleeps on the edge of Table Rock Lake. "We have been to her home in the Turkey Mountain Estates. She is not there."

"Glad to see ya didn't pass the buck and did some of the research yourself,"

Billy complimented. "The first step is always locatin' their hometown and seein' if they can be found at their home."

"What do you know about her life beyond Shell Knob where she lived?" Jason asked.

"She's a housewife!" Tilly exclaimed in total disgust with her hands on her hips. "She spent her whole life serving a man! To top it all off, she had nine children and five baskets of clothes to wash everyday."

"Probably life theme of caregiver," Luke surmised.

"Horse feathers! Raisin' a brood of little ones is workin' hard!" Billy countered. "Well that's down right respectful!"

"Did you check the homes of her children?" Jason methodically asked.

"None of them," I stated as Tilly unwrapped a second stick of gum.

"That is a lot of work left undone," Jason stated. "Did the two of you actually even work on the project?"

"Let's keep movin' down the list," Billy directed as he flipped to look at the second paper attached to the clipboard. "Next is Ryan Smith."

"I can save you a little time," I sighed. "We didn't find Ryan either. He isn't home."

"Who is the third?" Jason asked eyeing Tilly who had made her way around Luke towards him.

"We haven't done anything with Brain Stanford," I stated. "Sorry!"

Once again the three of them were looking at each other and clearly holding back a chuckle. Luke looked away so as to not make eye contact with us.

Jason asked, "He didn't...?" He held out his hand for the clipboard and flipped to the last page. "Guess he did."

Tilly stood watching them and blowing bubbles. We were clearly on the outside of their inside joke. Tilly interrupted, "Cut the inside joke and let's get going. I've got to have time to do my nails later!"

"Time to divide and conquer," Luke chimed in.

"I reckon that's a good plan!" Billy agreed as he reached for the clipboard. "Jason and Luke, ya'll get hot on the trail of Mrs. Diamond's children. If you locate the gal at her home or at one of her children's homes, wait until we are together to help her cross over." He handed them the first page attached to the clipboard. He then turned to us saying, "We'll be workin' on Ryan Smith. Move 'em out!"

Jason was once again moving away from Tilly as he said, "Sounds great to us!" With a glance at Luke they quickly stepped away making their way across Elephant Room towards the double door leading to the portals.

"Alright gals! We know Ryan isn't home," Billy began as he looked at his clipboard. "What else do ya know about the feller?"

"He is a much more interesting subject than the other two," Tilly spit out with a tone of annoyance. "The other two are boring!" She had put off finding our three ghosts as long as she could. The inevitable had come, and she was forced into accomplishing our retrieval.

"How so?" Billy questioned.

"He was a manly man," Tilly dreamily stated. "A strong police officer who was tall, physically luscious and any girls dream."

"Life theme of justice," Billy added. "Looks may or may not be important, at least to the rest of us."

"He grew up in a small town, married his high school sweetheart, and worked for the police department of the same small town," I stated trying to give more background.

"What did ya'll miss?" Billy asked. "Nothin' on the Earth Plane is that perfect."

I knew what Tilly hadn't seen when we were at the Hall of Records. Thank heavens I paid attention. She was too busy dreaming about the police officer. "After about ten years of marriage, he had an affair with a fellow police officer. The betrayal led to their divorce," I said. "He threw away his life."

"How did the feller die on the Earth Plane?" Billy asked.

"He was killed in the line of duty not too many years after his divorce," I answered.

"Abruptly killed," Tilly added.

"Do ya'll reckon the feller would be a hanger or denier?" Billy inquired.

"Hanger," I answered.

"Denier," Tilly countered my answer.

"Why a denier?" Billy asked Tilly.

"He was strong and a very capable police officer," Tilly stated. "He trusted his ability and never dreamed he would be killed."

"Arrogance, bein' focused on one's self only leads to a path of destruction," Billy answered. "If the feller were a denier, you would find him walkin' within his life. For awhile, he will go about his normal day oblivious that no contact was made between him and others. As with all deniers, eventually they put two and two together. They might continue to deny their death and ignore the bright light of their portal. However, doin' this too long will allow the denier to slip into becomin' a ghost." Billy paused and turned to me, "Why would he be a hanger?"

"Reading his full story," I began. "You have to read the great love story of his life. He met his wife, Emily, in Kindergarten. As they grew older, he fell head over heels in love with her. For his life, there was never anyone that he loved the way he loved her."

"This is your reasonin' for believin' the feller is a hanger," Billy surmised.

"Yes," I stated. "He shouldn't have done what he did and spent the rest of his life after his divorce regretting it. Upon his death, he left everything to Emily."

"You believe he was a hanger, don't you?" Tilly asked.

"I believe he once was," Billy answered. "The second step to findin' a ghost is to research where they invested their time, energy, and emotions on earth. If this fellers love was as strong and true as you described, he probably was in the beginnin' a hanger."

"He was hanging on to visit her," I surmised.

"Probably," Billy stated giving me a warm grin. "Usually they will go visitin' and then return to their portal to mosey on home. When they go visitin' and stay, they become a ghost."

"You don't happen to remember where the ex lived?" Tilly asked. I shook my head no. "Great! We will have to go research her address."

"No," Billy stated. "Rhett wrote it down here." Billy pointed to his clipboard.

"If he already did the research, then why the million questions?" Tilly retorted as she threw her hands up.

"This is the class work ya'll were suppose to do," Billy stated. "Rhett went ahead and did it for today because he runs a tight ship and doesn't like wastin' time. However, makin' you gals go through the steps is how ya'll will learn to do this!"

"A tight ship," Tilly mumbled as she rolled her eyes. "Like I've said a couple times, lets get this over with!"

With Tilly's suggestion, we started making our way across Elephant Room. Strolling through the double doors leading into Elephant Room were Andy and Mike. On Andy's arm was Tiffany and Janelle was leaning over on Mike's. Even though Tilly and I both were preoccupied with gawking at the group, I knew we both had very different reasons. Tiffany had obviously forgotten all about Dustin, Janelle had forgotten Rodger, and Andy had obviously forgotten all about Tilly. There was no doubt that this scene had crawled under Tilly's skin. She wasn't used to being spurned by any man.

Since we had slowed our walk to stare at them, Billy had gained a few paces ahead of us. We sped up our pace to catch up and passed through the double doors into the glaring white corridor. Another man approached Billy as he turned to see if we were following him.

"Did you see that?" Tilly spewed. "What does she think she is doing?"

"What she is doing is forgetting she has a boyfriend?" I questioned in an exasperated, but hushed tone. "Dustin deserves better!"

"So does Andy!" Tilly spit out with a sigh. "Or he will have. I've let this go to long. I've ignored Andy too long."

"I take it your not going to ignore him anymore then. What's next?" I asked.

"Part two of my plan," Tilly said with a grin.

"Part two?" I repeated.

"I need to leave no doubt in his mind that I am the one for him," Tilly said.

The man talking with Billy parted ways leaving me no opportunity to respond to her. Tilly and I fell silent as we followed Billy. She seemed to be enjoying whatever Andy related thoughts were running through her head. The thought of part two of her plan scared me a little. It was sure to be radical! We made our way through the corridors which seemed endless. We passed many golden doors which were evenly spaced down the sides of the corridors. Each announced by the electronic sign above it and led to its own destination. Since Springbrook has a population of around 500, it took awhile for us to reach it.

Billy turned to us as we neared our door, "Zip up!"

Tilly and I obeyed and zipped our coats in preparation for the portal. Billy opened the door and I looked upon the familiar black hole. He typed the address into the control panel, pressed save, and the star lit up on the electronic sign above the door. Billy then turned to us, "Ready?"

"As ready as we will ever be," Tilly sighed.

"Be my guest!" Billy said as he held his hand out for us to go first.

Tilly marched into the darkness. As I began to step down the first step following Tilly, I said to Billy who was holding the door, "Thank you."

In the darkness, I let my hand run down the cold, damp walls to steady myself as the cool breeze coming off the water shower hit me. With a deep breath I inhaled the fresh air and stepped off the third step. The ice cold, invisible water shower hit my skin as its bone chilling cold left me shivering. The sound of the water hitting the rocks below was deafening. Feeling frozen, I hurried down the remaining three steps and out the door at the bottom.

As I peered around, we were standing in the living room of a cabin. I peered through the windows lining the room and could see that this house set on a beautiful lake with woods surrounding it on either side. I could never get over the feeling of astonishment when I looked at my feet which were resting on an invisible ground about a foot up. It appeared I was standing or floating on air. Billy exited the portal into the room asking Tilly, "Are you okay?"

"I'm fine," Tilly replied. Her short skirt left her legs exposed to the cold and numbing water shower. She looked cold and had goose bumps.

Billy took Tilly at her word and began to peer around the room. When he began to move down the hall, a voice asked, "Who are you?"

"I reckon ya must be Ryan?" Billy questioned backing up with a warm smile.

"How did you break in?" Ryan asked as he moved aggressively though the hall towards Billy. "No thief is going to break in here and get by with it!"

"Aah, shucks," Billy began. "We aren't here to plunder nothin'."

The man burst into the room. Since he was walking on thin air about a foot up, I instantly knew he was Ryan, our ghost.

"Look at that," Tilly began as she pointed to his feet. "You are walking on air too!"

Billy's head instantly spun around as he gave her a warning glare. It was too late. Ryan zoned in on Tilly.

"You shouldn't be here," Ryan said as he stared at her. "You're intruding! Go away!"

"Tell me about Emily," I interrupted as I stepped towards him diverting his attention. I wasn't sure Tilly could work her wiles on him.

Ryan peered at me and you could hear a pin drop within the room. "How do you know Emily?" He asked.

"Can you see the light?" I asked pointing in the direction of it.

Ryan appeared caught off guard that I knew about the bright light which he could see. He retorted, "What does the light have to do with you knowing Emily?"

"Everything," I replied as I glanced at Billy unsure as where I should be going with this.

Billy smiled at me before saying, "The light…"

"I'm not dumb," Ryan interrupted. "When she mentioned the light, I knew you were here to persuade me to go to the light. However, it's not my time. This is the home I am choosing."

"The jigs up! Ya already know ya no longer belong here," Billy stated. "It's time to be movin' on home!"

"I belong where she is," Ryan said pointing to a picture on the mantel. "I will not leave without her!"

"Death is not leavin' your gal," Billy calmly stated. "Death is goin' home and waitin' for her to join you in the light. If this gal's your soul mate, she will love you once more there!"

"Do I have others waiting for me?" Ryan questioned.

"Ya do, but I reckon ya already knew that though," Billy answered with a warm and inviting smile on his face. "Those waitin' for ya miss ya as badly as you will miss her."

"I still don't know how I could leave her here alone," Ryan countered looking pained at the thought. "I'm her protector!"

"You shouldn't be hesitatin' because you worrin' about leavin' Emily alone,"

Billy said. "You see, she ain't alone. She has family here and family waitin' for her in the light."

I could see this didn't satisfy him. "Once home, you can visit her till she comes Home or crosses over," I added. "I bet she doesn't hear you anymore." I paused and it was clear that I had hit a nerve. He must have been trying to talk to her, but had been unsuccessful. "When you visit her from home or within the light, you can talk to her and she will hear you."

Billy once again smiled at me for my effort.

"I owe her an apology because I really messed up our whole lives. I never told her and now she can't hear me!" Ryan stated looking deeply regretful. Then he sighed and asked, "I could really talk to her and she would hear me if I enter the light?"

Billy reassured him, "Yes, if your gal is open to communicatin', she will be able to hear ya."

"If you are open to communication?" Ryan questioned watching us intently. His expression read that he thought we were playing word games with him.

"Does she dream?" I interrupted.

Ryan shook his head saying, "Like at night."

"Yes," I replied.

"She dreams about me," Ryan said with that pained look on his face.

"How do you know she is dreaming about you?" Tilly asked.

"She is always saying my name," Ryan stated. "I keep trying to tell her I'm here."

"She is looking for you," I stated. "The problem is you aren't home to communicate with her. She's looking for you in the world of dreams."

"Are ya ready to be headin' on home?" Billy asked. "To cross over and start sendin' her your messages. Let her hear ya in a dream?"

Ryan turned, looking side to side, and held up his arms as if feeling some type of breeze. He then watched something in the distance which none of us could see. He took a couple steps and I was startled as he began to fade. Tilly started to say something and Billy shook his head no and put his finger to his mouth to signal for us to be quiet.

Within seconds Ryan was gone and a poof of air rushed across the room blowing our hair. "Why did that rush of air not move anything?" Tilly asked as she was looking at the unmoved papers on the counter edge.

"The closin' of a portal can only be felt by someone on the same plane as the portal," Billy stated as he moved towards the front door to open it.

"One down!" Tilly happily stated realizing our work with Ryan was done. "Two to go!" She moved to the door and passed through it and rushed up the stairs.

Billy held open the door for me as I passed through and I rushed up the stairs myself. As I reached the top of the staircase, I saw the corridor before me moving. I held onto the door frame and realized it was the door in the wall moving. The whole portal was moving!

"Jump!" Tilly demanded. "Elizabeth, jump!"

I followed her advice, jumped out into the gleaming white corridor, and fell to the floor. Peering back towards the portal, Billy appeared in the door-way. He held on to the frame until the portal shuffled to the right and shuddered to a stop.

"What was that?" I asked as Billy stepped out into the corridor.

"A change in population," Billy stated in amusement. He held out his hand to help me up out of the floor saying, "Let's go find the guys."

Tilly rolled her eyes as we followed Billy down the corridor. She leaned over and whispered, "This is taking forever!"

"You have something else to do?" I returned.

She gave me a devilish grin which answered my question. She always had something more important than training.

"We'll be done in two shakes of a monkies tail!" Billy stated as he glanced over his shoulder. "Don't peter out on me yet!"

We followed Billy in silence knowing he was listening until we stood before the portal leading to Shell Knob. Jason and Luke appeared to be relaxing and waiting patiently. They were leaned against the golden portal door shooting the breeze.

"I reckon y'all found our gal Staci?" Billy asked.

"Didn't take long," Luke said as he smiled at Tilly and me. "Alright ladies, do you think she is a denier or hanger?"

"Give it a rest," Tilly stated. "It's on the clipboard!"

"A hanger," I answered trying to speed things up for Tilly's sake. Tilly moved to stand next to Jason. "She can't be a denier since she wasn't found walking in her earth life."

"A real whippersnapper!" Billy stated with a friendly smile. He turned to Luke and Jason, "This gal doesn't pass the buck."

"Did you read anything which might have led you to believe she would hang on for any particular reason?" Jason asked. It was like he was checking off a check list in his mind.

"Not that I can think of…," Tilly sweetly stated from beside him. Now, she was suddenly interested since she wanted his attention.

"We noticed that in her children's homes we visited, they had pictures of her displayed," Jason stated as he gave Tilly a wary glance. "In each photo she wore a huge cross which was always prominently displayed."

"So she stayed for religion?" Tilly questioned as she batted her eyes at Jason. Tilly believed boys liked to show off. She was allowing Jason, in his own way, to do that. Thus, her game plan.

"She did stay for religion," Luke stated as Tilly ignored him.

"The third step to be taken if ya have a denier or hanger which ya can't locate in their current life on the Earth Plane is to look at their individual history," Billy began. "Each person who goes to the Earth Plane has their own individual history which is a part of the overall Earth Plane history."

"In Staci's case, it was her religion, or history, in a previous life which was holding her," Luke stated. Then he watched Tilly with a fascination that screamed he thought she must be nuts.

"She was a nun in her previous life," Jason stated. "She went back to the hospital where she served a lifetime!"

"Was that on your clipboard?" Tilly questioned clearly annoyed that the man tricks weren't fazing Jason.

"When we do research, we always list their home address, relative's addresses, and employment. Anything pertinent," Jason answered looking directly at her.

"We also list the last couple of lives they lived," Luke added.

"Again, Rhett's runnin' a tight ship," Billy stated. "Havin' that information ahead of time…"

"Saves time," Tilly finished his sentence. "This is all nice, but can we just get on with it!"

Luke and Jason exchanged a look between themselves.

"The Staci gal already crossed over, didn't she?" Billy asked studying his clipboard of information.

"When she saw us, she just went," Luke stated.

"Great!" Tilly stated. "Two down. One to go!"

"That leaves Brian Stanford," Billy stated with a smirk.

"We haven't done any research on him," I admitted.

"It's all on your clipboard," Tilly stated as she rolled her eyes.

"Do we really need to go through the motions?" Luke asked Billy.

"We better have a go at it," Billy stated. "This is their trainin' work which they will be receivin' a grade on."

We began to walk down the corridor. "Brian is unique!" Luke said shaking his head.

"Unique how?" I asked.

"He hangs around a hotel," Jason chimed in.

"Why?" I asked.

"He's likin' the room service," Billy said with a chuckle as he began to stroll down the corridor.

Luke and Jason followed with their focus turned to their work for the afternoon. Billy had a small spiral notebook which he pulled from his coat pocket. They were going name to name and discussing updates and the plan of action for helping them cross over. By the long list of names, I felt a twang of sorrow for them. Rhett had them chasing after us when they had a lot of serious work to do.

I glanced over at Tilly who was searching Rhett's coat pockets. Apparently she had found a pair of men's sunglasses which now graced her face. Annoyingly, she was fiddling with a flashlight and banging it on her hands trying to make it come on. With a shrug she shoved the pint sized flash light back into her pocket. She then pulled another small spiral notebook out of the opposite pocket. She began to thumb through it.

I elbowed her mouthing, "Tilly!"

Her attention turned to me as she shrugged giving me her best innocent look and mouthed, "What!" Her smile turned to a devilish grin as she shoved the notebook away. To my dismay she then began to dig in an inside pocket. She looked disappointed when she pulled out an aged pair of gloves. With a sigh she shoved them away too. She was going through Rhett's personal possessions in the coat.

The trio of guys stopped and looked towards the golden door, marked Eureka Springs. Population roughly 2,300. Billy opened the golden door and typed an address into the keypad just inside the door. He didn't even look at the clipboard. This would be a doozy since he knew the address by heart. He turned to us, "Gals, you're takin' the lead." He held out his hand towards the door for us to go first as all three of them grinned at us.

Tilly smiled her best flirtatious smile at Jason as she passed him. I followed her into the portal feeling it was extremely frigid, damp, noisy, and windy. I held my breath as I rushed through the cold, numbing waterfall. Ghosties were crazy! Who would want to do this day after day? A girl would spend a fortune on skin crème to combat the portal's effect on her skin.

I stepped out into the lobby of a huge hotel. The guys weren't far behind us as we moved towards the center of the massive room. A loud plaid carpet extended to the sitting area across from us. The walls were a Victorian pink which blended with the massive wooden columns. The ceiling was a marvel to behold with its exposed beams running across.

Individuals on the Earth Plane were coming and going freely in and out the door. Busy to everyday life, they were oblivious to our intrusion into their world. I turned to Billy and asked, "What now?"

"Be patient," Luke stated. "Brian is a curious soul."

"He'll be along," Jason assured us while once again moving away from Tilly.

To pass the time, I leaned against one of the massive wooden columns and watched those in the dining room eating their meal. A little girl eventually caught my eye. She was playfully going from table to table with all the adults ignoring her. Casually, she would walk up to each table, reach around whoever was seated, and steal the spoons and shove them into her pocket. I could hear her giggle as those served soup would look for their missing spoon. It wasn't until she sauntered to the table in-front of the dining room door that I realized why no one had noticed her. This was no normal child. She was walking on thin air about a foot off the Earth Plane ground. Sadness swept over me as I realized she was a ghost child.

As she turned to skip down the hall she stopped dead in her tracks, having seen me. Then with a poof of air, she disappeared leaving the missing spoons to clamor to the floor in the place where she had been. A ruckus ensued with the staff rushing to pick up the spoons and those on the Earth Plane rushing to take photos excited that this was a ghost sighting. Naturally, I always believed ghosts knocked photos from shelves, played with light

146

switches, or blew candle flames out. Maybe it all was true! This one messed with spoons.

It was then I noticed the teenager leaning against a column across the room, staring at me. Instantly my eyes shot to his feet which were perched a foot off the ground.

I started to cautiously approach him asking, "Are you Brian?"

"Who wants to know?" The teenager retorted.

"I have an important message for Brian," I replied hoping to catch him in a moment of curiosity. "I can only speak to him."

He moved towards me with piercing eyes. "If I were Brian, what would you be telling me?"

"I would say your death on the Earth Plane is simply using your portal to return to home," I stated.

"Another pesky, do-gooder, intruder," Brain sighed appearing disappointed. "I thought we might be able to have some fun together! I haven't talked to a good looking girl for awhile."

"Do you see the light?" I pointedly asked.

"Why does it matter to you?" Brian defiantly retorted. "It's just my luck. I finally get a girl who sees and hears me and she's one of those light pointers!"

"I only want to understand you!" I stated firmly.

"The only thing to understand about me is that I don't want to go anywhere else!" Brian stated. "I have too much fun here."

"You are choosing not to cross over and use your portal then?" I questioned out loud.

"Get over it hotel waiter or laundry boy!" Tilly shouted from beside me. "You are dead and you know it! Go to the light! Quit wasting our time so we can all go home."

"Is this good cop, bad cop?" Brian said. He pointed at me saying, "You I like!"

"Get real!" Tilly said. "You are a lame, lazy boy who wants to play Halloween everyday and doesn't want to go function in the real world!"

"I'm just not interested in the light," Brian stated. "I like this existence!"

"Why?" Tilly sarcastically questioned. "You have some tourists to scare or a beautiful girl hidden away in a mop closet somewhere?"

"Actually... yes," Brian stated with a smile. "I enjoy the looks on pretty girl's faces when they order room service and I make their food seemingly disappear."

"Seriously?" Tilly questioned with a look of awe and disgust. "Beautiful girls are around you and that is the best you can offer in ghostly flirtation?"

"What's wrong with having some fun?" Brian retorted to Tilly. "Being a pretty female doesn't have to be about mulling each other. He then peered over at Billy, Luke, and Jason who were still standing just inside the door.

Luke held up his hand saying, "We still want you to cross over. However, the three of us are fully aware of your feelings. We like pretty females ourselves and you do seem to have the corner on the market here."

"Then why did you bring them here?" Brian asked with an outstretched finger pointing at us.

A smirk came over all three of their faces as we all stood there.

"I get it. How insulting! You brought fresh meat to try to talk me over." His fun, easy going, slouching teenage bravado was no longer present. Replaced by anger, Brian stepped towards us red faced and spewing, "I won't tolerate your intrusion, sarcasm, and snide remarks in the home of my choosing, nor your insults concerning my relationship with females here."

Shooting across the room in ghostly fashion, he stopped directly in front of me and peered eye to eye. "The good cop. Hmm..." He placed his hand on his chin while thinking. "Although I don't trust you, I will spare you today since I believe you to be a green, but wise soul and I like ponytails." He pointed over his shoulder adding, "You are green because you let the three of them bring you here." With the rage of a raging bull he yelled in my face,

"Don't come back! Next time you won't find yourself so lucky. I'll tie your ponytail to a door handle."

He then moved towards Tilly as she spewed, "Oh yes, yell at me too. It takes a real man to yell at a woman. Why should I be left out?"

Stopping directly in-front of her, he looked a bit amused. However, you could still see cracks of anger. Tilly always took bravery to a new level with each situation that arose. She wasn't likely to cower to anyone. As Tilly stared Brian down I could see a hint of panic growing in our three guides. They motioned vigorously for me to come and stand with them at the door. I firmly shook my head no. My place was standing next to Tilly, even if it ended badly.

"You are mouthy!" Brian stated as his hand ruffled his hair.

"I'm not the only one with a big mouth. It takes one to know one." Tilly retorted loudly in a carefree manner while fearlessly smacking her gum.

With that, Brian rushed Tilly as she jumped backwards. He was like a deep sweeping wind, which no amount of jumping backwards was going to thwart. He moved through her body leaving ice-cycles hanging from every surface of her body, hair, and clothing.

Tilly's hands turned into fists as she screeched, "You iced me! Show yourself Brian because when I get my hands on you!"

An eerie chuckle echoed off the walls of the massive room. "Girls," Jason called. "We need to go now!"

I stepped towards the portal door when suddenly we were rushed by an array of ghosts. Our three guides disappeared just inside the portal door and began to watch as the ghosts whirled around us.

A young adult wearing a wedding gown was screeching at us, "Came to take my room, did you?"

I tried to answer her saying, "No." However, she was gone into the swirling mass surrounding us.

Next a small boy with pop bottle glasses asked, "Interested in playing hide and seek?"

The girl from the dining room appeared and answered, "I'll ask Charles."

"Who is Charles?" I asked as they both turned to look at me. With that they too re-joined the swirling mass.

A young man stepped out of the swirling mass and did a double take, looking at me. He held up his hand as if gesturing to the others to stop swirling. As the wind died down around us, Tilly and I found ourselves in the center of a circle of ghosts.

Brian was standing beside the annoyed bride. The boy and girl were happily playing peek-a-boo around the other ghost's legs. In addition to the young man, there was a soldier wearing an ancient uniform, a doctor with a stethoscope around his neck standing with a nurse, and an older gentleman in Victorian riding clothes.

The young man stepped out towards us and appeared mesmerized by me. He eventually stated, "Not this one!"

"Charles," whined the little girl.

"No," Charles sternly stated never taking his eyes off me.

With that the group formed a single file line. Brian smiled as he peered around those in-front of him. Tilly and I began to back quickly towards the portal door. I leaned over whispering to Tilly, "I think they intend to ice us!"

"Not us," Tilly countered. "Me!"

Then it all happened fast. Tilly turned and sprinted for the door. The rushing wind they created blew my hair as they rushed past me towards her.

Jason appeared through the portal door holding out his hand for Tilly and yelling at me, "Elizabeth run!"

Before Tilly reached the door she was once again iced by one of them. They were moving so fast I missed seeing which one. I did see Jason pull Tilly speedily and safely into the portal. As the group of ghosts turned to look at me, fear spread through my body.

Charles stepped forward saying, "I think it is best if you leave too." He extended his hand towards the door in a gentleman fashion. I ran past all of them and crowded into the portal with Billy and Luke who were waiting for me on the bottom step.

The two of them looked at me and then each other. Luke shook his head asking, "Have you ever seen them do that?"

"Nope," Billy stated as he began to move up the stairs. "But their strange birds. I was tellin' Rhett earlier we needed to be findin' a way to have ourselves a ghost round up. That group is outta control!"

Luke waited patiently for me to go ahead of him. I was already chilled from the swirling wind and ran back up the six stairs as fast as I could. Bursting out the door, the bright light of the corridor was hard on my eyes. I squinted towards Tilly who appeared shivering and miserable. Jason had put his coat around her and was now paying her all the attention in the world. Tilly however, was too cold and irritated to enjoy his attention, now that she had it.

We began to walk in silence down the endless corridors. My thoughts centered on the group of swirling ghosts. They were a scary sight. Not to mention, as a group they were powerful. I couldn't help but ask, "Is it normal for ghosts to work together like that?"

"Ghosts sometimes dwell in the same place together," Jason stated from beside Tilly who was beginning to drip since the ice was slowly melting. "But in general, they don't form gangs."

"That's why we haven't been able to get Brian to cross over," Luke added. "He feels safe with his group."

"Out of the group of three, he must have been the denier," I stated.

Billy gave me a warm grin. "Your cookin' gal!"

"He died accidently from a fall," Jason stated. "He didn't think he was dead at first. He denied the fall ever happened!"

"Now he knows and chooses to be a ghost," I surmised.

Warm grins from our three guides issued as we once again began to walk in silence. Relief washed over me as the double doors leading to Elephant Room appeared. Once through the doors, Luke made a bee-line for Rhett's office. As suddenly as he had entered, he exited with a grinning Rhett and pressed guy in tow.

I hurried across to give pressed guy his coat back. "Thank you for allowing me to borrow you coat," I said to the pressed gentleman as I passed the coat to him. "If you ever need a return favor, I owe you."

"You are welcome. Thank you for not getting it iced," he said with a warm smile. "Call me Conrad."

"This one's a whippersnapper," Billy chimed in as he walked up behind me, slapping me on the back.

"I'm sure she is," Conrad stated while watching me with a look of fascination.

"I see Tilly met Brian," Rhett stated as he stepped out of his office with an I got you smirk written all over him.

Instantly, Billy and Conrad smiled as they turned to look at Tilly who was still covered in ice which was melting slowly.

"She's not very happy with you!" I whispered as the smirks faded from each of their faces.

Rhett shrugged. You could see behind his eyes that he had set Tilly up to get iced. Hmm... Maybe this plan was to discipline her. As Tilly chattered, Rhett grinned.

CHAPTER TWENTY

Tilly

"Where's Trevor?" I asked Eddie as I walked up beside him.

"Hey!" Eddie greeted me. Then he looked to Elizabeth grinning and exclaiming, "Crash!"

Elizabeth smiled at Eddie as I again asked, "Trevor?"

"I don't know," Eddie stated. "He didn't come to class today."

"Right!" I giggled to myself. Trevor wouldn't miss class with his red-headed Ruthanne watching his every move.

"I'm not joking," Eddie reprimanded me. "He received a note and left like a jet saying he'd catch up with me later today."

"A note?" Elizabeth hesitantly asked. She paced back and forth a couple times and appeared to be losing it. Always the worry wart!

"Was it a love note from Ruthanne?" I asked adjusting the buttons on my blouse.

"Not unless Ruthanne knocked on our door in the middle of the night," Eddie answered. "I think he's got another chick in the closet somewhere."

"It can't be a love note," Elizabeth mumbled. "Come on, Eddie. Trevor is nuts about Ruthanne."

"Sorry Elizabeth, it still could be," Eddie disagreed. "It could have just been delivered by one of the other guys on our floor. Speaking of the devil."

I turned to see Trevor heading our way with a young man that I didn't recognize. He didn't look carefree today, but appeared to have the weight of the world on his shoulders. The young stranger and he split up. I met Trevor half way asking, "Is something wrong?"

Those true eyes peered into mine saying, "Everything is okay."

"Bro, where ya been?" Eddie asked.

I will still searching Trevor's worried face for some hint as to what was wrong when he answered, "I needed a day off, so I took one!"

"Who is that guy?" I asked as I pointed to the stranger who appeared to be mulling around in the distance.

"I met him today. He's cool. He invited me to play basketball sometime," Trevor stated with a shrug of his shoulders.

"The note?" I questioned. "Are you getting notes from someone other than Ruthanne?"

Trevor tried not to look at Eddie. No luck. Eddie instantly held up his hand saying, "Bro, I've told you that your chick problems were going to catch up to you!" With a smirk he placed his ear buds in.

I read it in his face. Trevor wished Eddie hadn't said that in front of me. Trevor's gig was up! Maybe Ruthanne wasn't as much a fixture in his life as everyone thought. I could live without Ruthanne. I definitely missed having Trevor's full attention.

"We had an exciting morning," Elizabeth hinted to Trevor raising her eyebrows slightly and giving him a you know what I mean look.

"How so?" Trevor asked as he kicked at something on the floor avoiding Elizabeth's eyes.

"You haven't heard?" I asked in astonishment. "Where have you been hanging out? On the moon?" I couldn't help but think Ruthanne was slowly distracting and keeping his attention occupied and distant from our usual loop.

In true Trevor form, he simply peered at me taking in my sarcasm. He was a smart man and knew better than to attempt sarcasm in return. He got my drift.

"Someone put hundreds of frogs into the Administration House bathroom!" Elizabeth blurted out nervously breaking the news to him.

"Really," Trevor stated still avoiding her looks.

I began to giggle noticing that Trevor looked away from Elizabeth's prying stare. As my laughing lightened, I asked, "Why aren't the two of you laughing? What's going on between the two of you?" I could tell by both of their body language that they had a secret.

"They blamed you didn't they?" Trevor seriously asked avoiding Elizabeth's looks.

"Yes!" Elizabeth replied firmly before I had the chance to. "You tell me how the two of you managed to get boxes and boxes of tree frogs moved and emptied?"

"That's even a funnier story," I stated. "You are right Elizabeth! We would have to be wonder women to accomplish that!"

The rehearsal room door flung open before I could continue. Kim entered and was standing and peering at us. The demon in curls was probably making fun of poor Kim again. My story, or lack of a story, would have to wait. I strolled past Kim and into the rehearsal room for Harmony practice. This was my new home. The personal challenge had come from those who didn't believe I could lead Harmony. I would prove them wrong.

The crowd in the room fell silent when they noticed my arrival and began making their way to their chairs. I knew they were secretly shocked about the direction I wanted to take Harmony. However, I needed them to give it a chance. I had never really made an effort to befriend any of them, now I needed them to give me a chance. My mind was already made up. Together we could be amazing as a group. As I made my way to the front of the room, I unwrapped a perfect piece of bubble gum and popped it into my mouth. I slowed my pace to allow a few moments of comforting bliss with my gum.

You can't sing with gum in your mouth, or so my mother always told me. I could hear my mother scold me saying, "You can't talk or sing with gum in your mouth. Spit it out!"

Standing before the podium, I had a perfect view. The double doors at the back of the room opened with all of Administration House filing in through the doors. Then I spotted my nemesis. The demon in curls. Who exactly who did they think they were? Two thirds Harmony group was wearing yellow T-shirts which read, Tiffany for conductress. The demon in curls broke off from the very group who were standing against the back wall. She had Ruthanne in tow and she seemed distraught. Maybe Ruthanne heard about the love note.

When Tiffany neared me, she spoke loud enough that the microphone broadcast her demand, "The Administration House is here to practice our song. Professor Presnell has given us permission to dedicate our time to our own song."

"Why do you think you are special?" I growled. "Let me remind you that you are no longer conductress."

Tiffany turned and plucked another mike from its stand and turned it on. She then proceeded to turn before the room saying, "Harmony, Tilly has reminded me I am no longer conductress. After trying to sabotage our efforts at our last performance and embarrass us all, Tilly was made conductress." She paused giving me a devilish grin. "Tell me Tilly, didn't they say you needed to learn some responsibility?"

Two could play at this game. "Harmony members. Let me ask you. Did you prefer the conductress who berated all of you and felt everyone was second class to her and her cronies? I might ask you to remember the snide remarks, dirty looks, and teasing. None of her snobbishness had anything to do with the running of Harmony. She was high on power!" I paused to give her my own wicked grin before adding, "People who treat others like trash deserve to receive what they dish out to others. The sound system was tampered with, but not to embarrass any of you. The embarrassment was all yours, Tiffany."

"I wasn't embarrassed," Tiffany defiantly stated.

"You didn't run with your tail between you legs crying to Professor Presnell," I taunted. "Saying I had ruined all your hard work?" I turned to look at the crowd who stood dumfounded as to how to respond. They were scared to support me because if Tiffany regained control in the future, they would pay. "Don't all of you see? The hard work she claimed credit for was your hard work. With her, you never got credit. She did nothing more than place all of us where she wanted us on stage and pick robe colors."

"Bravo! Bravo!" My nemesis taunted. "Great speech. However, everyone in this room doubts your crazy plans. Look at them all," Tiffany pointed to the crowd with her arm held out. "When you fail, I will be the conductress to pick up the pieces and put the group back together."

With that Administration House began to cheer, "Tiffany! Tiffany! Tiffany!"

I was shocked as Trevor suddenly stepped to my side holding his hand out for Tiffany's mike, demanding, "Hand it over."

Tiffany shook her head no with an evil grin and clutched the mike tightly.

Trevor then abruptly plucked the mike from the stand before me. Instantly he turned to the crowd saying, "My fellow trainees and fellow Harmony members. I have something to say. As I see it, we have two options. As a group we can support Tilly as conductress, sing the familiar music we all know for the next performance, and then follow the new path Tilly will be leading us on. Stepping out of the traditional box would be work but rewarding and probably fun." Trevor paused as all stunned eyes were watching him. "Our other option is not to take the new path. Tilly's failure to lead us would be our failure as well. I do agree with Tiffany that she would regain control of the group."

"I am the natural leader of Harmony," Tiffany said under her breath.

"Option one, Tilly and success. Option two, Tiffany and failure. With Tiffany, everything will go back to exactly the way it was," Trevor concluded. The crowd still frozen with fear just stared at the three of us. "I know you are all scared. Sometimes in life though, you have to take a stand."

"I'm with you bro!" Eddie stated from below as he moved to stand before the rehearsal stage.

"Count me in," Elizabeth said as she stood next to Eddie and they joined hands and held them up in a unison gesture.

"I'm going with Tilly!" The piano boy yelled. "She will need a keyboardist." As he made his way to the front, he ushered his group of friends with him. They joined hands with Eddie and Elizabeth.

Slowly the group at the front was growing, leaving only Team Tiffany in the back.

It was Ruthanne who shocked me the most. She left her place behind Tiffany where she had been standing quiet as a church mouse. She grabbed Trevor's hand as if making her last stand. Her eyes then darted to Tiffany's as she pulled Trevor off the stage to stand in front of the still growing group. Without moving her eyes from Tiffany she said, "I choose to stand with Tilly." Ruthanne closed her eyes and raised her and Trevor's hand in a gesture of unity.

"Trader," Tiffany snapped. "When Tilly fails to lead you, I will once again take the reigns. Don't worry, you won't be plagued with her for long."

I grabbed the mike from Tiffany and demanded, "Get off my stage. Also, remove the yellow T-shirts or you will not be allowed to participate in Harmony's practice."

"No problem," Tiffany stated in a sticky sweet voice. "Administration house will practice their song in Grand Hall nightly.

"Why do you think you get to practice in Grand Hall and not in the rehearsal room?" I questioned.

"We are meant to be on stage!" Tiffany said in a sticky sweet voice. "Professor Presnell approved our song and where we could practice." With a devilish grin she walked to the edge of the stage adding to Ruthanne, "You can play with Tilly after you practice with your house in Grand Hall."

Ruthanne suddenly looked unsure. Truly, she was the one with the most to loose by taking a stand tonight. I needed to cut her some slack and talk to Trevor about his fooling around with love note girl. I liked a person who knew how to take a stand!

CHAPTER
TWENTY-ONE

Elizabeth

As I walked up the Dogwood Trail leading to Rhett's home, I was relieved to be away from all the madness. Tilly had Harmony practice our usual music for the upcoming performance. Then she held an organizational meeting for the band. Everyone stayed. Tilly was either loved or hated. I wasn't sure which. Curiosity got the best of them all.

Tilly announced a few key positions. The keyboardist was to be piano guy. It was no surprise that Ruthanne was selected to be manager. Technicians were to be Trevor and Eddie, and a back-up third boy from Record House. The one position I assumed would be solely Tilly's, was the singer. I was shocked to learn she planned to share this honor with three other people. Each house was to nominate their own singer. This part of her plan was crazy. By doing this, she wasn't creating one band, she was creating four. Tilly spouted something about every great band had opening acts. The other three houses would be her opening acts. Everyone else in the group would be backup singers. I planned to stand as far in back and away from any microphone as I could be!

A few key positions were left unfilled, the bassist, guitarist, and drummer. Basically, she needed a whole band. If it were anyone but Tilly, I would think she had bit off more than she could chew. However, Tilly always pushed the envelope.

As I was attempting to leave, Tilly asked Trevor to make her a destination card for tonight. She wanted to go to The City on a date. Trevor's radar was on red alert since Tilly hadn't asked for two cards. He insisted to know who she was going with. This went over like a lead balloon. Whomever Tilly was meeting, she clearly didn't care to share it with Trevor. The tense look on Trevor's face was just too much for me. I excused myself and left them to battle it out.

Reaching the A-frame house, my steps faltered. The appearance of this house was a run down shack standing lifeless under the moonlight. However, to anyone who could look below the surface, you could see a vibrant and lively home within. Each added on room jutted off here and there. The little additions screamed character with each a new paint color. I meandered down the deeply cracked and partially missing sidewalk thinking that a little kid would have trouble riding their bike over them.

I tapped on the door and could hear steps as someone was scrambling to open locks to greet me. When the door opened there was Marvin smiling down at me. I could tell he was as happy to see me as I was to see him. I fell into him with my arms wrapping around him. In an instant his arms were wrapped around me as he kissed the top of my head. "I'm so exhausted," I mumbled. As my head rested against his chest, I could once again hear the soothing sound of his heartbeat. In his arms, I felt the world fading away.

"Come on in!" I heard Rhett calling from the Living Room, interrupting my peaceful, blissful moment.

"We gave up on playing the Astral Time Travel game and started watching history," Marvin sighed.

"I'm sorry I'm late," I replied. "Tilly and the whole lets make a band thing."

Marvin smiled down at me and gave me another warm, comforting hug. I sighed when he released me. I would have been perfectly happy to stay wrapped in his arms all night. With his hand on the small of my back, he ushered me down the long, darkened hall leading to the bachelor's living room as I yawned.

Rhett was seated in an oversized chair to the side of the couch. He started to stand as I waved for him to sit with my hands. "You made quite and impression today on Billy," Rhett stated as he paused the history movie. "And on some of the others." Rhett's eyes flashed to Marvin's saying you know who I mean.

"Overall, it wasn't as bad as I thought it would be," I stated noticing Marvin appeared like the last comment had crawled under his skin.

I hadn't made the connection today. However, by the look on Marvin's face, I knew. I once again had overlooked the obvious. No wonder pressed man looked me over head to toe. "Conrad is your father?" I thought out-loud.

"Yup!" Marvin stated as he shook his head yes. "If he wanted to meet you, all he had to do was ask."

"Like I told you earlier," Rhett stated as he turned back on the history movie. "It had nothing to do with the two of you dating."

Rhett's words clearly meant to end the conversation. I smiled at Marvin who returned my smile. He wasn't upset with me and I was simply too tired to worry about it. We moved to the comfy, oversized couch and I plopped down. The history movie itself was boring. I nuzzled my head over on his shoulder.....

I awoke to Marvin gently shaking me saying, "Elizabeth."

I squinted under the bright light, finding that I was snuggled up to Marvin with my head still resting on his shoulder. I had fallen asleep. I raised one arm and stretched a little while yawning.

Marvin watched before asking, "Are you feeling okay?"

"I'm okay," I said as I peered at him. "I'm just tired."

Rhett was standing at the television, retrieving his movie. As he turned, the smirk on his face was visible as he said, "Ghost hunting really exhausted you, huh?"

"Causing me nightmares," I said off the top of my head.

Rhett's eyes flashed to mine as he gasped, "You dream?"

"Yeah all the time," I mindlessly stated.

They both seemed to look at each other in a strange way.

"What?" I asked.

"Nothing," Marvin said shaking his head.

"You don't dream?" I asked.

"No!" Marvin said with a smile.

"Whenever you are ready, I'll walk you back to the Hall of Knowledge," Rhett stated.

"There's no need," I disagreed. "Marvin can walk me back." Rhett started to disagree as I held my hand up to stop him saying, "I already told you, I can get past Professor Zirak."

Rhett turned serious as he warned, "Tilly and you are going to be in serious trouble if the professors figure out you are coming and going without their permission."

"Probably," I agreed. "Tonight though, I'm too tired to worry about it."

Rhett shook his head as he made his way out of the room.

"He's right," Marvin said as he stood. "I am causing you to break rules to see me."

"Not you too," I whined as I stood, putting my arms around his waist and snuggling into his chest. "Please... Not tonight."

With a deep sigh, he gave in and his arms were soon around me. I knew he had more to say, but was surrendering to my begging whine.

"Love birds," echoed down the hall as Rhett called. "You better get going."

"Let's go," Marvin said. His hand rested on the small of my back as we moved down the hall.

As we passed the kitchen, Rhett was fixing himself a late night snack. He looked up, "Good night guys."

"Good night," Marvin replied.

"See you later," I added as Marvin opened the door for me.

The cool night air washed over my skin as we sauntered down the cracked sidewalk towards the Dogwood Trail. "You are quiet," I said to Marvin.

"Your not feeling well reminds me of Mrs. VanCues," Marvin stated.

I stopped and looked him directly in the eyes, "I already told you, I feel fine. It has just been a long day! Why in the world would I remind you of Mrs. VanCues?"

"She's been sick this week," Marvin said with a sigh and a look that read there was more.

"And?" I questioned.

He put his hands in his pockets while the suspense built in the silence. He began, "Mrs. VanCues says she hears us all the time. I know that others think she is…" he seemed to stop not wanting to say the obvious word, crazy. "I believe that she does hear us and I have a theory about that."

"A theory?" I asked.

"I know those on the Earth Plane can hear their assigned Keeper if they listen for them," Marvin began. "But I also believe Humlings and Keepers here can sometimes hear each other while here at Home. When I was in training, Mrs. VanCues often talked about learning she could hear us while being here in the afterlife, as she calls it."

Marvin paused and rattled whatever was in his pocket and shuffled his feet. There was something so simple in his demeanor when he was nervous.

"I have never shared with anyone my real reason for wanting to work with Mrs. VanCues. Everyone has thought I was crazy for wanting to work with her." His eyes flashed to mine as he spit out, "I hope to go see her on the Humling side of Home when she returns to see if she can still hear me. I want to prove my theory."

"How do you plan on getting to her on the Humling side?" I questioned, amused by his seriousness. Going to the Humling side was a piece of cake for Tilly and me.

"I will never get clearance to travel outside of the dome to go anywhere near her. I'm going to the Hospital wing when she arrives. It is the only place were we can be in the same place together at Home. I plan to stand far enough away so that I can send her my thoughts and see if she reacts to them," Said Marvin.

My mind flashed back to the first time I saw Dustin. Was he checking to see if I could hear his thoughts when I arrived in the hospital wing? At that time, I felt so drawn to him. He seemed to exude safe and secure. I was frightened, confused, and alone. I had thought he knew me on that first night in the Hospital. I had wondered why he seemed to want to protect me from harm, whether it is Mrs. Farris, Tiffany, or what he perceived as harm from Marvin.

"Elizabeth?" He questioned to regain my attention.

"This is why you didn't think I was crazy when I told you I could hear others?" I spit out.

Marvin smiled at me as we stopped on the bridge overlooking the river in Spring Park. "I suppose, you now think I am the crazy one?" Marvin asked as he leaned on the railing.

"No, you're the sanest person in this crazy world of mine," I said as I too leaned against the railing. "Can you promise me something?"

He looked wary when he said, "Depends on what it is?"

"When the time comes to test your theory, may I come along?" I asked.

He paused and I could tell he was wondering why I would want too. Puzzled he answered, "I guess."

"I just think it's interesting," I added resting my hand on top of his as we leaned on the bridge railing eyeing the beauty of the landscape beyond the bridge.

"Mrs. VanCues is getting old!" Marvin seriously said. "I think the time is close."

As if on cue, I could hear the familiar sound of wheels rolling against the pavement, approaching Spring Park. I peered over my shoulder and waited for the skater to come into view. I had to wonder what Tilly was doing out on her board at this time of night. Up to no good, I was sure. I was totally surprised that Trevor was rapidly approaching. After seeing us, he dug the heel of his board into the pavement and skidded to a stop.

"Hey," Marvin greeted Trevor.

"Hey," Trevor returned with a look on his face which screamed he had been caught. "What are the two of you up too?"

"I'm walking Elizabeth home from Rhett's," Marvin stated.

"We watched history movies tonight," I added. "You aren't waiting up for Tilly?"

"She's already in," Trevor shortly stated.

"Where are you heading?" Marvin asked with a serious look on his face.

Trevor sighed deeply before answering, "I needed a little fresh air."

"Were the two of you still arguing over…?" I paused as Trevor seemed to avoid our eyes. I looked away from Marvin's peering eyes. How careless could I be? Thank goodness Marvin knew nothing about the destination card maker. He really wouldn't approve. Trevor was nervous because he thought I was spilling the beans.

With another big avoiding sigh Trevor said, "No, she got her way. She always gets her way. This time I'm right though! The guy she sneaked off to see tonight is too old for her."

There was only one man I could think of that was too old for Tilly. "The guy with the bow tie?" I asked feeling Marvin's stare.

"Yeah," Trevor said. "His name is Barrett and he walked her up to the bottom of the ladder tonight."

"Your way around the professors is a ladder?" Marvin surmised. "Classic escape route. They probably wouldn't dream your method would be so simple."

"Simple," Trevor stated with exasperation. "Dude, it's not simple. Someone keeps cutting the thing. I keep repairing it. You have to put it out and take it in each night. I have to stay up until everyone is safely in for the night."

"Set your alarm clock and pull it in," Marvin suggested. "There is no need to lose sleep."

"Let me ask, why are you walking Elizabeth home?" Trevor pointedly asked.

"Point taken," Marvin conceded with a true look of understanding for Trevor's predicament. "You want to know Tilly is in for the night."

"Not only do I have to worry about her making it in," Trevor sighed. "Now, I have to worry about her dating that predator! She won't be sneaking off anymore to meet Barrett at..." He paused suddenly mid sentence. He didn't want to spill the secret of the destination card maker.

I could see Marvin tense up beside me. He knew we were both leaving out where Tilly had gone tonight.

"Look, it doesn't matter if you're right or wrong about the guy being too old for Tilly," Marvin stated in a reasoning voice. Marvin placed his arm around me and continued, "Man, if you've dug a hole with Tilly, give her a little space tonight. Apologize tomorrow."

Trevor nodded as if taking in Marvin's advice. Trevor and I both knew you couldn't talk Tilly into thinking like you did. It was like trying to give a cat a bath.

CHAPTER
TWENTY-TWO

Elizabeth

After a boring and sleepy morning learning how to properly access a Keeper's portal with Professor Zirak, I was headed up to our office to log a few of Mrs. VanCues requests and how they were answered in her dreams. As I entered the line approaching the turn-style in the lobby of the Keeper Complex, I couldn't help but notice Dustin standing on the opposite end of the turn-style. His tall body was leaned up against a wall and those pale, long fingers were picking candy out of a clear bag and popping them into his mouth. I quickly looked away as he glanced at me and our eyes met. Darn, I was caught red handed staring at him.

"Wow, does she look ill today," I heard Dustin's mind say.

Subconsciously I pushed the loose wisps of my hair back behind my ear and tightened my pony tail. I was a little tired, but not sick. What was he talking about?

I moved through the turn style and began to walk briskly past Dustin as I heard, "Not even going to say hello today?"

I stopped and looked into his smirking face. I asked, "Won't your girl-friend care that you are talking to the enemy?"

"Who cares what she thinks!" I heard his mind retort.

His face turned serious as he held the bag out for me, "Want a piece?"

"What is it?" I asked.

"Ginger candy," Dustin replied.

"No thank you," I said as I looked back over my shoulder at the lift.

"You should try it before you knock it," I heard him think.

"You do know I'm trying to be nice!" Dustin stated as I turned back to look at him. The bag was still extended for me to take a piece.

Reluctantly, I grabbed the bag from his hands and reached in. The candy had the consistency of dried fruit. Not hard, but not soft. I held the brown murky candy up and looked it over.

Dustin grabbed the bag back saying, "It's not poison!" With that he reached in with his slender pale fingers and plucked a piece from the bag and tossed it into his mouth.

I followed his lead. To my surprise, the candy was good. I savored the sweet, tangy, goodness! "What did you say this was again?" I asked.

"Ginger," Dustin stated looking at me oddly with those deep brown eyes. Almost like he was studying my reaction.

I had to admit, "It's actually…"

"Yummy," Dustin finished for me with an I told you so smile. He extended the clear bag back my way, "Take it. I'll get more for myself."

It was simply too good to pass up. I took the bag from him asking, "Who are you waiting for?"

"Waiting for my love," I heard his mind reply.

He shrugged, looking away and running his fingers through his spiked hair.

"Well, I had better get to training," I stammered as I once again looked to the lift doors. Being caught by Tiffany talking with Dustin would be gravely dangerous.

"Yeah," Dustin sighed. "Later."

"Thanks again," I added holding up the clear bag as I turned to stroll over to the lift.

I popped piece after piece of candy into my mouth, enjoying each succulent bite as the lift took me to my office. The minute the door dinged, I was greeted by a smiling Marvin who looked genuinely glad to see me.

"Were you just hanging out by the lift to greet me?" I asked in a teasing manner.

"Actually, I was waiting to give you something," Marvin hem-hawed. With that, his hands held out another backpack.

I sheepishly smiled at him. I didn't think he had noticed my missing backpack.

"Take it!" Marvin stated as I took it from his hands. "I ran into one of the other girls from your house. I thought she had your backpack."

"Well, you see, it's a long story," I began as I stared at my feet.

Marvin placed his finger across my lips saying, "I can't blame you for helping another trainee who didn't have a backpack."

My eyes darted to his as my mind screamed What!

"She explained how badly she needed one and, of course, you understood her need for one," Marvin said with a shrug. "I get it. However, that doesn't mean I want you to do without. I'm just sorry it took me a couple days to get you a replacement."

I flung my arms around his neck overcome with his understanding and generosity. Of course, I would need to thank Destiny for this special moment. Who would have thought she would craft such a good story to cover for me.

Someone cleared their throat and we both turned to see Mrs. VanCues Head Keeper, Jacob, standing with disapproval all over his face. He stated, "We have work to do today."

"Yes sir," Marvin stated. I nervously shook my head affirmatively as we both began to move towards Marvin's desk.

"Logging dreams today?" Marvin asked.

"Yes, I'm hoping to get as many as possible today." I unhappily responded.

"Where's Tilly?" Marvin asked frowning. "Tell me you are not planning to log dreams for you and Tilly?"

"Well, she is busy with Harmony," I responded as I shoved my bag of ginger candy to the bottom of my new backpack.

"No busier than you are with attending classes and working at the Hall of Records each day," Marvin retorted clearly put out. "Not to mention Tilly has turned your one hour a day Harmony practice into three hours every night.

He had given me a glimpse into his mind. He was frustrated with our practices which were running long and depriving us of our time. "We have to practice. If Tilly doesn't succeed, Tiffany will once again become conductress," I responded. "Who wants that? Actually, who could live with that?"

"She should do her own work," Marvin scolded despite my practical response.

"You know, she helps me out in her own way. It is give and take between us," I replied.

With that, Marvin sat quiet and returned to filling out his paperwork. His silence said he didn't agree. However, I couldn't concentrate on his evaluation of the situation.

I made my way to the locked shelf which contained the recorded sections of Mrs. VanCues life on the Earth Plane. Dale, the second in charge in this office, sat beside the locked shelf. I interrupted him while he worked as I asked, "Excuse me, would you mind to open the shelf for me."

"Why do you need in there?" Dale asked as he looked up from his paperwork.

"In training this week, we are to record different types of dreams," I began. "Professor Zirak told us to do the research on the Humling we were assigned too."

"Hmm…" was all Dale hummed in response. He began to pack up the paperwork from several files which were sprawled over the top of his desk cluttering it. Once they were neatly stacked, he stood and dug a large ring of keys out of his pocket.

"Are all of those for here?" I asked off the top of my head.

"Everything in a Keeper office is kept under lock and key," Dale responded as he shoved a small silver key into the lock on the shelf. With a quick turn he slid the glass door to one side and began to dig through the small, bound recorded sections.

I was shocked to see that there were so many of them. They didn't resemble the chapters found in the Hall of Records. I couldn't help but ask, "There are so many of those, how will they be combined and turned into one, single chapter?"

"All of these smaller volumes will indeed turn into one larger chapter!" Dale assured me. With a sigh he added, "However, I'm sure it will be one of the heaviest stored in the Hall of Records." With a slight grin he continued, "Haven't you noticed that chapters use rolodexing?"

"Rolodexing?" I repeated with a confused expression.

"Miss Cantrell, have you not been paying attention in your Records training?" Dale seriously asked. With a shake of his head he continued, "All chapters have an invisible rolodex inside them. Chapters are the exact same size on the shelves at the Hall of Records. Each contains exactly one hundred pages. However, they may contain hundreds or thousands of actual pages. Depends on the Humling."

"The more you thumb through them, seemingly endless pages appear," I stated as my mind drifted to the Art History book in Mr. Farris's private library. It had been incredibly heavy for such a relatively small book. I barely got it to the desk before realizing its appearance was deceiving. Rolodexing.

"Maybe you aren't sleeping through your training then," Dale said under his breath while he pulled several volumes from the shelf.

"Without someone really telling me about chapter's rolodexing, how would I know they did this?" I questioned. Before he could respond I added, "I thought only those who the chapter belonged too could open them. So how would I discover this?"

His face turned stern as he glared at me. "Don't even try to tell me you never reviewed your file upon returning Home. These…" He held up the volumes in his hands. "Are reviewed in the file upon returning, then they are sent to the Hall of Records with your signed file to be processed into their final chapter." He stood slightly shaking his head awaiting my response.

"Oh yeah," I stated shaking my head in agreement. Maybe I had never done this? I certainly didn't remember doing this. Maybe this was why my chapters were blank.

"As far as us reviewing them within this office," Dale continued. "Anyone can. We are all authorized to view these until they are turned into the official chapter to be stored in the Hall of Records. Then yes, Mrs. VanCues would be the only one able to access them at that point. That is, without Council permission."

"I guess that clears it up," I stated desperately wanting out of this conversation.

With a sigh which screamed he was frustrated with our whole conversation he asked, "Do you know how to use the viewer?"

"We have a viewer?" I returned.

"In Jacob's office," Dale said shaking his head yes and pointing towards the one office door I had never been invited into. He handed the three volumes over to me and added, "Don't take these out of the office and I need them back before you leave today. Again, you do know how to use the viewer."

I shook my head yes as I reluctantly took the volumes from Dale's hands. "Thanks."

"You're welcome," Dale stated as he closed the clear door to the shelf and locked it back with his small, silver key.

Jacob's office was always a hub of excitement with those coming and going all day long. He was almost a recluse inside his office, taking it so far as to eat every meal in there. Tilly and I neither one had ever been invited into his office and rarely saw him. Uneasy was the only way to describe walking up to his door. I stepped up to the door and knocked.

"Come in," the voice bellowed from inside.

I opened the door and made my way inside. Instantly, I wondered how so many fit into this small place. This room could best be described as a closet. A narrow work center ran the length of the room along the wall. It had three stools pulled up to it, one of which Jacob was sitting on. One stool set in front of the viewer and the other was in front of a work space that was stacked to the ceiling in papers. The other side of the wall was covered in an array of bulletin boards with a green chalkboard in the very center. Instead of cleaning off the bulletin boards, it appeared they simply added new ones and stacked papers on top of old papers on the current boards. The floors under the work center were full of boxes with papers haphazardly sticking out of them. The ceiling had shelves suspended from it with more boxes. In contrast to the clean, orderly office environment beyond this office, this room was a disorganized mess.

"Welcome to the hub, Miss Cantrell," Jacob stated gaining my attention. "I know it's a little messy."

"You run such a tight ship out there," I said off the top of my mind in unbelief that the office outside the door looked like someone with O.C.D. managed it. Versus the office I was standing in appeared like a hoarder lived in here.

He chuckled and disagreed, "No, Dale runs a tight ship. He likes order. I have too much to do with Mrs. VanCues to worry about cleaning and filing." He paused and then asked, "What can I help you with today?"

I held up the volumes saying, "I need to view these. I'm logging dreams for an assignment."

"There's the viewer," he said pointing towards the machine next to him. "Have at it!"

I plopped the volumes down on the desk and pulled out the stool and climbed up on it. I opened the first volume to thumb through the pages and noticed a slightly raised red page marker. Instantly, I flipped to the page and found it marked a dream.

I must have made some type of noise because Jacob answered my unspoken thoughts, "We often have trainees come to view her. It helps to pre-mark the sections they will need. Since Mrs. VanCues has many volumes, we don't always have time to help them find what they are looking for."

I nodded and flipped through the second volume noticing several pages already marked with the slightly raised red markers. "That certainly saves me time," I added.

"You certainly lucked out on this assignment," Jacob agreed before returning to his paperwork.

I loaded the first volume into the viewer and it began to play. The arm of the machine came out over the chapter and began to skim the words. On the white wall the machine projected a small moving scene in vivid color form.

Jacob interrupted as he asked, "Would you mind to use the headset."

His hand was pointing to an old, raggedy looking pair of black headphones. I picked them up answering, "Sure."

He took the cord and plugged it in for me as I placed the headset on. Now I was lost in the dream which I was beginning to watch.

The Mrs. VanCues which I was accustomed to watching always wore slacks and a fashionable coordinating top. Everything she wore complimented her snow white hair. It was a shock to be viewing Mrs. VanCues as a young person in her thirties wearing jeans and a sweatshirt.

She was standing on a tarmac viewing an airplane making pre-flight preparations. You could see the confusion on her face as to why she was standing there. Eventually, she lost focus on the workers and the plane as she began to watch colorful tree leaves falling and blowing around the outskirts of the airport. It was a marvelous, sunny fall day. She turned rapidly as if looking at landmarks she suddenly recognized. This is when she must have realized she was standing on the tarmac which serviced her hometown.

She had missed the beginning of the line of those who had begun to climb the mobile staircase from the tarmac to the airplane door. All the individuals were military in identical fatigues and crew-cuts. As she caught a glimpse of the men, a look of pure panic crossed her face. She began to concentrate on the faces of those passing her. She mumbled, "Please don't let him get called up. Not him."

As fleeting as this thought was, she moved on to the next moment. A soldier who was standing at the top of the mobile staircase was waving and trying to get her to see him. He was lovingly staring down at her as her eyes blinked away the tears upon seeing him. I had seen photos of him hanging in her house and I knew this was her husband. With a deep breath she dried and reopened her eyes to see his arms outstretched as if he was ready for her to run into his arms. His left hand began to wave wildly an American flag. A moment of pure pride for his service seemed to sweep over her.

The plane began to fade and suddenly she found herself standing within a graveyard. She closed her eyes and was very audible when she said, "Not him. Please don't take him." I understood she didn't want to open her eyes for fear it would be her husband lying in the casket.

She didn't see her husband because it was not him lying there. All the mourners were crying as they looked upon her father-in-law. The last thing she focused on were the silver dollars placed over his eyes. The shock was too much and all of a sudden, Mrs. VanCues awoke.

I stopped the viewer machine, pulled the volume out, and took off the headset. I then proceeded to write down the dream while several others entered and dropped off paperwork, placing it between Jacob and myself. Each time he thanked them and went right back to work, ignoring me. As I wrote my last word, his pen dropped to the table.

He peered at me and asked, "What type of dream was that?"

"A fear dream," I answered.

He shook his head no while I recognized and thought it might be a wish dream. "Is the dream a prophecy?"

Do you understand the difference between them all?" Jacob asked.

"Well, yeah. A prediction dream foretells the future, a wish tells the Humlings deepest desires, and a release dream lets go of worries or concerns buried deep within them," I rattled.

"Good way to put it," Jacob answered. "Since both the wish and release dreams are from the Humling subconscious, they instigate those. These are avenues of understanding for us. We can see their deepest desires and truly understand their worries. To help them, you must be able to understand both of these avenues."

"Only the dream of prediction comes from us," I surmised.

"Yes," Jacob answered. "We use this type of dream to answer their questions or concerns, tell them about future joys, or warn them about future problems. This type of communication is vital between the Keeper and Humling."

"So you were warning her in this dream," I said as I held up the volume.

"Yes," Jacob stated. "There would be turmoil leading up to and falling afterwards from this happening in her life. To an outside on-looker like yourself, it might be seen as a fear dream. That is why knowing your Humling is so very important."

A beeping noise sounded as Jacob smiled a weary smile saying, "I'm on!" Go ahead and stay to view those." He stated pointing to my remaining two volumes.

"Okay," I returned.

I watched as he pulled open a door which was buried under the bulletin boards. It wasn't until now that I even noticed the door handle. With a smile he stepped into the darkness of the portal. This had to be the offices missing dream portal.

CHAPTER
TWENTY-THREE

Tilly

Life was great! Friday night had finally come! I was awaiting Elizabeth in the Hall of Records and extremely happy to get away from the office and Marvin the square. He didn't like Elizabeth logging a few dreams for me and had purposely seen to it that they kept me all day. To make it worse, Mrs. VanCues was sick and I simply couldn't stand to listen to her whine. That was when my spur of the moment plan fell into place. I was always so brilliant!

They gave me those boring volumes and sent me into Jacob's disorganized office to watch them on the viewer. Jacob seemed to be out, which was odd. Someone said something about his son was leaving today at the Hall of Babies. Mrs. VanCues was going on and on about her guy being missing when she didn't feel well, thus the whining. My being a firm believer that when the cats away the mice should play, I did what any bored trainee would do.

I had no intention of watching the dreams on the viewer. It didn't matter how long they required me to sit here. No matter which stack I dug in, or which box, all the papers in this small office revolved around Mrs. VanCues. Boring! That is when I happened to hear the whining coming from behind the wall. I moved to the other end of the long, small office and discovered a door. Not just any door, it was a portal door. This was too good to be true.

I stood looking down into the dark portal thinking I should just do down and tell her to give it a rest. Her whining and whaling was simply on my last nerve. I went down the six steps in the dark holding onto the walls. At the end, I was surprised to find I couldn't step out. An invisible barrier was barring me from it.

I could hear her crying and thought for a moment that I shouldn't interfere. That is when she noticed me. I had never considered that she could actually see me. I should have though. She was perceptive.

I don't know what overcame me, but I in a moment of panic began to attempt to sing the lullaby Mrs. Summors had always sang to me when I was upset. I discovered as I moved my mouth, nothing came out. I could hear the song in my head and it seemed as I thought the tune, Mrs. VanCues began to lay her head over. I was surprised. Communication between worlds must be telepathic. Mrs. VanCues fell asleep with the singing in my head.

Once she was asleep, I could feel the invisible barrier disappear before me. Of course, this was a dream portal. I now was free to walk beyond the barrier. I had not one ounce of interest in messing with her dreams. I tiptoed back up the six steps and back into the small office. I took my seat before the viewer and enjoyed the quiet. She slept very peacefully the whole afternoon. Marvin was gone when I exited Jacob's office. I was disappointed not to be able to ignore him and to show my displeasure with him. The square.

However, the tide had turned. By the looks of Elizabeth exiting the lift with Marvin, I was going to get my chance. I got up from my place at the table and began to make my way over.

"Marvin, I really insist. Take the team to their tournament and don't give me a second thought," Elizabeth was saying.

"Elizabeth, this is your first home weekend," Marvin replied.

"I know, but the team is your and Jessie's responsibility. What would everyone think if you didn't go?" Elizabeth reasoned.

"What are you going to do for the weekend?" Marvin asked.

"I don't know," Elizabeth playfully responded. "I could always terrorize Tilly's family." She turned to smile at me for obviously eavesdropping on their private conversation. Marvin raised his eyebrows and Elizabeth answered him, "What? She did invite me."

"You do realize I would take you with me," Marvin stated. "But, Dad can't request a pass for you."

"Elizabeth doesn't need you every waking moment of every day," I butted in and then blew a big pink bubble.

Ignoring me, Marvin pulled Elizabeth close to him and I thought I heard him mumble, "I wish I didn't have to leave you."

"Stop being silly," I mused. "It's just two days and Elizabeth won't fall into a black hole while you are gone."

The lift door dinged and opened to reveal Marvin's friend, hairy legs. He strutted out into the room with his backpack slung over his shoulder. He smirked at the sight of Marvin and Elizabeth as he asked, "Ready?"

"Yeah," Marvin sighed as he leaned over to peck Elizabeth on the lips. She gave him a lost puppy dog smile as he turned to walk away.

"What about me?" I threw out. "No goodbye for me?"

"Bye Tilly," Marvin said with a wave of his hand.

"Good luck!" Elizabeth bid them as they entered the lift.

"The plan for tonight is dinner at my house," I said interrupting Elizabeth's stare at the lift. "My mother is having one of her parties."

"You don't have to take me home with you," Elizabeth responded.

"And leave you pinning away in our room by yourself?" I asked. "Her parties generally aren't that bad. There will be great food, her friends will ignore us, and we can sneak out early without her noticing."

"You are not going to take no as an answer, are you?" Elizabeth asked.

I smiled and simply said, "Thank you, No!"

"A thankful Tilly? Turning over a new leaf?" Asked Trevor with a chuckle as he strolled up with Ruthanne in tow.

Elizabeth answered, "She was thanking me for agreeing to face…"

"The Queen," I finished her sentence.

A hint of a grin flashed across his face but was gone in an instant. "What time do you want us there?"

"Us?" I questioned. Then I looked over at Ruthanne who looked paler than normal and nervous under my glare. He was bringing her and hadn't asked me.

Ruthanne began to answer, "Hopefully, you don't mind that Trevor…"

I held up my hand to stop her. "The more the merrier," I stated. Trevor gave me a glare. I added, "I would love for the two of you to come around six."

"Why not suffer right along with us," Elizabeth stated from beside me in a teasing voice. Ruthanne shyly smiled at her.

"Dinners there usually aren't that bad," Trevor stated. "Considering they are at the Ice Castle."

He was kind.

CHAPTER
TWENTY-FOUR

Elizabeth

We followed a meandering sidewalk along the golf course. I was discovering a new territory I had never wandered out towards the other side of Spring Park. A road forked to the right and I followed Tilly down it. This road was lined with stately homes, huge trees, and well manicured lawns. The houses along this road gave Mr. Solliday's estate a run for its money. They were magnificent.

"Don't look so in awe," Tilly stated.

"All of these homes are impressive," I stated doing a little rubbernecking.

"Not really," Tilly retorted. "They are all show. With only a couple of exceptions, the majority of those who dwell in them have no substance."

"Pine Hills Country Club?" I questioned as we passed a sign with an arrow painting.

"Yeah, it sets just down the pathway," Tilly said as she popped a piece of gum in her mouth.

We walked past a couple more houses as Tilly slowed before a wrought iron fence surrounding a colonial home with six white pillars lining its front. In its bare state, the yard looked much different than those surrounding it. There were no trees, bushes, flowers, or life. Only rocks.

I hesitated, "Tilly, it's so…"

"Cold and impersonal," Tilly stated. "Mother had the trees moved long ago. Then they hauled in all that rock. She likes rock gardens and it fits her personality." She shrugged, pointed, and added, "Trevor's home is the big two story Victorian with the huge front porch at the end of the street with light and love shining from its windows."

I peered down the street, but couldn't see his home. Tilly was holding open the wrought iron gate for me. We walked up the walkway to the massive wooden front door. Tilly's mother was awaiting our arrival and standing stiff and starchy to greet us.

When we reached the front door, Mrs. Bradford put both her hands on Tilly's shoulders saying, "Welcome home dear!" Then she pulled Tilly towards her and gave her an overly dramatic embrace.

"Hey Mother," Tilly returned as Mrs. Bradford let her go and granted passage into the house.

"Miss Cantrell," Mrs. Bradford paused trying to decide how to greet me. Now I could see the room full of others beyond her and understood. This was to be a show. "Welcome to my home!" I was given an embrace as well.

"Thank you for inviting me," I mumbled. "Your home is grand and beautiful."

"I would certainly hope so," Mrs. Bradford returned. Then she whispered in my ear, "Don't do anything to embarrass me tonight." Then she pulled back and gave me a super sticky sweet smile looking me over from head to toe. "Mathilda, can you find your friend something more appropriate to wear for our dinner party?" I didn't particularly think I looked frumpy today in my uniform slacks and blouse. Mrs. Bradford sighed and added, "That hair. Mathilda, see it's brushed."

Tilly grabbed my hand asking, "Dinner at six?"

Mrs. Bradford gave Tilly a serious look saying, "Is that the only reason you came home? To eat?"

"No," Tilly said. "I just wanted to ensure that I had time to add the additional place settings for my additional guests."

"Why do you insist on bringing that boy?" Mrs. Bradford whispered, not wanting her guests to hear.

"Boys," Tilly corrected.

"Why of course," Mrs. Bradford spewed. "He insists on bringing that slacker cousin of his."

"Tonight, Trevor will be bringing an additional guest as well," Tilly added.

"Honey," Mr. Bradford interrupted walking up with a smile giving Tilly a hug.

"Hello Father," Tilly answered.

"Trevor is coming," Mr. Bradford surmised. "Why don't you all sit down by me tonight? I would love to hear how training is coming."

"There wouldn't be room for the number of place settings Mathilda will be adding down by you," Mrs. Bradford nervously countered wringing her hands.

"Is something wrong dear?" Mr. Bradford seriously asked.

"Absolutely not!" Mrs. Bradford retorted. She looked at Tilly and you could see her holding back whatever was willing itself to slip off her tongue. I was right that she was putting on a show for her friends. "Mathilda, please give me more notice the next time you decide to add to my guest list."

"Honey, if Mathilda is coming, you should expect Trevor and Eddie," Mr. Bradford stated. "Now we have Miss Cantrell with us as well." Mr. Bradford started to give me a warm smile, and then he noticed Mrs. Bradford staring bullets at him. "Good evening."

"Hello," I returned.

"What I expect is for everyone in this family to respect my wishes," Mrs. Bradford stated.

With this, Mr. Bradford took a huge drink from the glass he was holding, and then said, "Yes dear."

With the cowering tone, it was something I was sure he said a lot to Mrs.

Bradford.

"Don't worry Mother, I will retrieve the additional settings right now since six is almost here and help the staff reset the table," Tilly said as she pulled me beyond her parents.

As we walked straight down the center of the massive, stark white, formal living room, people bunched in pairs or groups would wave politely at Tilly and me while obviously whispering about us. Actually, probably about me since I seemed to look so unacceptable. Tilly whispered a few times to me their names or jobs they held. They must, as a whole, be a group of aristocrats. Did it really matter if I fit in?

The far side of the living room gave way to a classic, long dining room. The lengthy wooden table invited you in and seemed to run forever down the center of the long room. It was long itself with armed chairs on either end of the table. The two end table settings were formal dripped with gold, while the rest were just as elegant, only silver. Tilly was busily taking out matching plate settings from the massive china hutch as I began to wonder where she would be placing them on the table. I didn't see any chair which didn't have a place setting in front of it.

I began to walk around the table peering at the place cards. Each was exquisitely rendered in fancy calligraphy writing and included the guests name and employment. I knew Mr. Bradford worked at the Administration Complex, however I had no idea he was the complex administrator. "Tilly, your dad!" I blurted out as I pointed at his card.

"Yeah, he was just promoted," Tilly sighed dejected. "Why wouldn't he be promoted? He has spent nearly every waking hour there for my whole life." She instantly went to pulling out the silver spoons, forks, and knives and haphazardly placing them on top of the stack of plates.

I continued to walk around. There were several council members, high ranking complex associates, community members, and unfortunately close friends whom would all be present. "Did you know Tiffany is coming? More interestingly, did you know she is bringing a date?"

"Oh, I'm sorry!" Tilly stated and turned to look right at me. "Yes, Tiffany always comes with her parents, but I had no idea she was bringing a date." Tilly paused, "Dustin?"

"Bingo!" I stated exasperated with my luck.

"Are you planning a game to spice things up around here?" A gentleman in a chef's hat asked as he appeared in the dining room.

"Dalton!" Tilly squealed.

He gave her a friendly grin and then looked at me.

"Dalton, this is Elizabeth," Tilly said as she pointed to me. "Elizabeth, this is Dalton."

"Hello," I said with a wave of my hand.

"It is nice to meet you," Dalton said as he tipped his head and chefs hat.

"Where's Jill?" Tilly asked.

"Jill didn't come tonight," Dalton said and looked away. "She's still at the country club."

"Why?" Tilly demanded.

"Your mother asked me to bring Rowan," Dalton stated. "She also asked me to set the table for you." He walked over to take the plates and clearly didn't want to tell us the full story. Tilly stared him down. He leaned over and whispered, "Stop by sometime if you want me to elaborate."

"The Queen always gets what she wants," Tilly sighed.

"Indeed she does," Dalton replied.

The first members of the dinner party were beginning to huddle around the dining room entry arch. "Tilly, we need to go freshen up. Guests are heading for the table," I started to point. I had no idea where her room was in this massive home and I couldn't go on my own.

Tilly smiled, waved, and answered, "Come on. You are right, we better get changed or the Queen will have a melt down."

"She didn't object to your appearance," I added.

"She did," Tilly disagreed as we moved out the arch on the other end of the dining room which leads away from the guests and living room. We walked past a pristine office, a bathroom, and several closed doors. Our journey ended as the hallway spilled out into a commercial kitchen. Towards the back of the room, a staircase jetted off on the left. Tilly stopped before it saying, "Welcome to the private entrance to my wing within the Ice Castle."

"Ice Castle?" I repeated. "I though this was perhaps the entrance to the servants quarters."

"Ouch! Servants quarters," Tilly stated looking serious like I might have stated her mother's obvious low opinion of her. "Trevor and I named my parents home, the Ice Castle, long ago," Tilly said with her face turning devious. "The house is cold and in general and unfriendly place. However, my wing is full of life and warmth, plus I have access to the kitchen. Mother hates it! We call it the bubble gum wing. You first."

I began to walk up the staircase noticing the wooden wanes coating and bubble gum pink walls. It screamed clean, warm, and most definitely Tilly's color.

The staircase gave way to a small, cramped living area. I was amazed at what I saw. The wanes coating had been painted bubble gum pink as well as the lower half of the walls. The upper half was covered in an array of pictures which all seemed to be glued directly to the walls in a mismatched manner. Many smiling pictures were of Trevor, Eddie, and Tilly all doing different activities. There were some family photos and some photos of persons I didn't recognize. A few photos included those I knew including Mrs. Summors, the chef downstairs, and others from our training. Snapshots of Tilly playing tennis, basketball, and golf were scattered everywhere. Then there were photos of Tilly playing the piano and attending dance class. The walls looked like full pages of what could only be described as pages from a yearbook. All four walls were plastered with her life memories. All were displayed to welcome any guest who came up.

The black ceiling left this room with a cave like feeling. There was no carpet in a traditional sense. It was foe, black fur with glimmers of pink here and there. The only furniture was a small, black couch and huge television. A gaming system appeared to be hooked up to the television with a basket full of games setting next to it. On the other side of the gaming system in the corner was a pile of glass vases from flowers. I couldn't even guess how many were piled there as souvenirs of men and boys who had sent her flowers.

Tilly passed me and stood in the middle of this room asking, "You haven't said anything yet. Don't you like it?"

"It definitely has your style," I said off the top of my head. "You are right, it's warm and friendly."

She walked away from me and through the only door in the room. I followed her. The next room was incredibly more shocking than the last. It was almost psychedelic. The walls were painted hot pink with the same black ceiling and foe, black fur floor. A wooden, four poster bed set in the middle of the room with pink and purple draping hanging from it. Her pink and black plaid bedspread was crumpled and discarded on the floor, revealing her black, silk sheets. Behind the bed, a mosaic of bubble gum wrappers that swept up, across the black ceiling, and down the wall on the other side of the room. Hmm… trash hanging on the walls. A huge make up counter, the kind you would see in a movie stars dressing room was across one wall.

I walked up to check out the monstrous beauty parlor pit. Photos of all the boys Tilly dated hung around the mirrors edge. I was sure I was looking at the ghosts of many brokenhearted boyfriends. The photos were falling off at places and piling up on the floor. Thinking about the comments made by Mrs. Bradford, I pulled my ponytail holder out of my hair and let my long hair fall over my shoulders. I brushed it out and shoved the pony tail holder into my pants pocket.

"Come in here!" I heard Tilly bellow from the depths behind another door.

I stepped into a massive closet. The clothing in this room could rival a small store with the clothes hung by type and color. Tilly held up a bubble gum pink dress asking, "Do you like it?"

"Not really," I said wanting to run if that was what I had to wear.

"Yeah," Tilly sighed. "I thought you would say that." She ruffled through the clothing behind her pulling out another dress. Orange. "Is this any better?"

"You want me to look like a nectarine?" I retorted.

"No," Tilly replied. "But I have very few dresses which are long. I could always let you wear something with a little more flare. We could spice things up a bit!"

"My choice is between the two then?" I questioned ignoring the comment about flare altogether. Tilly shrugged and shook her head.

"Let me have the pink one," I sighed as she handed it over. "How does my hair look to you?"

"I'm sorry about her comments," Tilly sighed. "Concerning your hair and clothes."

"It's fine," I said. "It is her party."

"I know," Tilly stated. "But, you're a guest. That isn't how you should treat a guest."

"Don't worry about it," I reassured Tilly. "I'm going to get changed."

"I want the opportunity to shower," Tilly said. "Can I meet you downstairs?"

"I'll make my way down," I said as I smiled at Tilly.

I changed into the bubble gum pink dress which seemed to mold to my body. As I peered at my reflection in the mirror, I had to admit I didn't actually look bad in this dress. I paced, looked out the window, and tried to pass the time to wait for Tilly. I wasn't sure about facing the crowd downstairs alone. Finally, I had to go on without her.

When I came down, I was surprised to find the seats around the table were almost completely taken. There were two empty seats across from each other. One next to Trevor and one next to Dustin. I was trying my best not to look at Dustin. He hadn't noticed me and was seated next to Tiffany. They appeared to be happily amusing to each other. This evening was going to be awkward if I had to sit anywhere near them.

I walked past Mr. Bradford who was already seated at the end of the table. I approached the seat next to Trevor who was already seated.

It was Eddie who waved at me saying, "Ooo, la, la." Then he pointed to the seat next to him, and said, "You are next to me Crash. See!" He held up a place card with my name on it.

I felt absolutely sick! I was to be sitting between Dustin and Eddie. I glanced down at the place setting and place card next to Trevor. It was Tilly's. The empty seat to her other side was designated for Scott. Tilly's father hadn't given up hope that Tilly would one day date Scott. At least her night was shaping up to be as awkward as mine. I smiled at the grinning Eddie and returned, "Great."

That is when Dustin seemed to notice me. He appeared taken back by my appearance, but not in a good way. I felt awkward in the borrowed pink dress. His look at me wasn't one which stated I looked fabulous.

I heard him in my head say, "This is going to be a long night."

Now I felt subconscious knowing I didn't look as good as I thought I did in Tilly's dress. Eddie also seemed to be staring. However, he was so laid back he wouldn't begin to know good taste. He probably just objected to the color.

Trevor looked up and greeted me, "Hey."

I smiled at him and Ruthanne and then greeted them, "Hello."

Ruthanne sheepishly smiled an extremely nervous smile back at me. I turned to walk around the long table. I chose to walk past Mr. Bradford's end versus Mrs. Bradford's. I was in no mood for her critique. In my slow dawdle around the table, I missed Scott's entrance altogether.

He was seated when I arrived at my chair. To ignore Dustin, I concentrated on greeting Scott, "Hello Scott."

"Ignoring me," Dustin's mind stated.

"I didn't expect this," Scott mumbled turning his face away from Tilly.

Mrs. Bradford began to clank her spoon on the side of her glass as she stood, demanding everyone's attention. "I would like to make a toast."

189

"I didn't know we were having breakfast?" Eddie seriously stated nudging me slightly with his elbow.

Trevor and Ruthanne both grinned at him while I picked up my glass of water trying to keep a straight face and ignore him. He could be amusing at times.

"Cheesy," I heard Dustin say in my mind.

"As you all know, my dear husband Thomas was recently promoted to the position of Administration Complex Administrator. Thus, the reason we are celebrating tonight."

"Probably paid for the position," I heard Dustin think.

Polite clapping came from around the room.

"I would like to propose a toast to my dear husband for his leadership and dedication to everything he tackles," Mrs. Bradford said.

"To Thomas!" The crowd chanted. "To Thomas, to Thomas." The clinging of crystal came from around the table as a late Tilly appeared in the doorway.

"To Thomas," Dustin stated from beside me turning and clanking his glass to mine.

That's when his intoxicating smell floated to me. Instantly, I held my breath and used my napkin to fan what appeared to be myself. In truth, I was attempting to fan away Dustin's scent which seemed very potent tonight.

Tilly sauntered under the archway and stood behind her father. I was certain she was trying to make her mother pay for the comment about my clothes not being appropriate. She was wearing high heeled boots, black fish net stockings, a way too short, bright pink skirt, and a black and pink stripped shirt which was way too tight with the upper buttons undone. She accessorized her look with what looked like a studded dog collar. Her hair was frizzy and her makeup loud.

"Did she think this was a Halloween party?" I heard Dustin think.

With every eye staring, I could tell Tilly was drinking in the moment.

190

Then she spied Scott and seemed to be pleased by his surprising presence. In true Tilly fashion, she turned the charm on. She smiled, batted her eyes, and sauntered over to gently touch his arm. Should I expect anything less? She saw him as her date for the evening. When she finally peered across the table, she almost did a double take when she saw Dustin sitting next to me.

Before anything could be said, Trevor stood with his toasting glass in his hand. Mrs. Bradford made a loud choking sound when she saw him standing and hid her mouth in her table napkin.

"This is sure to be good," Dustin spoke in my mind.

"I would like to make a toast of my own!" Trevor stated. "I'm sure many at this table..." Trevor paused to look at Mrs. Bradford who appeared to be squirming in her chair. "... Are not aware that Tilly has been made conductress of Harmony. I propose a toast to Tilly."

Shocked faces politely smiled and nodded. Each guest around the table repeated, "To Tilly! To Tilly! To Tilly!"

Again Dustin raised his glass to toast with mine. I quickly, purposely turned and moved closer to Eddie saying, "To Tilly."

"What was that about?" I heard Dustin question concerning my snubbing him.

The only negative response came from the Raderton family. Tiffany leaned forward to stare all glass clinkers down and then settled her glare on Trevor who simply smiled at her.

"Changed your mind?" Tilly sweetly asked Scott while rubbing his arm. "Did you ask for the seat next to me?"

"Can I barf now or later," Dustin said in my mind.

"Your Dad invited me over," Scott stated as he pulled his arm out from under Tilly's touch and placed his napkin in his lap.

"Then, I should assume you didn't know I would be here," Tilly added.

"No," Scott snapped. "I would prefer a seat next to Tiffany!"

"Would you have come tonight if you knew I was here?" Tilly softly questioned ignoring his Tiffany comment.

"Probably not..." Scott truthfully answered slowly and emphatically.

"Crash and burn!" I heard Dustin say in my mind.

The raw look of determination on Tilly's face scared me. He rejected her. No one did that.

"Water or tea?" The serving maid asked.

"I'm fine with the water," I answered over my shoulder.

This is when I noticed Dustin adding a drop of something to his water. He looked over at me perched as close to Eddie as I could be, "Want some?"

"What is it?" I asked.

"What else, ginger," I heard his mind answer.

He smiled a goofy grin as I answered my own thought, "Ginger."

He leaned over and placed a couple drops into my water saying, "It makes it like ginger ail."

Again, I caught a whiff of his cologne. I closed my eyes and let the intoxicating smell travel deep into my body as I breathed. Sitting still, I could feel the tingling between us. The drawing of my soul to his.

"I'll give that a try," Eddie stated interrupting my tranquility as he took my glass and took a sip.

I just simply stared at him. Did he not know how rude that was?

"Does he not have any manners?" Dustin's mind questioned.

"Yuck!" Eddie stated as he made spitting sounds, drank and sputtered from his own glass, and attempted to wash the taste away. "What did you say that was again?"

"Ginger," I repeated as I scooted a little away from him.

"It's awful!" Eddie added as he pushed my glass back towards me. "Crash, I though you had better taste!"

"You are one to be commenting on those who have bad taste?" Dustin's mind stated.

"How long have you liked ginger?" Trevor pointedly asked me.

The maid set my salad in front of me as I answered, "I hadn't ever tried it till Dustin gave me some ginger candy the other day." I looked over my shoulder, "Thank you."

"Oh, she just didn't say that," I heard Dustin sigh.

"Why would you be giving Elizabeth candy?" Tiffany demanded to know from the other side of Dustin.

"Because she happened by," Dustin retorted in his mind.

Instantly, I knew I had inserted my foot in my mouth. Dustin was not mine and shouldn't be giving me anything, including candy. Off the intoxication train, I scooted closer to Eddie who was appearing mesmerized by my sitting so close.

"A better question is why Dustin would want to date you?" Tilly butted in. Her eyes shot to mine and I knew she was trying to deflect the unwanted attention away from me.

"Maybe you should ask yourself why Scott has no desire to date you," Tiffany retorted. "He seems to be rejecting your obvious flirting tonight. But then again, even Andy seems to ignore you. Have you lost your touch?"

"Harsh," I heard Dustin say in my mind.

"Andy," Scott repeated in a short laugh and now looked angry all over again remembering Tilly's betrayal.

"You can't seem to land and keep yourself a boyfriend," Tiffany taunted Tilly. "Isn't your nickname? One date Tilly?"

193

"If it weren't for me dating her, Tiffany would have the same problem," Dustin thought.

With that, silence fell over everyone. Eddie was the exception. He leaned over and asked, "Want your croutons?"

I began to pick them off the side of my plate and place them on his. His grubby hands began to help me and I felt totally grossed out about his hands being in my food. So much for the salad. I placed my salad fork on top the plate and waited for the maid to pick it up. I then watched as the exact scenario played out with the lady sitting on the other side of Eddie. She seemed as appalled as I had been.

The center of the table where we were seated was void of talking. Even Dustin's mind seemed quiet. Silently, salad being eaten and glares being given. Eventually the lady on the other side of Eddie asked Trevor about his parents. Trevor, Eddie, and Ruthanne fell into an easy conversation with her. Occasionally, Trevor would glance at Dustin. For the most part, the adults ignored the tension between all of us younger ones.

By the time the salad plates were picked up, I had decided this was the longest dinner of my life. Tilly had moved her focus from Tiffany to Scott. I was sure her missing hand had to be on his leg under the table since he appeared really uncomfortable and squirming in his chair. The regular dinner plates were systematically being placed in front of the guests and I was now practically sitting in Eddie's chair. Dustin seemed to be slowly moving his chair nearer mine. What was I, the filling for a sandwich being thrown and smashed like a grilled cheese sandwich? I was sweating and melting just like cheese.

The silence was broken when the extra servant from the country club placed a bowl in-front of Tilly saying, "Miss Bradford, Rick sent you mac-n-cheese."

"Lucky you," Eddie chimed in salivating as he glanced her way.

I looked over at him in disbelief. It was Trevor who answered, "The mac-n-cheese is delicious and not a normal menu item. I'm sure it is a gift in recognition of her being made conductress."

"I'll share with you," Tilly said to Trevor.

"Three ways?" Eddie asked with a hopeful smile holding up his plate.

"Everyone have a little," Tilly sighed as she dipped a little onto her dinner plate and passed it down to Eddie.

"Dustin, which part of the dome do you live in?" Trevor out of the blue asked.

"What's the angle?" Dustin questioned in his mind.

"I share a small apartment with a friend," Dustin said with a shrug. "Your parents are neighbors of the Bradford's aren't they?"

"My home?" Trevor repeated.

"Cat and mouse!" Dustin thought.

"Down the street," I interjected off the top of my head. "Trevor lives down the street."

"Biggest Victorian on the street," Eddie chimed in with a carefree manner. With another glance at me, I suddenly felt his hand on my knee. I jumped in my seat and jarred the table. Instantly, I looked at Eddie. What was he doing? I shook my head a slight no. He shrugged with an I had to try look.

"What did he do?" I heard Dustin question from beside me.

"No," Trevor disagreed peering at me strangely as I suddenly scooted my chair and myself closer to Dustin. "My house isn't as big as the rest."

To this Tilly rolled her eyes at Trevor in exasperation.

Trevor added, "My home may be actually big in square footage. However, it is small since the whole Stillholm gang lives there. Square footage per person is small."

"That's right," Tiffany spewed from beside Dustin. "Everyone knows the Stillholm household is full of cousins because they only marry their cousins."

"Ouch!" I heard Dustin's mind grimace at Tiffany's words.

"Tiffany, you take that back," Tilly demanded with her fists on the table.

"Are we in kindergarten now?" I heard Dustin's mind question.

"Or what?" Tiffany questioned staring Tilly down.

"You can say what you want about me," Tilly began. "But my friends are off limits."

"The line is drawn," Dustin thought.

Trevor placed his hand on Tilly's arm in a calming effort. Tilly was already fuming and angry.

Tiffany leaned forward looking at each of us with a smirk. Then she peered down the table at Mrs. Bradford. As with Tilly, I could see the wheels spinning in her devious mind.

She smiled a super sweet smile at Tilly saying, "You couldn't stop me from unloading his room of personals and embarrassing him. You couldn't stop me from getting you into trouble with my crying routine. You can't stop me from dating the boy your room mate has the hots for. You are powerless to stop me from causing Ruthanne grief. Most of all, you can't stop me from saying whatever I want!" Then she held her finger up adding, "You also can't stop your mother from wishing I was her daughter and not you."

The last comment was too much. It was like slow motion. Tilly placed both hands on the side of her plate. In one fluid motion, she stood and flung the plate and its contents at Tiffany.

Trevor tried to grab Tilly's moving plate while yelling, "No!"

Dustin moved to fling himself in front of Tiffany.

Scott stood and grabbed Tilly's hands which were going for his plate to fling next.

In her one act, Tilly had managed to hit Tiffany with her plate and dowse her with everything on her plate including her macaroni and cheese.

"What do you think you are doing?" Mrs. Raderton shouted as she popped up comforting Tiffany. "You're a monster!"

"A monster with a good shot!" I heard Dustin think while I could physically see him shaking his head.

Tiffany had macaroni in her hair, gravy and potatoes down the front of her, and food in her lap.

"I'm so sorry," Dustin said to Tiffany. "Here, take my napkin!"

From under Dustin and Mrs. Radertons's protective stance, I could see a hint of a smile. Tiffany had certainly crawled under Tilly's skin and set her up to be in trouble. As I looked at Tilly, she didn't appear worried. Both girls were happy with themselves!

"All that wasted food," Eddie mumbled from beside me.

I was scared to look at Mrs. Bradford. I slumped down into my chair. Somehow, I knew I was going to be blamed for this altercation along with Tilly.

"You uncouth, ill mannered brat!" Mrs. Raderton screamed. "I told your mother years ago you should have been sent to boarding school. You have always needed more discipline and they would have given it to you!"

With that said, Tilly picked up her glass. You could have heard a pin drop in the room.

"Go for it Tilly," I heard Dustin think.

As if Tilly could hear too, she flung the glasses contents in Mrs. Raderton's face. She then carefully placed the empty glass back on the table looking quite smug with herself.

"So much for the party!" Scott mumbled from beside Tilly as he plopped down in his chair.

Trevor looked down towards Mrs. Bradford's end of the table. She wasn't there. He seemed startled as he heard her heavy controlled breathing directly behind them, "Mathilda Bradford, how could you do this at your father's celebration party?" She took a huge deep sigh as she noticed Trevor staring at her. In a lowered voice she whispered, "You need to disappear from my sight before I say something I fear I will regret."

"I was bored to tears anyway!" Tilly defiantly stated as she peered at Scott.

Instantly, I glanced down the table at Mr. Bradford who quietly cracked his knuckles at her comment. Only Tilly could cause such a big scene. The scene didn't faze her. She only seemed to be concerned with the guy she wanted to notice her, hadn't. Only Tilly's father would be disappointed at the lack of a love connection between her and Scott and be unconcerned about the catty food fight.

Tilly left her chair and happily bounced the length of the room, passing all the other guests. She stopped before her Father saying, "Sorry Daddy!"

I looked at Trevor who was still watching her bounce away. As he glanced at me, I knew he thought the same thing I did, the show must go on. Anyone who really knew Tilly understood she didn't call her father daddy.

"Dale... Rose... I'm very sorry," Mrs. Bradford instantly apologized. "I will see that Mathilda writes you a note of apology."

"Mathilda is crazy!" Mrs. Raderton loudly stated for all to hear. "She continuously picks on my Tiffany. She's mental!"

"Hold on," I said as I stood. "Tilly is not crazy. She..."

"Here we go," I heard Dustin sigh in my head.

"Like you are one to talk," Mrs. Raderton interrupted me. "You go right along with Tilly's bullying."

"You actually have it all wrong," I disagreed putting my hands on my hips.

"Keep digging your hole," Dustin again sighed in my head.

I could see Trevor shaking his head no. He had slumped way down in his chair and I could feel his leg kick me from under the table. I glared back at him as he mouthed, "Sit down!"

With my ignoring him, Trevor made a loud, huffing noise and peered over at Ruthanne. I knew he had looked at her for permission to follow Tilly. Trevor reassured Ruthanne, "I'll be right back." Ruthanne nodded as Trevor stood and took off following Tilly.

"That's interesting," Dustin's mind stated as he looked between Ruthanne and *Trevor.*

"Dale, we're leaving!" Mrs. Raderton demanded as she pulled Tiffany away from under Dustin's arm. She took a few more steps, pulling Tiffany along, saying, "Don't expect us to ever come to any party where that hellion will be present."

"She's not a hellion!" I yelled as I stomped my foot.

Dustin stared me down as I heard in my head, "Taking it to the end."

Mrs. Bradford's attention now turned to me. The party was over for me. "Mrs. Bradford, I want to thank you for your hospitality," I stated to the shock of those around the table. They didn't view me any better than Tilly after my outbursts. "I would like to apologize to you and your other guests for my outbursts. I just couldn't stand the lies. I hope you will all understand."

"So you are not going to eat your food?" Eddie questioned. I looked at him like he was mad and pushed my plate towards him. He said, "Thanks!"

Mrs. Bradford pointed towards the door which the Raderton's and Dustin had just disappeared through. The dinner itself had been painful, however I wouldn't have imagined it would end in this fiasco. The walk of shame was painful with everyone staring. I walked slowly. I didn't want to catch up to the Raderton's.

When I finally made it to the stark white living room, I could see a maid approaching me. I stopped and waited to see what she wanted. I assumed it was the dress I had on.

"Miss Cantrell?" She asked.

"Yes," I responded waiting to hear whatever Mrs. Bradford had sent her to say.

"This is for you!" She said as she held out a single brown envelope.

I held out my hand to retrieve the familiar envelope saying, "Thank you. May I ask who gave this too you?"

"A courier dropped it by," she answered and turned to hurry into the dining room.

I walked out the front door and sat on a step between two of the pillars. The brown envelope had my name neatly printed on the outside. I sighed as I ripped open the envelope and pulled out the journal entry.

Journal Entry #207

Today I was called before Deward. He wanted to discuss a new assignment for me. He made a deal with the neighbor that I would go into the world of the Humlings as her son. She would then ask her family within the dome to raise me as theirs, telling them she wanted more for me than she could offer in the world of the Humling.

Once inside the dome, I would need to blend in with the Keepers. This included living a life on the Earth Plane which Deward assured me they would send someone to make it short. The overall goal would be for me to become a Keeper and begin to look for Bethany. I would have access to their records which would make finding her easier.

I agreed to go and was actually relieved to get away from Tina. I just can't watch anymore. She is dreadful and slowly becoming Piper's other half. She already seems to have more influence over Piper than Deward. I believe it is her idea to find Bethany. She seems to spew venom when her sister is brought up in conversation.

Journal entry #210

I haven't written since the final plans were made for me to leave. I arrived, with the help of my new locket, to the neighbor. She arranged, as promised, for me to live with her sister in the Keeper dome. It took a few days for us to set up my entrance into the world of the Keepers. We met her family at the Humling entrance to the Administration Complex. I played my part, hugging her, calling her mom, telling her how much she would be missed. Her sister seemed to believe it and has taken me in as her and her husband's child.

They are different than anyone I have ever known, more like Grace. They are compassionate, gracious, and caring. They seem to be accepting me as one of their own. Upon arrival at their home, I was given a comfortable room. They were accommodating and kind.

I am not getting side tracked, though. I have requested to go to the Hall of Babies tomorrow to begin my planning and charting for, as they put it, my one life. I assured them I did not want to be a burden. I wanted to start living my one life and come back for my training. They seemed pleased with my ambition. If only they knew the real reason for it.

I was right! Dwellers were traveling into our world. This was the proof! Maybe I was getting these journals because somehow this boy had something to do with my life. But what?

CHAPTER
TWENTY-FIVE

Tilly

Who was pounding on my door at this time of morning? I pulled the covers over my head and loudly yelled, "Go away!"

Incredibly the knock had turned to a loud hammering. I pulled the covers down and was furious with whoever was on the other side of my door. Didn't they know what an extremely busy evening I had last night?

I threw my legs over the edge of my bed and stomped to the door. I flung it open and was greeted by a grinning Destiny, "Good morning."

"What do you want?" I demanded. "It's early."

"I know," Destiny agreed. "Marvin is downstairs asking for Elizabeth."

I peered over at my still sleeping room mate. How in the world had she slept though Destiny's attack on our door?

"What does he want this early," I asked.

"He's her boyfriend," Destiny stated trying to peer past me at Elizabeth. "I don't have a clue, but he's in swim trunks and flip flops."

"Alright," I said as I shut the door.

I jumped up on Elizabeth's bed and began to jump up and down to wake her. She mumbled in irritation, "Tilly, give it a rest! It's Sunday morning and we can sleep in!"

"Okay," I said as I jumped down. "I'll go downstairs and see what Marvin wants."

"Marvin?" Elizabeth repeated sitting straight up. "What is he doing here?"

"Don't look at me," I mused. "I thought he was coaching the kid's basketball team at a tournament." I moved to my closet and began to dig. Just when Elizabeth and I would have a free day together, the square shows up. It was as though he had built in radar.

Elizabeth interrupted my thoughts as she asked, "Did you tell him I'd be down?"

"Me?" I questioned with a grin. "No, I didn't tell your square anything. I don't know if Destiny went back down to say anything to him or not. You better hurry or he may get tired waiting on you and take Destiny out instead."

"She is so nosy," I heard Elizabeth mumble as she jumped up seeming to be a little panicked.

There it was! "You'll need this," I said as I tossed Elizabeth my bubble gum pink two piece bathing suit. Even though, I never really went swimming. I didn't like to be in the water, sun bathing was okay.

Elizabeth held it up and stared at it like it was from a different world mumbling, "What in the world is this?"

"Earth to Elizabeth," I sighed. "A bathing suit?"

"Why would you think I needed a bathing suit?" Elizabeth retorted.

"According to Miss Nosy, your boyfriend is in swim trunks and sandals," I answered.

With that Elizabeth plopped down on her bed deep in thought.

"Are you going down or not?" I questioned. Then I surmised swimming must not be her thing, once again proving we were more alike than anyone knew. "Just go down and see what he wants before you get all in a tizzy!"

Still in her comfy yellow T-shirt and sweat pants, she ran a brush through her long hair. I handed her the toothpaste which she ate a little of to ensure good breath. Then, I followed her down the stairs, past the professor's dark office, and watched her pass into the common room where Marvin was seated on the couch.

From my place, leaning against the wall of the hallway I saw Elizabeth greet him, "Hey, it's early."

Marvin was staring intently at Elizabeth as she moved towards him and he pulled her down to sit next to him. He reached out to caress her cheek and push her long flowing hair behind her shoulder, "You are truly beautiful in the morning."

Oh please! All that mushy. Elizabeth was buying it though. She was lost in his gaze. Didn't she know to ignore half of what a man said?

"Thanks, I guess," she shyly answered. "Why aren't you with the team?"

"Are you not happy to see me?" Marvin seriously asked.

"Don't be silly," Elizabeth returned. "I just thought they had games all weekend."

"They lost the first couple games in the tournament," Marvin said not looking unhappy.

"You don't look sad," Elizabeth challenged.

"I wanted the boys to succeed," Marvin began. "When they didn't... Well, I just knew it meant that I got back to you sooner than later."

"Hmm," I hummed. He really was in love with her. You could see it in his gentle touch and hear it in his words.

Marvin looked over to see who was intruding on their otherwise private moment saying, "I didn't expect to see you though."

"I had a little food situation with Tiffany," I began as I moseyed into the room and sat in one of the comfortable recliners. "Mother was..."

"Food situation?" Marvin asked Elizabeth.

"She had it coming!" I declared.

"At the dinner party," Elizabeth began.

"You did decide to go then," Marvin surmised with a look that screamed he knew there would be trouble.

Elizabeth fondly smiled at him and continued, "Tiffany was being herself and when Tilly had enough…"

"It was the last straw!" I declared popping my gum.

"Tilly threw her plate of food across the table at Tiffany," Elizabeth said cringing a little wondering what his reaction would be.

Marvin gasped and looked at me with those big eyes.

"You forgot the best part," I added with a devilish smile twisting a lock of my uncombed hair.

"She also threw a glass of water in Mrs. Raderton's face," Elizabeth responded to my queue.

"You didn't," Marvin again gasped.

"Oh, I did!" I replied. "Mother is very angry. The heat was too hot in the ice castle so I returned to my nice quiet room here at the Hall of Knowledge. My mother actually thought she was going to punish me. Imagine."

Marvin sat tongue tied, watching me. The square was shocked. "Seriously, you should close your mouth and put your eyes back in your head!" I stated.

Marvin started to respond but Elizabeth side tracked him asking, "What are we doing today?"

"We're going to the lake," Marvin said still shaking his head in disbelief.

"Sounds fun…" Elizabeth said in a less than enthusiastic voice.

This captured Marvin's attention as he explained in a gentle voice, "I want to spend a special day with you."

My friend, the awkward and frumpy Elizabeth, had more luck in love than anyone I knew. She had found love despite herself. If only I could sift through the sea of men and pull out the perfect one for me.

CHAPTER
TWENTY-SIX

Elizabeth

T he body of water I was standing before was breathtaking. "What is the name of this lake?" I questioned as I looked out over the pristine, crystal clear waters nestled between mountains on either side.

"Table Rock Lake," Marvin answered with a smile as he walked out onto the rickety looking boat dock.

"Like on the Earth Plane?" I questioned.

"I suppose," Marvin replied. "Most landmarks at Home are reminiscent of landmarks on the Earth Plane."

"Does it extend beyond the dome?" I questioned.

"The Silver Forrest backs up to the dome and extends into the Ghost district," Marvin stated. "It's a long mountain range with several lakes. The lake outside the dome is called Beaver Lake and it feeds Table Rock Lake."

A bald eagle with its brown body and white head and tail was soaring overhead making chirping whistles. I watched as it swooped down and snatched a fish out of the water. I mindlessly said, "Magnificent!"

"There are a lot of eagles on the lake," Marvin stated as he stepped into the fishing boat tied to the dock.

I jumped as I felt a cold nose touch the back of my bare leg. I turned to see a dog wagging its tail. I held out my hand and the dog sniffed it. Then I petted the friendly dog's head. It trotted past me and out onto the dock. When Marvin rose up from what he was doing, the dog began to run and jump at the docks edge as its tail wagged frantically.

"Hey boy!" Marvin said as he stepped back out of the boat and ruffled the dog's fur. The dog held up its foot to shake Marvin's hand.

"Your dog, I assume?" I questioned as I stepped onto the dock and knelt down to again pet the dog.

"This is Banjo," Marvin sighed looking intently at the dog's dirty foot.

"What's wrong?" I asked.

"Banjo is dirty," Marvin stated in complaint form.

"So…" I retorted. "He's a dog."

"Mom doesn't like Banjo tracking in dirt," Marvin stated. "And Banjo doesn't like to take a bath."

By the look on Marvin's face, I knew there was more to the story. I was getting so I could read him.

Marvin asked, "Would you mind to wait here while I put him back inside?"

"I could help you," I suggested turning towards the dwellings behind us.

"No!" Marvin quickly said. "There's no need. It will only take me a minute to put him in the basement."

I shrugged and watched as Marvin walked towards the row of massive homes all setting in a row along the lake side street. Each structure appeared to house five or six, two story townhouses. He walked up and around the front corner and disappeared from sight.

I hopped into the boat and waited for him to return. Relaxing, I passed the time by watching a boat pulling a skier back and forth, two men fishing from a stationary boat not far from shore, and the amazing landscape.

When Marvin came jogging back down the hill towards me, I was ready to boat out on the water.

"Banjo getting a bath?" I asked as he stepped into the boat.

"Dad let him out," Marvin said seeming to speak his thoughts. "Mom did insist he have a bath." With that said, Marvin gave a little shrug.

"Where did you get this boat?" I questioned to change what had become a sore subject according to Marvin's body language.

"It's my dads," Marvin replied while untying it from the dock.

"Which house is yours?" I asked as I pointed up the hill. My knowledge of his family and how they lived was limited. He didn't share much about them.

"My family's townhouse is in the blue structure straight ahead," he answered as he moved toward me with what appeared to be a yellow life jacket and forcibly placing it over my head.

"Where's yours?" I questioned as he snapped the strap around my mid section.

"It's below the seat. I swim like a fish, I don't need one," Marvin replied as he snapped the second snap on my life jacket.

"And you assume I do?" I questioned as Marvin began to push the boat away from the dock.

"Do you remember if you can swim?" Marvin seriously questioned as we floated out onto the water.

"Good point," I replied. I began to peer back at the blue house, "How many families have townhouses next to yours?"

"Each townhouse has two floors. Roughly every couple of windows is a different townhouse," Marvin replied. "Ours complex holds six townhouses."

"Really?" I questioned trying to count the windows. "Are all the houses along here townhouses?"

"Yes, this is the Department of Ghosts Living District," Marvin said as he looked at me. "We all live in townhouses."

"There are living districts?" I questioned.

"Yeah, my parents live in the Ghost living district, Keepers live in the Keeper living district, and so on, so on," Marvin replied as he started the outboard motor. "You will one day live in the Keeper district. "

"One day, you will leave the Ghost District," I added matching his smile.

"Yes," Marvin said as he grabbed my hand with his free one. "It will seem odd not to return to here, since I grew up here. However, I look forward to my future."

I could feel his heart rapidly beating as mine kept pace with his in his warm grip on my hand. I could see us together in the future. He could feel it too. I simply sensed it in my gut.

"The Department of Knowledge, which district is that located in?" I questioned.

"It is in the Administration District," Marvin said. "That district runs down to the Administration Complex"

I sat watching the blue structure of condos disappear and asked, "Is that why you have never wanted to bring me home? Because we are Keepers?"

"Oh no, that has nothing to do with it," Marvin corrected me as he revved up the engine and sped off. We could no longer talk. The roar of the engine loudly drowned our voices out.

We sped across the water with the wind blowing my hair, my mind drifted as to what I could only hope would come in my life. I could see Marvin and me starting a life together in the Keeper District. The only time we would be forced to leave each other would be when we went to work.

We would have dinner parties. Not like the uptight one at the Bradford's house. Ours would be with close friends who loved us for who we are. We would invite Tilly and whoever she was dating, Trevor, Ruthanne... Actually, if Trevor and Ruthanne were together, would they live in the Keeper district or the Administration district? Would they live in the house with the other Stillholm family members?

We would also invite Marvin's family and friends, including Jessie, Rhett... Hold on! Why did Rhett live in the Administration district? He was a Ghostie. Hmm... He was different. He had no wife and lived in the A-frame just off Mr. Solliday's property. His homes dark windows kept the outside world separated from what went on in the house. Rhett was like the boy from the journals. He didn't quite fit in, one more question unanswered.

We made a few circles in the boat around an island which rose in the middle of this lake. Marvin began to slow the motor as he asked, "Want to jump in?"

"Sure," I said patting my life jacket which totally covered Tilly's revealing bubble gum pink swim suit. I was sure I didn't look overly attractive.

Marvin chuckled at me a little. He must have been able to see my nerves concerning my appearance.

"You have told me your Uncle Rhett is smart enough to be a Keeper," I began as the boat motor made its final sputter. "Has your uncle ever been a Keeper?"

"No," Marvin said as he attached an orange flag on the end of a pole attached to the back of the boat.

"Marvin, how does Rhett live in the Administration Living District when he works for the Department of Ghosts?" I asked.

Marvin replied, "He moved there after living with Mr. Solliday."

"How does he know Mr. Solliday?" I asked.

"Ready?" Marvin pointed towards the water seeming impatient to get.

"How is Rhett related to you? Wait! Are you related to Mr. Sollilday?" My mind was racing as I sarcastically added, "Is he really your uncle?"

With that, Marvin's smile disappeared. I had hit a nerve. He stood back from the edge of the boat and moved to sit back in the captain's chair across from me. "Uncle Rhett tutored me. He is a brilliant and can indeed answer any question you throw at him. He definitely is smart enough to be a Keeper. If he hadn't tutored me, I would have never made Keeper," Marvin began. He seemed to peer past me. "Technically, I'm not actually related to him by blood. He grew up with my mother and he lived with Mr. Solliday when they were younger."

"Like Trevor and Tilly?" I questioned.

"Sort of… Yes," Marvin answered. "He has always been Uncle Rhett. I never give much thought to the fact he is not actually my uncle. No one ever asks, because Mom always introduces him as her brother. I'm not sure anyone realizes he isn't. You are the first to ever pin me down and directly ask. He is steady, dependable, and has lived in the A-frame for as long as I can remember." Marvin paused deep in thought and a million miles away. When he came back to me, he seemed impatient with my questions adding, "He is at the top of his game! Does it matter which district he lives in? He's a workaholic and rarely home."

"Are you saying he isn't usually home in the evening?" I questioned.

"He has been home a lot lately," Marvin said with a growing irritation. "He used to only come home early on Tuesdays. That has always been our guy night."

"I wonder why he is suddenly spending more time at home?" I pondered out-loud.

Marvin looked uncomfortable, "I think he doesn't want to leave us in his house, unsupervised."

"Silly isn't it," I added.

"Is it?" Marvin questioned me. "Is it so silly for him to think we shouldn't be left unsupervised? I am a man and you are a woman."

To this I had nothing to say. I had waded into an uncomfortable area.

Marvin placed his hand on my bare leg sending pleasant chills all over my body. "Why are you asking me fifty questions about Rhett?" Marvin asked.

"I'm sorry," I replied to his irritated glare.

"Well, it seems there are three of us on this date," Marvin sighed.

I sat silently. How could I recover? He had come home early, and I was stressing the fun day he planned.

"Elizabeth, I don't know why you are so focused on my uncle," Marvin began. "There is no one else I trust like I trust my Uncle Rhett."

He was speaking from his heart. As much as he trusted Rhett, I trusted him. Rhett had been fair with me and I had no reason to suspect that he had anything to do with the journal. He was still a mystery though.

"I brought you out here so we could slow down and appreciate the small stuff together today," Marvin softly replied. "Like the eagles you noticed earlier and the crystal clear water. I want to enjoy the day with you!" He leaned over and our lips met as he gently kissed me. I could feel my heart flutter and the world melt away. When he pulled back he looked at me so lovingly. Then he asked in a pleading voice, "Okay?"

"Okay!" I responded. "I promise no more Rhett talk. It will just be the two of us on our date."

"Great!" Marvin replied as he stood and hesitated. Then he proceeded to take off his shirt and hang it on the back of his captain's chair.

Whoa! I knew Marvin had an athletic body type. However, his muscular body was incredible. Well defined abs was flanked by strong arms. He was scrumptious and hot. In my thinking, Rhett should be chaperoning this date.

He turned to me, "Let's get in!"

With that said he stepped on his captain's chair and dived over the side of the boat into the blue water. I moved and watched him surface. His hand pushed his wet hair back as he kept afloat saying, "Jump on in!"

Here goes nothing! I followed his lead and placed my clothes on the back of my chair. After viewing Marvin's amazing body, I felt self conscious in this bright, pink Tilly bikini. I was happy to put the life jacket back on to cover my pale, blotchy skin. What did Marvin see in me? I didn't come close to matching Marvin's physique. I quickly moved to the edge of the boat wanting to jump in as quickly as possible and hide myself in the inviting black water. I closed my eyes, gave out a squeal, and jumped. The whole time, I was wondering if I really could swim.

CHAPTER
TWENTY-SEVEN

Elizabeth

" Good evening," Professor Zirak stated from the head of the table. "Due to our home weekend, I know everyone in the room is tired. We will keep this short and sweet this evening."

I was relieved that this session would be quick. I was exhausted after swimming all day with Marvin and slightly uncomfortable from a mild sunburn. I would wear a T-shirt to cover my suit the next time.

"Let's begin by passing in the paper due on the life theme of leader and the paper due on your successes of your life theme," Professor Zirak stated.

Papers shuffled from all around the room as they were passed from person to person eventually reaching the professor. In the middle of the chaos, from the chair beside me Trevor whispered, "Is something up between you and Eddie?"

"Miss Cantrell, have you come prepared to share your life theme and plan?" Professor Zirak asked before I could fathom why Trevor would ask me that.

I shook my head thinking about how I had given Eddie mixed signals when seated next to him. At the dinner party I was practically sitting in his lap. However, it was only because I was trying to distance myself from Dustin. No one would understand this though. Eddie...

"Great!" Someone across the table mumbled returning me from my thought.

"Very well," Professor Zirak stated. "For the next week please write an essay on the life theme of healer. In addition, please write an essay on your failures within your life plan. Please include how you learned from your failures. Everyone in the room has Miss Cantrell to appreciate for the extra assignments."

I was aware that the extra assignments weren't making me any friends, but I ignored the glares and huffs from around the table. I was too tired to really care. I leaned towards Trevor and protested, "Have you ever eaten dinner next to Eddie?"

"You better write down your assignments," Trevor advised while scribbling in his own notebook. I followed his suggestion and found a blank page to begin to write.

"Moving right into the material, can anyone tell me the three main types of dreams?" Professor Zirak questioned.

"Release, wish, and prediction," Tilly spouted without raising her hand and smacking her gum. She blew a huge bubble and popped it nonchalantly.

Trevor scribbled on the bottom of my paper, "I'm sorry you got placed next to him."

"Thank you Miss Bradford!" Professor Zirak said. "Tonight we will answer the questions as we go around the table. Miss Ventine, please explain a release dream."

All I could think about was his hands in my food. "He eats like a pig," I whispered back to Trevor who was holding in a chuckle.

The professor paused and stared at Trevor. "Mr. Stillholm, is something funny? Would you like to share?"

With the smile wiped off Trevor's face, the satisfied professor held his hand up towards Shannon for her to start.

"A release dream is the Humling letting go of something bothering them," Shannon stated as she continued to glare at me.

"Mr. Stillholm," Professor Zirak called on Eddie. "Please give us an example of a release dream you logged this week?"

Trevor, seeing that Eddie was paying no attention, jumped right in saying, "Eddie and I…"

"Not you," Professor Zirak sternly interrupted. "Him!" The professor pointed at Eddie and waited for him to acknowledged having been called upon.

When he didn't, Shannon elbowed him hard and pointed towards the professor. Looking stunned Eddie looked up at the professor, then lowered his hoodie and took out his ear buds saying, "Yes sir?"

"You will not listen to your head set while we are meeting!" Professor Zirak spouted in an angry tone. The professor walked around to Eddie's spot and demanded, "Give them to me, now!"

Eddie reluctantly took off his ear buds and player, handing them over to the professor. As the professor began to walk back to the front of the table Eddie asked, "Dude, when can I have them back?"

The professor spun around, "What did you call me?"

"I meant… When can I have them back, sir?" Eddie recovered.

"We will talk about that in my office," Professor Zirak returned. "Mr. Still-holm, please read from your paper an example of a release dream."

"Mine is dreadful," Eddie murmured in protest.

"We're waiting," Professor Zirak impatiently countered.

"Trevor and I viewed Mrs. Uplit," Eddie began. "She woke to see two blond haired little girls playing and dancing merrily around in a circle in her living room. Something heavy was on top of her and she could hardly breathe. Suddenly, she realized she needed to move out from under whatever was holding her down. As she wiggled her way out, she realized it was the bodies of her fallen family members atop of her. In shock she stared down at her family. They were all dead!

As the two blond girls circled the heap of bodies, they noticed her. Instantly they began to yell and ran off in a flash. Fear overtook her as she looked at her family and peered down at herself. She was covered in their precious blood. There was no one left and she was meant to be dead as well.

She ran out the front door of their massive colonial home as fast as her small legs would carry her. She looked down the tree lined dirt road leading to her house. She peered at the fields on either side of the road. The family's horses grazed on grass as if nothing had transpired. She ran down the three porch steps and peered into the woods which lied a few hundred yards to the side of her home. That is when she heard them coming for her. She dashed across the yard that separated her from the tree line of the woods. Many had tried to escape through this exact route in her short lifetime. She knew there would be no hope if she tried to escape through the open land which lay the other direction. Once behind the tree cover, she ran through the untamed trees and sticker bushes as they tore her skin and smacked her body as she passed. Her father had never cleared the woods and it was no wonder why all those before her had been unsuccessful. When she stopped, reaching the river, she could still hear the men loudly working their way towards her. They were relentless in their pursuit of her.

For a fleeting moment, she thought maybe she could reason with them. She could promise her silence if they would just let her go. She turned to fully access the group of men chasing her. Soldiers, they were all Yankee soldiers. Her Daddy feared this would happen after the war. The confederates lost and their slaves had been freed. Now the Carpetbaggers had came to take her home. They had killed her family. There would be no bargaining with them.

She ran for the rope swing which her brothers had always swung out over the river on. As a hand lunged for her, there was not time to even swing. She flung herself over the cliff into the rushing water. She was heavy with all the clothing she was wearing and struggled to keep her head above the water. The men stood and watched feeling sure that she would drown in the rushing water."

"Did she?" Shannon asked.

"Yup," Eddie chimed in.

"Why was this a release dream?" Professor Zirak questioned.

"Her dream is releasing a fear stored deep away in her heart and mind," Trevor answered. "The fear of loosing loved ones. It carried over into the life she is now living on the Earth Plane. She has nightmares of loosing her mother and children, anyone close to her."

"She also keeps reliving this freakish nightmare over and over," Eddie stated.

"Mrs. Uplit's subconscious is telling her she needs to face this fear head on," Professor Zirak stated. "She needs to come to an understanding that this fear will only affect her life she lives now if she lets it."

With this Eddie shoved a whole cookie in his mouth. Why had I never noticed his eating habits before? I leaned over and questioned in a whisper, "His eating habits are normal for him?"

"Very," Trevor muttered back with a smile. "He eats everything in sight."

"Mr. Shepard," called Professor Zirak. "Can you explain a wish dream?"

"A wish dream is what your heart desires," Piano boy stated mimicking a girly high pitched voice. The girls in the room giggled at his imitation.

"That's enough," sighed Professor Zirak as if this was the response he always got when he asked about this. "Miss Jennett. Do you have an example of a wish dream?" Professor Zirak demanded.

"I do," she hem hawed looking at her feet.

"Well," Professor Zirak hummed. "Go ahead."

"I viewed the Humling in my office in an actual dream this week," she hesitated. "He dreams of being held… Um… of making love to his wife." She paused looking up at the professor.

"You are viewing him wishing to have more of a physical relationship with his spouse," Professor Zirak stated.

"His dreams quite honestly embarrass me!" She retorted.

"All a natural look into his innermost feelings," Professor stated. "Moving along. Miss Nabor," Professor Zirak called.

"A prediction dream is a dream in which we try to help our assigned Humling stay on their path. We attempt to lead them in the direction of their life plan, chart, etc. We send the prediction dream through the dream portal in our office."

"Very good!" Professor Zirak agreed. "A prediction dream is used to answer their direct questions or concerns and to give those answers and guidance for future joys or problems."

I was totally surprised when the stuttering Stone girl sheepishly raised her hand. Professor Zirak seemed taken back as well. He had probably started with Tilly so we wouldn't make it around the table to her. She wouldn't be forced to talk before the group. It wasn't like her to volunteer or interject herself into any conversation or discussion.

Professor Zirak called on her, "Miss Stone."

The stuttering Stone girl took a deep breath and removed her thick, coke bottle glasses. Since she couldn't see us, she seemed to have no anxiety. She easily looked at her paper which she held at arms length to read.

She took one deep breath and began, "I observed something the Head Keeper in my office said happens repetitively with whom I am viewing. She receives predictive messages through the dream portal at the Hall of Babies from her grandmother." Kim paused smiling as if there was an inside joke we weren't aware of. I had never seen her laugh. Usually, she was too scared to open her mouth for fear of stuttering. Another deeply inhaled breath and she freely rattled, "Her grandmother, a non-keeper, doesn't think her Keeper is communicating enough. She takes it upon herself to communicate regularly."

"You are viewing a Keeper," Trevor asked interrupting her.

Tilly gave him a stern glare. All I could think was she sounded enthusiastic about whatever gossip she had listened in on.

"No," Kim answered as her new found confidence seemed shaken. "I have two examples of prediction dreams which I would like to share with all of you."

"If she's not a Keeper, why is she allowed in the Keeper office?" Trevor interrupted more concerned it seemed with security issues for the dome.

"Exceptions can always be made by the Council," Professor Zirak shortly answered to hush Trevor. The professor understood the gravity of Kim volunteering to talk. His attention turned back to Kim as he said, "Miss Stone, be our guest. Tell us about your assigned Humling and your take on prediction dreams."

"She was sitting in her big, comfy green reclining chair in her living room. It was dark outside and she sat down to eat a bowl of soup and watch television. To her surprise, when she looked up her TV stand wasn't setting in front of her. Instead a huge pen-ball machine loomed in its place.

As she placed her bowl of soup on the end table, she rose and moved closer to look at the massive pin-ball machine. She was startled to see her grandmother standing at its side. Her grandmother had been deceased for roughly a year. She beamed at the visitation. Her grandmother smiled in a warm loving look and pointed to the game.

She was sure her Grandmother wanted her to play the game. She pulled back the lever to release the ball. It ran up its long track on the side and started falling down. She pushed the buttons to hit the blue ball back up, keeping it in play. However, as with all pin-ball, the blue ball eventually rolled right down the center and she was unable to keep the ball in play.

Her grandmother gestured for her to try again. She did and another blue ball began to whiz, hitting this and that, adding points to the scoreboard. Eventually slipping past her flippers, it to fell down and out of play.

All of a sudden her cousin, who lived hours away, strolled though her back door. Her grandmother told her, telepathically, it was her cousin's turn to play. She stepped aside. Her cousin happily stepped up and played her first ball. Instead of blue balls, her cousin played with a pink ball. She played several times and only with pink balls. A doorbell rang! She woke finding that she had been dreaming in her green recliner. Interestingly enough, this was the first vibrant communication between her and her grandmother."

Kim took another huge, deep cleansing breath. Her nervous energy turned into a huge smile that went across her face. "This was a prediction dream! Her grandmother was showing her she would have two boys and her cousin would have a slew of girls."

"Miss Stone, I would like to point out something you said," Professor Zirak stated. "You said her grandmother communicated telepathically with her."

"Yes," Kim answered.

"I hope each of you learned while logging dreams this week that the majority of communications through dream portals are done telepathically," Professor Zirak said. "Spoken words are used sparingly." Nods came from all around the room. "Thank you Miss Stone. Your answer and opinion is the best the class has had to offer today!"

Kim once again raised her hand. When the professor looked at her astonished, she said, "I'm not through!"

"Oh," Professor Zirak hummed. "Proceed! Class listen up. Perhaps you slackers will learn something."

Returning to her dream, "It was almost dusk as she drove her car away from her grandmother's house on Thoman Street. She was very sad because she had knocked on the door and no one was home. It dawned on her that her grandmother had died a few years before and was no longer there. A forgotten grief overtook her as she suddenly felt the need to go to church and pray. Her car seemed to be on auto pilot as she turned on a small street connecting her to a thoroughfare called Atlantic Street. Normally, she would go right. However, on this day she wanted to go to church and went left. Although the direction felt right, it crossed her mind that she didn't know there was a church to the left.

She drove past closed up Mom & Pop store fronts of yesteryears, beyond a trailer park, past a commercial lot, beyond a housing project, and then stopped at a four way stop by the a gas station.

As she looked across the four way stop, she was confused. There was an unfamiliar hill to go down. She pondered if the hill had always been there. This wasn't the best part of town or four way stop to be pondering at. It was getting dark.

When she rolled through the four way stop and began the descent, there stood her church. What a funny place for it to be since her church was in another town many hours away. However, that detail was unimportant. She was relieved to see the comfort her church would offer her.

She pulled into the church's parking lot and into her usual space at the back of the building. As she exited her car, the pastor caught her attention. He was standing at the edge of the parking lot, peering further down the hill.

He grinned at her as she approached. Following his gaze over the valley she felt overwhelmed by the sight of a huge garden. The pastor then looked at her and told her it was all hers.

She began to walk through the vines which had abundant fruit and vegetables growing. She was overcome with joy. You see, the fruit of the vines were hers. The dream predicted that she would be spiritually blessed and wealthy."

"Thank you Miss Stone," Professor Zirak stated. "Very good!"

I watched as Kim placed her glasses back on her face. The smile disappeared from her face when she could see every eye peering at her. She retreated back into her reclusive world.

"I want to complement those who have answered," Professor Zirak stated. "You did a great job of sharing the dreams you logged. Please pass your logs to me. Let me see… You also should have a paragraph about how your offices use the portal and a paper logging five verbal requests the Humling made and the five corresponding answers given to them by the Head Keeper in their dreams. Pass them all in."

Again the papers shuffled around the table.

"Can anyone explain exit points to me?" Professor Zirak questioned looking around the table.

Eddie popped another cookie in his mouth and instantly made a gagging noise. I glanced at Trevor who was locked into a stare with Tilly. It seemed she had forgotten to smack her gum as she sat perfectly quiet. What was up with her? Awkward glances and eye rolls came from around the table. Why was attention focused on Tilly? Had she been called on? What was going on?

"This should be juicy!" Destiny mumbled.

"An exit point is when you leave the Earth Plane to come home," Tilly mindlessly answered never taking her eyes off Trevor as though she were relieving a nightmare played on the screens of his eyes.

"You plan several in an earth lifetime. When you soul is done learning its lessons, it can exit," Trevor added.

"We have the point," Professor Zirak stated observing the looks around the table. "I would like each of you, including you Miss Cantrell, to write a paper explaining your planned exit points. I would like you to include which one you took to come Home."

Trevor and Tilly were still staring at each other. Eddie was shaking his head slightly.

"I've been looking forward to this!" Shannon said out loud while staring at Tilly.

"As I promised, short and simple this evening," Professors Zirak said. "Everyone is free with the exception of Mr. Stillholm." The professor turned to Eddie continuing, "I will see you in my office!"

Trevor jumped up, closely followed by Tilly. I followed both of them as they walked towards the hallway. They better not think of leaving me out of whatever was going on. Exhaustion was suddenly overtaking me and I didn't want to chase them down.

I was just about to exit when Destiny stepped out in front of me saying, "I have something for you."

"Not now," I told her. She could be so annoying!

As I stepped to my left, she did too. "I think you are going to like it," she whined.

I could see Tilly and Trevor hovering by the front door of Keeper house. They seemed to be attempting to wander off by themselves. What in the world was going on?

Again, I stepped the opposite direction, to my right. She matched my steps. "Elizabeth, I…"

"They're leaving," I said in an exasperated tone. "Get out of my way!"

With this, Destiny stepped aside. As I was passing her, she said, "Fine. Go after them. Maybe I'll read this mysterious love note with your name on it. You don't seem to want it!"

I stopped dead in my tracks and turned around asking, "What did you say?"

Destiny retrieved a familiar brown envelope with my name scrolled across the front from my discarded backpack she now carried. "I found this today in the laundry shoot." Destiny said. "I don't know how it got there."

I did. I was lucky Destiny had discovered it and not Tilly. She had cleaned our room today out of boredom. It had to have been hidden in my bedding. Whoever left a note for me at the Bradford's must have came and left one on my bed as well. I wasn't crazy when I felt uneasy the other night all alone in our room. Destiny was waiting for my response while waving the envelope. I smiled holding out my hand saying, "Thank you for finding it."

She didn't make a move to hand it too me. With a catty grin she said, "When are we going to watch that real life you promised we would see?"

I really had no desire to spend time with her. "Destiny, I've just been busy," I hem-hawed.

"Friends are never to busy for each other," Destiny stated in a huff. "I've been a friend to you. It is time for you to return the favor."

"Destiny, I'm so tired. I don't feel well," I countered as I held out my hand. "Please! I really don't have the energy for this."

Destiny let the envelope fall into my hand saying, "You did promise... that's all. A Keeper is only as good as their word."

"Thank you," I said hoping to ignore her comment as I wrapped my fingers around the envelope. As I started moving towards the staircase, I added, "I'll see you in the morning."

I didn't hear a response. My tired legs carried me up the stairs, through the girl's floor hall, and through my door. I flung myself into a chair under the window and ripped open the envelope.

Journal Entry #221

I am back. As promised my earth life was short. I dreaded the process, but it wasn't so bad.

Upon re-entry, I found myself taking a dreadful test in which I knew very few answers. It was an important test to determine which department I would work for. Of course, I must work for the Department of Keepers, to fulfill my duty. It is not uncommon for us to communicate through our thoughts, with no words spoken, where I come from. Since here in the dome, it has been quiet with my hearing no others thoughts. So, I was startled while taking my test when I heard loud and clear a voice in my head, Tina. She came to help me answer the questions I did not know. I should have known Deward would have a plan for this test. Although I was glad to hear the answers flowing so freely in my thoughts, I wondered were she was in the dome.

I am now a training Keeper and my Professor's name is Zirak. He asked to talk with me this evening. He went to training with the two that are posing as my parents and knows they are indeed not my parents. I was forced to tell him about who was supposedly my mother and I followed the line as to why I was sent into the keeper dome. Have a better life, more opportunity, etc. He bought it and offered to help me in any way possible. I fear I will now be his pet project.

Just as I feared. This Dweller had fit well into the society inside the dome. He infiltrated the Keepers and was walking amongst us. The only person to suspect had bought his lie. Professor Zirak knew who he was, but had no idea what he was. I would need to work out a devious way to ask.

I had quizzed Marvin today about Rhett. Who was as odd as this boy I was reading about? Now I knew there was no way he was the person in this journal. However, he had a secret too. I felt it!

CHAPTER
TWENTY-EIGHT

Elizabeth

"Hello again," Leo greeted me as I entered the lift. He smelled of fresh gingerbread and had a spot of flour on his nose.

"Are you having a good morning?" I asked.

"Fine," he said as his smile disappeared from his face as he saw Tilly.

"Destination Two," Tilly said over my shoulder. "For both of us."

Leo turned to me and said, "Thank you!"

We stepped to the back of the lift. I couldn't get Rhett out of my mind. My gut screamed he was hiding something. All of a sudden, so much didn't add up. Why was he an older and unmarried to a soul mate? Wasn't this rare?

"Tilly, have you ever thought or wondered about Rhett's unusual life and position in the dome?" I asked as we moved to the back of the lift. "He does strange things."

"What are you talking about?" Tilly asked.

"Like his inability to catch that old ghost," I answered.

"He's strange because he can't get one ghost to cross over?" Tilly said in a huff. "He's top dog in his field!"

"What if he is not catching the old ghost on purpose?" I thought out loud.

"What are you on today?" Tilly asked. "A ginger high from all those cookies?"

"It's not only the old ghost!" I returned.

"Destination two, Department of Administration," Leo stated as the lift dinged.

Tilly marched out of the lift irritated. I, as well as everyone else, had been put on a short leash. She had been in a foul mood ever since last night and everything seemed to agitate her today. Whatever was going on between her and Trevor would work itself out in time. Actually, since it seemed to revolve around exit points, it would work itself out probably by Sunday. Would we all survive until then? I had to ask, "Are you actually irritated with me over this? Are you standing up for Rhett?"

"What?" Tilly questioned in return popping her gum.

As we walked across the complex foyer, I could feel the warm sun on our skin as rays of bright light flooded through the glass walls and roof.

"Elizabeth, don't be crazy!" Tilly said shaking her head. "You are my best friend. I would never stand up for Rhett over you." Tilly paused and popped a second stick of gum in her mouth. "Listen, you are like a leach on this subject and are sounding paranoid again. Honestly, I don't get it. Why are you obsessing with him after all the time you've spent at his house with Marvin."

Suddenly two hands covered my eyes from behind and a voice I recognized said, "Guess who?"

"An annoying best friend," I stated hoping he hadn't overheard our conversation about Rhett. As his hands were removed I turned. "Jessie."

"Hey," Jessie greeted both Tilly and I. "Where are the two of you headed?"

"We're viewing the Council today," Tilly stated.

"Forth times the charm?" Jessie returned to Tilly with a pure smirk.

"Whatever," Tilly said as she hurried up the marble staircase.

"What did you mean fourth time?" I asked Jessie.

"You don't know?" Jessie seriously countered. "You live with her as your room mate and you don't know?"

"Never mind," I answered him.

"Don't go getting in a sour mood," Jessie said as we began to climb the grand staircase. Jessie broke the silence when he asked, "Elizabeth, do you have gingerbread?"

Instantly I peered over at Jessie responding, "Why would you think…"

"I smell it," Jessie said giving me a knowing look.

"In my backpack," I sighed.

Once at the top I proceeded to walk down the corridor. Jessie asked walking beside me, "You don't know where the Council is located, do you?"

"No," I answered half embarrassed as I stopped to look at him.

He pointed to the first hall off the grand staircase smiling and saying, "Come on, I'll walk with you. I will only make one request."

I questioned, "That would be…"

"A piece of gingerbread," Jessie said with a grin.

"Where were you going?" I asked as the backpack slipped off my shoulder.

"I was going to the engineering office to register a complaint about our dream portal," Jessie stated.

"It's not working?" I asked off the top of my head as I unzipped the backpack.

"It certainly needs a little work," Jessie said. "I was trying to send a dream message through about a health issue. The message went through as car issue."

"Not good," I said as I shook my head. I unwrapped a piece of gingerbread and handed it to the grinning Jessie.

"Thanks!" Jessie said as he broke off a piece and shoved it in his mouth.

I peered back towards the first hall off the staircase, I asked, "Showing me the way won't make you late?"

"Na," Jessie mumbled with a full mouth as we turned the corner into the corridor. "Did you have fun yesterday?"

"I did!" I replied. Marvin and I had indeed had a fabulous day. I would give anything to be lost on a lake island with him. We would be hermits just enjoying the water, mountains, and the boat with no distractions. Swimming, talking, and being held by him would be heavenly. I was tired today and crawling into his protective arms sure sounded good.

As if reading my thoughts, Jessie said, "You know he couldn't wait to get back to you." A smirk crossed his face as he added, "Or maybe it was the blond ice cream gal."

I play slapped his arm as I countered, "Blondie is out of luck!"

Jessie gave me a knowing look and said, "Here we are." He pointed to a massive set of wooden doors.

"Thank you for keeping me from getting lost," I said to my food loving laid back escort.

"The pleasure was all mine!" Jessie said as he held open the door for me in a gentlemanly fashion.

I walked into a long hallway with a series of benches along both sides. I joined the group of trainees huddled around the massive wooden door. Professor Presnell was already standing keeping an eye on the already quiet group. I joined them and stood quiet watching those coming and going down the hall.

Professor Presnell addressed us, "Trainees. I would like to remind you that we will be viewing the Council in session today. We are granted access for training purposes only. Information you hear is confidential and should not be repeated outside these walls."

A prim and proper lady appeared through the doors and stated, "We have seating now for your group."

"Single file!" Professor Presnell demanded. "No talking or making noise of any kind."

I closed the gap between myself and Tilly just in time to hear Professor Presnell say, "Miss Bradford, no gum chewing or popping."

Tilly spit her gum out in her hand and held it out for the professor. "Yes ma'am, it's all yours."

The prim and proper lady who was holding the door stated, "Miss Bradford, how nice to see you again."

"It's always a pleasure," Tilly returned still holding her gum out between her fingers.

"Let me dispose of that for you!" The prim and proper lady said with an outstretched hand.

Tilly's devious smile was suddenly gone as she dropped her gum into the ladies hand instead of the professors. I smiled at both the ladies as I stepped into the room.

The space looked like any courtroom would. There were two sides, one for the plaintiff and one for the defendant. Chairs were placed behind each for the corresponding parties to be seated in. The front of the room held judges seats for nine instead of just one. Glaring bright lighting, lots of massive, old wood work, and neutral paint colors loomed. This room made me feel nervously uncomfortable.

I filed into the row with Tilly and took a seat. The judges entered through their chamber door located to the side of the long judge's desk. They ranged from thin and plump to young and old. Six of them were men and three were women. They all wore the same glowing white robes. I leaned over and asked Tilly, "How do you know which ones are Humlings?"

"There is no way to tell!" Tilly whispered back.

"Ladies," a voice from behind us reprimanded.

I turned and Mr. Solliday was having a seat behind us. He gave me a warm smile and placed his finger to his lips to remind us to be quiet. When did he arrive? I hadn't seen him come in probably because he used his special door. I smiled back at him.

When I turned back to the front, a gentleman with a stack of folders appeared and placed them on the plaintiff's desk. A sinking feeling in my gut was overwhelming. This wasn't a peaceful place. He opened the first file and briskly walked over to the massive door, opened it, and called out, "Mr. Pierce."

A small, gentle looking man appeared at the door. He walked in alone and nervously took his seat at the defendant's desk wringing his hands and beads of perspiration on his forehead.

The prosecutor stood before the judges saying, "Mr. Pierce is concerned there are discrepancies recorded in his chapter of his previous earth life. He has requested to come before you to discuss it."

If he was that nervous to approach this group which he asked to come before, I was right to feel uptight, hot, and flush.

"The man sitting in the middle politely said, "Mr. Pierce, please tell the Council what is incorrect."

The nervous man stood and began, "I would like to start by thanking the Council for hearing my concerns." He paused and shuffled a paper before him. "You see, I went to the Earth Plane with my soul mate, as law dictates."

"He's a Humling!" Tilly leaned over and whispered.

"The problem is my chapter says I exited with another, not my soul mate," the small man complained.

Tilly seemed to be squirming in her chair.

"You are in hot water with your wife and you want us to fix it?" The judge asked.

"It's more than hot water," Mr. Pierce complained. "Doing so goes against the principle of soul mates. She feels we have made a mistake!"

"Did you exit with another?" The judge sternly asked.

"Absolutely no!" Mr. Pierce answered adamantly shaking his head.

"Did you collect the real life?" The judge asked the prosecutor.

"I have the chapter," the prosecutor said.

"Could you retrieve the raw footage from the archives?" Asked the judge.

"Yes," the prosecutor said. He then scurried off like a rat running from rising water.

The judge peered into the back of the room asking, "Is she ready?"

"Yes," said a voice from behind us. I turned and could see a woman flanked by three burly men who had to be guards. She appeared dejected, but re-signed for what was to come. My hands began to get sweaty. It was more than feeling hot. Maybe I was getting sick or something.

"Mr. Pierce, while we wait on your footage, could we ask that you wait in the hall?" The judge questioned.

"Yes sir," Mr. Pierce said as he retrieved his paperwork and hurried to the door. One look towards the lady in the back made him appear more ner-vous than he was before. He almost tripped over his own feet as he glanced towards the judges.

"We will recall you momentarily," the judge politely stated.

As the door closed behind him the guards walked the lady up the center isle to stand before the Council.

A judge on the left side stood announcing, "Mrs. Diane Jane Baker, you have been sentenced to the Black Arch for your crime."

The room was silent as the lady's weeping could be heard.

I didn't want to watch this. All I could think of was the cruel world of the Dwellers. If she was weeping here, what would she do there?

"Do you have any last words you would like to say?" The judge asked.

Silence beyond her weeping is all that could be heard. I wanted to ask where the justice was for her. Sending anyone to those animals was an injustice.

Was this how Tina went? Weeping? This lady had no idea what was in store for her on the other side of the arch. I only knew what I had read and it wasn't a happy place. Was it really necessary for anyone to be sent there? I could feel my heart rapidly beating in my chest. My lungs felt heavy and unable to breathe. Then the room began to spin. I told Tilly, "Doesn't anyone understand what a dark place the world of the Dwellers is?"

I faintly heard, "Elizabeth… Elizabeth…"

Also by JJ Hull...

The Keeper Saga

Forever and a Day (Book 4)
Things Left Unsaid (Book 5)
Smoke and Mirrors (Book 6)
Letting Go (Book 7)

Available at

www.paranormalcrossroads.com

Visit The Keeper Saga

www.thekeepersaga.com